Herding THE *Wind*

RICHARD LAYH

ISBN 978-1-63814-185-3 (Paperback)
ISBN 978-1-63814-186-0 (Digital)

Covenant Books, Inc.
11661 Hwy 707
Murrells Inlet, SC 29576
www.covenantbooks.com

For the four points of my compass, my grandchildren:
Austin, Avery, Savannah, Charlotte.

Love is like the wind. You can't always see
it, but you can always feel it.
—Nicholas Sparks

The human heart is a very curious thing.
—Lee. J. Richmond

But in your dreams…whatever they may be…
dream a little dream of me.
—Gus Kahn

1
CHAPTER

"Dee?"

The man looked up from *The Economist* he was perusing while the bootblack was polishing his shoes.

"Morning, Bryce. What can I do you out of?"

"We have sights on a new sales assistant. We like her, and I'd like you to give her the once-over. You know, the whole whoop-a-dap-adoo."

The man smiled. "Do I detect some altruistic stance up your sleeve toward this old coupon chimp?"

"Dee," Bryce Mckenna said, "you're the best at pegging people, and since you are also an ardent admirer of female pulchritude, I figured...why not. Just want to make sure the tuning fork is still on pitch."

Dee chuckled. "I may have to talk to legal about you plagiarizing my lines."

Bryce smiled. "Just give me the seal of approval and she'll be on staff."

"Okay." Bryce handed Dee her resume.

"What's this?" Bryce said, "Another...another shine? Those shoes look new."

"And so they are. I'm not a factory luster guy. I like the Real McCoy. Besides, the kid needs work."

"The kid? Tony's fifty-eight years old! He's probably the oldest shoeshine guy on the Street...maybe the only one left."

Dee laughed. "Last of the bootblacks with the last of the coupon chimps. So goes the legends."

7

"Say, Tony," Bryce said. "How many parking lots you own now? One? Two?"

Tony smiled up at Bryce, flashing a gold-capped incisor. "Three."

'You see, Dee. This guy owns more prime real estate than me and you put together. Let's put him in touch with Trump. Tony's mogul status."

Tony chimed in. "No Trumpa. His papa…good… Trumpa." He then blew a Bronx cheer. "Bott longa mista Dee needs a shina… I gib'im a shina. Dere!" He snapped the polishing rag like a whip. "Afinish."

"The man's on a mission, Bryce," Dee said. "A horse trader from the old school." He handed Tony a twenty and waved his hand indicating no change. He picked up *The Economist* again and said, "Send in the lass for inspection. Whenever. I'll get out my jeweler's glass." Bryce left Dee's desk.

Dee reviewed the resume, got up, and went to the restroom to freshen up. While urinating, Craig Zimmer, head of government bond trading, came in. "Dee. How's it coming out?"

"Like a water cannon."

"By-product of a beer binge?"

"No," Dee said. "Just two tall coffees."

Zimmer looked in the mirror, rearranging several commas of hair, picking, curling, and fluffing them with great care.

"Zim. When the hell," Dee said, shaking himself dry and zipping up, "are you just going to slick it back and quit that disheveled Hugh Grant hairdo shit?"

"Professionally coiffured, I might add," Zimmer said.

"At what cost? A s'teenth on an odd lot trade? You keeping a beauty parlor position?"

"Dee," Zimmer said, finally satisfied with his hair, "kindly fuck-eth thyself."

Dee smiled. "Appreciate the suggestion. I'll give it my best shot. Then I'll let you know how I make out."

Zimmer chuckled. "Really great to have you back, buddy. The place wasn't the same without you."

"Thanks," Dee said as Zimmer walked out.

Dee looked at himself in the mirror and was going to fumble with his tie knot but saw that it was already straight. "Yes," he said out loud. "I did lose weight. But it's damn good to be back."

He saw strain on his face. It was the same look he had in Vietnam when he was on watch too long.

How he had gotten through the last six months was a miracle and a blur. If it wasn't for the efforts of his daughter Becky and Bryce Mckenna, he surely, he thought, would have been in some loony bin or found floating facedown in the Atlantic.

He had always thought of himself as a survivor. He had survived Vietnam, two stock market crashes, 9/11, a financial meltdown, and being married to a redhead for nearly forty years—until that redhead was snatched from him in a white-hot flash. Then it seemed that his survival skills had vanished.

That horrible excruciating cry. "My head... God! My head"—the last words he ever heard her say. His beloved Carlotta, that vivacious redhead...the rush to the hospital...the opening of her skull... and the devastation the exploded aneurysm did to her brain...like an internal claymore mine, he thought. And then, even before he was capable of coming to terms with the whole idea, he was thanking people for coming to her wake and funeral.

And the aftermath bubbled rages of anger...mad-dog viciousness—he fought with everyone. He just wanted to be alone—alone with his thoughts and confused feelings. He wanted to iron everything out himself, but he couldn't, and that only increased his anger. He felt weak and empty, two very real and very tangible feelings he trafficked with eons ago and, like then, had difficulty contending with them.

He didn't eat. He didn't drink. He didn't read. He just sat and looked at the ocean...and, impetuously, on several occasions, ran into the waves and swam out as far as he could because he heard Carlotta calling him, and when he got to the spot, or so he thought, he found himself alone—she wasn't there, and he was too far out, and he became scared. Through the bob of the waves, he saw his daughter on the beach, and with aching effort, he swam back to shore and fell to his knees exhausted. "Daddy... Daddy, you're too far out"—he saw her tears—"you'll get a cramp. A shark might even get you, goddamnit! You're not on the New York AC Water Polo team anymore. You're not forty years old!"

He understood and cried bitterly, and his mother's voice came to him. "When you're sick, you need sleep—that will heal you—but when your sickness is a cry of the heart, you need to pray till you sweat bullets and get busy till you hurt like a canker sore. Work will help you through it. It won't cure it, but it'll form a scar that will be tough and hold it together, and the pain will ease, for God works in mysterious ways."

Bryce and Becky had gotten him back into the fold. He had purpose. He had set himself up as a limited partner now. He involved himself now only in special situations. The trading room banter distracted the black moments, but he did have his moments, and when they broke through the barbed wire of his defense, he took a walk to Battery Park to look at the water. That always seemed to calm the furies. His days seemed to go quickly, and his sleep was less fitful.

He washed up, dried his hands, and stepped out of the restroom.

As he walked through the trading room, the din, the clatter, the open outcries, and the creative profanity started to well up. The slamming of phones, nano-arguments, and momentary laughter followed him to the office between quick greetings from the various trading desks. To Dee, the trading room was a musical suite. It was something, he felt, that you could almost dance to.

He saw Bryce and the young lady looking down from his office window at the Brooklyn Bridge. And when he entered saying, "Sorry for not being here when you came in," they both turned around.

When he saw her, he stopped dead, startled, almost imperceptibly inching back, his mouth formulating a word or a name that he held back. His eyes widened a mite.

Bryce noticed this immediately. He was Dee's trading partner for years, and he knew every subtlety, every facial nuance. He could read Dee assessing a situation, reformulating a strategy to delve into once he got a handle on the natural flow of action, always disposed to adjust as a necessity dictated, much like a surfer negotiating a hundred-foot wave. As Dee always said, "Trading is part technical, part 'seat of the pants,' part Zen."

The girl smiled close-lipped and moved forward, extending her hand just as Bryce introduced: "Mary Jo Barnes, this is Democedes Felico." Her hand was warm and had a good squeeze to it.

What Dee saw was his first love—almost an exact image—a girl he adored, a girl he wanted to marry, a girl he always wanted to be with, a girl who had broken his heart as only a twenty-year-old's heart could be broken. It was a vision of Beatrice Sharpe. He couldn't even fathom the last time he thought of her. It was a lifetime ago, and now, in his office, this flesh-and-blood person before him seemed to churn his inner most being and jellify his soul. This was a peculiarity his mother had told him ages ago. "Everybody has a double in this world, and sometimes, if you're lucky, or unlucky, it will pop up in your life, but either way, you'll have a problem." Beatrice Sharpe's specter stood before him.

"Wow," she said. "That was a mouthful!"

Bryce was taken aback by the affront, but Dee laughed out loud, quelling his nervous edge. "Yes. Democedes Felico. It's a lot of name. That's cause I'm one-third Greek, one-third Catalan, and one-third Sicilian."

"And 100 percent pirate?" she queried, her smile widening, enjoying her play at upper hand.

Bryce jumped in immediately, "Now, hold on now," stopping when Dee held up his index finger.

He smiled, viewing the same beautiful teeth, the same slight overbite, the same charming right-dimpled cheek. *God*, he thought, *the spitting image of Bea, just a little taller, even the lovely light brown wavy hair, the afterthought of makeup...*

"Bryce. Doesn't she look a little like Faye Dunaway?"

Bryce, still a bit upset, looked at Dee and said nothing.

"Now, Ms. Barnes," Dee said, "I'm kind of curious. What prompted you to say what you just said?"

"Well," she said, "a friend of mine forewarned me that if you were involved in a Wall Street interview, someone will throw you a curve ball, something that jars you, might even be inappropriate, just to see how you'll react, to see what kind of stuff you're made of and to see what kind of counter zap you can come up with." She paused and smiled again. "I just thought I'd lob the hand grenade first."

Dee clapped his hands, almost in a youthful glee. "Bryce. I think I'm going to have a fabulous chitchat with this one." He then turned to Mary Jo. "As my friends in Brooklyn say"—his finger pointing to his office couch—"sa' down, baby girl!"

She plopped down on the sofa, slightly bouncing with a muted giggle, as ordered.

Bryce left the office as Dee sat in a chair leaning forward addressing Mary Jo. "I've read your resume. Now tell me what it says, but more importantly, what it means."

Her eyes looked askance at the two plates on his desk. "Does that," she asked, "say what I think it does?"

Surprised, he said, "You read Greek?"

"Only the filthy words—'Cut the Shit'?"

"I am impressed. My favorite expression, especially in the morning meetings. The traders gave it to me."

"And 'Ace Coupon Chimp'?"

"That's another story. Let's talk about you."

"All right," she said as Dee gazed at her face and started to think about Beatrice Sharpe.

Bea Sharpe did not smoke or drink. She didn't do drugs even though they were in the Age of Aquarius. She was a vegetarian before it became a fashion. She tap-danced, swam like a torpedo, and had the libido of an alley cat.

2
CHAPTER

He met her in Creative Writing class in high school. The seating was done alphabetically and, by happenstance, they were placed next to each other.

She was not a head turner as in the prom queen class or the class sizzler that all the boys had wet dreams over, but she had a certain attractiveness—widely spaced tawny eyes, a very slight overbite that exploded into a dazzling smile, accentuating a dimple on her right cheek—and a certain self-assurance that seemed to give her a sophisticated air beyond her years.

He knew she had a boyfriend. He had seen her walking hand in hand with Liam Crosby, a somewhat effeminate art student, in the hallways.

They were both voracious readers and capitalized on the classroom discussions. This brought them into a friendly competitive association which opened up their intellect and their eyes toward each other.

Their final, a term paper on Horace McCoy's *They Shoot Horses, Don't They?* led Dee on a lark to suggest a joint effort to Bea comparing it to Camus's *The Stranger*. Dee felt there were a lot of similarities and felt that such a topic would blow the socks off the teacher and given them an A as well as a good college recommendation.

Bea had never read *The Stranger*. She borrowed his copy, read it in one sitting, and agreed that it would be one fantastic collaboration. They both approached the teacher and presented their topic. He enthusiastically agreed. "Boy," she said, "we have some difficult paper to write. Can we find any books on this? This is a little beyond me. This is first class college stuff."

"There is a library in my neighborhood. The librarian there really likes me…well, I think she loves me. She'll help us."

Bea cocked her eyebrow upward. "Loves you? How old is she?"

"She was," Dee laughed, "in silent movies. She says I look like Gilbert Roland. Maybe she had a fling with him back in the day."

She frowned, studying his face. "You don't look like Gilbert Roland. I saw him in *Beneath the 12-Mile Reef*. He had a mustache."

"In silent pictures he didn't. He always played the Latin lover."

She smiled slightly, looking deeply at him. "Maybe you should grow a mustache. I think I'd find that very interesting."

He felt a flush coming but he controlled it. "That might be an idea."

"Then, at least, I'll see whether you look like the Gilbert Roland I'm familiar with."

"Where do you live?"

"Jackson Heights."

"I'm in Astoria. Does next Saturday seem okay? We can get a good jump on this project. I can come fetch you…"

"No. Why waste a token? I'll take the el. Where do I get off?"

"Take it to Ditmars…last stop. When you come down the stairs, look for Mike's Diner. I'll be in front. Is ten thirty too early?"

She smiled. "Perfect. See you there." She took her books and left for another class.

The Saturday of the meeting she was right on time. She carried a folder with both books in it, along with a legal pad, index cards, and several pens. When they met up, Dee led the way to the library correctly on the outside closest to the street.

She noticed this gesture immediately. "I don't think the horse carriage will splash mud on me. But I do thank you for that gallant courtesy."

"I am impressed. You do understand." As they came to the corner of Ditmars and 31st Street, he said, "I must give you the lowdown on the librarian. Her name is Zelda Eisenstadt. She has yellow hair."

Bea looked at him. "Yellow hair? You mean blond, platinum blond?"

"No. Yellow. Yellow like Van Gogh's *Starry Night* yellow. Or, for that matter, goat-vomit yellow."

She giggled heartily. "Goat-vomit yellow. Now that's a good one."

"Get this: yellow hair, fire-engine red lipstick. She chain-smokes Old Gold's, smells of My Sin and Sen-Sen, and by"—he quickly checked his wristwatch—"about this time has cheap rye on her breath."

"Wow. A real lulu." They crossed Ditmars. "You said she was in the movies."

"Yes. Silent pictures. A couple of Buster Keaton films. If it was a successful film, there'd be a two-week party—basically a bender for the crew—and this during a Prohibition, a binge-fest. She never quite made it to the marquee. She was an extra who fizzled out pretty fast. Her stage name was Constance Cox."

She stopped and looked at him. "Therein lies the problem."

"You might have something there."

They were almost at the library. "You told me she loves you."

"Indubitably," he said.

"Is it because older women have better hormones, or is it because they are so grateful the morning after?"

"If you keep this up," he quipped, "I'll have you expunged."

They both laughed and entered the library.

When they walked into the reference section, Bea saw Ms. Eisenstadt. Dee had described her spot-on. She was reading Betty Friedan's *The Feminine Mystique*. Without even meeting her, Bea liked her.

"Good morning," Dee said.

Zelda Eisenstadt looked up through heavy-lidded eyes and immediately perked up. "Democedes Felico, my favorite library patron, what can I do for you, sweetheart?" Her voice sounded as if she gargled with ground glass. Her eyes shifted toward Bea. "And who is your little friend?"

"A classmate of mine. We are jointly doing a paper comparing McCoy's *They Shoot Horses...* and Camus's *The Stranger*, and we're wondering if you can help."

"My goodness. Of course I can. And what is your name, dear?"

"Beatrice Sharpe."

She smiled showing her nicotine-stained teeth. "Bea Sharpe, Bea Sharpe..." She put a bookmark in *The Feminine Mystique*, and then mused, "Sometimes be sharp, never be flat...but always, especially when you're in bed, be natural." She chuckled.

Dee said, "It's a music thing," looking at Bea.

"I know that," she said sarcastically. "I'm not from China, you ninny."

"McCoy and Camus. How interesting. Yes, I remember reading the McCoy when it came out in '35. In fact, I was in a dance marathon in the spring of 1930. Lasted nineteen hours till my partner caved in. I still think it's the reason I wear arch supports today." She laughed to herself. "Well, why don't you two busy yourselves amongst the shelves—but no hanky-panky, mind you—while I check some periodicals. I think I'll be able to cull together some stuff to support your thesis." She looked very tenderly at them. "Go on now. Explore. Let me go to work. I'll seek you out when I'm finished." She got up and went toward the periodical section, humming and whisper-whistling, a bit off-key, 'I'll String Along with You.'

Roughly a half hour later, Ms. Eisenstadt found them and said, "I've found some very interesting scholarly articles—seven to be exact, not long, some interesting observations and commentary. I think you'll find them supportive of your arguments, but you decide. They're in the small conference room. You can do your work there."

"I can't thank you enough. Is there anything I can do to repay you for your efforts?" Dee said in earnest.

"Well," Ms. Eisenstadt said, looking at Dee, hesitantly, "we're not allowed to accept any gratuities from the patrons. Library policy, you know. But if you can show me the final grade on the paper and any comments the teacher scrawls on it, well, I'd be thrilled."

"It's a deal," Dee said.

"Dear boy," she said, shaking Dee's hand.

"By the way," Bea said, breaking Ms. Eisenstadt's gaze on Dee. "I saw you reading *The Feminine Mystique*. What's your opinion?"

"Fourth time reading it! Truer than truth!" she snapped. "I'd put it as one of the books of the Bible. I'd tear out St. John's Revelation and put Friedan's work in as the true Revelation! That'd knock the apologists and the theologians on their ear with a Dempsey punch!"

"I heartily concur," Bea said.

Ms. Eisenstadt came out with a throaty Tallulah Bankhead laugh. "Be aware, I strongly advise you, Democedes, that you have a very smart, very brave woman in your midst. A revolutionary soul." She then turned and left saying, "Back to the salt mine of pedestrian readers."

They concentrated their efforts in the little conference room and, after a good five hours, put together a workable paper. Exhausted, he suggested they go to his home to have a quick bite since they had worked through lunch. She did not want to impose on his mother, but he insisted.

They ate at the apartment. Since Bea was a vegetarian, his mother made her a Greek salad, sending Dee out for additional feta cheese so she could have some girl talk with her.

When they finished, Dee said, "I'll take a ride with you. Keep you company on the way home."

"Don't be silly. It's a two-way trip for you and a one-way for me. Besides, it's getting late. I want to look over my notes on the train. I think we should both write the paper as if we didn't collaborate. Then, we can take the best of each paper and meld it into a finished product. How's that?"

"I'll buy that. Next Saturday, same time, same place for the consolidation?"

"Yes." She looked at him. "Mind walking me to the el?"

As they strolled toward the station, Dee asked, "While I was getting the cheese, you and Mom chatted?"

"We did." She continued to walk, saying nothing.

"Anything to divulge?"

She stopped and faced him. "Your mother is a real mother."

He did not know how to take this. "What do you mean?"

"She's looking out for her boy."

He said nothing and continued to walk with her toward the station. When they reached it, he said, "Get home safe. I think I'm going to work on this tonight."

"I'm going to sleep on it," she said. "I'll tackle it fresh in the morning after church. See you Monday in class." She smiled, close-lipped, at him and walked up the stairs without looking back.

When he went back home, he asked his mother what she thought of her.

"Do you have thoughts of going out with her?"

"Mom. She's a classmate. We're doing a paper together. And, by the way, she has a boyfriend."

"Well," his mother said, "if things turn around and you decide to go out with that Beatrice…" She paused. "Watch your step."

Every time his mother used the adjective *that* before an individual's name, he knew they were not held in high esteem in her eyes.

"I don't understand, Mom."

"She has pepper up her ass. You just watch your step." His mother then turned and busied herself with the dishes.

*****

The paper turned out to be the best the teacher had read in years. It earned them both an A+ and a glowing recommendation on their college applications. He also promised, since he thought the paper worthy of publication, he would make every effort of getting it into a scholarly journal. His intention was sincere, but with three months off a few days away, his effort on their behalf died a quiet death. Yet it boosted their morale and made them feel secure that college work was something they could handle.

Dee insisted that they give a Xerox copy of the paper with all the comments and accolades the teacher had written in the margins to Ms. Eisenstadt. When they gave it to her stating that it was dedicated to her, she was exuberant. With tears in her eyes, she said, "I have been saving a bottle of brandy for such a celebratory occasion. I will quaff, as a humble footnote, to your future success this evening, as well as to the memory of my sweet prince, John Barrymore, the gentleman who gifted me the bottle from his private stash ages ago. I cherish you both and your gift to me. Thank you, thank you, thank you, dear ones." She gave them both a rather slobbering kiss on the cheek, which she wiped off their cheeks with her thumb. "Sorry, dears. Think of the kiss as not being wiped off but being rubbed in."

When they left the library, Bea said, "So sweet of you to remember her."

"It gives her a good excuse for hitting the bottle. At least she's cracking the crock of some good stuff in our honor."

"Dee," she said, "how could you—"

"Let's be honest, what she's going to do tonight she would have done anyway, but you have to admit that we could not have done this without her. That's the reason I gave her the paper. She did our research and gave us direction. That's foremost. Everything else is incidental. We made her day. And I am glad of that."

"I agree. I was going to say something before, but..." She touched his arm. "Such a sweet gesture you did for her. I'm glad you didn't do it without me. Thank you."

On the last day of class, he gave her an envelope.

Smiling, and a bit confused, she asked, "What's this?"

"A little thing I wrote for you."

She began to open it, and he put his hand on the envelope in her hands. "What?"

"No, no," he said. "Not now. When you get home."

"Are you crazy? That'd be worse than water torture," she said as she ripped open the envelope and began to read the poem. As he watched her read it, he saw that she was visibly moved. When she finished, she sighed. "It's beautiful. Really. I'm...actually touched. When did you write this?"

"Last night. It gushed out of me. I think typing it out took longer than writing it."

"Now, how does Chopin's Etude in E Major go?"

He hummed three bars and she immediately knew it. "I think it's the most beautiful piece he ever wrote."

"I know the song. I have it on a classical album. But what I don't understand is this: you really see me in this music?"

"Yes. When I hear that music, I see you."

"Is it that you think of me?"

"No. Not at all. I actually see you. If I never saw you again for the rest of my life and I heard that piece fifty years from now, I'd see you…crystal clear," he said.

She was stunned. "You really see me in the music…now that you know me?" She was finding it very troubling trying to understand this. "And what did you see in this piece before you knew me?"

"Just the notes."

"I'm finding this so strange, beautiful, touching… I have no frame of reference."

"It's sort of like," he said, "if you smell some aroma, you remember where you were or who you were with. Something like that."

"Am I the only one you see with music?"

"In this particular Chopin Etude, I do, but I see other people with different pieces. And there's no change, no alteration. In this piece, it's you and only you."

"How exquisitely curious this is," she said. "So I am unique to this composition."

"Yes. You're correct."

She was totally overwhelmed. "What a romantic affliction you have." She gazed at him, seemingly studying his face for some answer to pop out and give her understanding of this unusual happening. "I've never…never come across this before."

"You've never met anyone like me before." She saw a beautiful tenderness in his eyes.

She reached over and kissed him on his right cheek, her palm on his left. She smelled of musk oil and coconut.

He suddenly said, "Just think on the bright side. You wound up with a Chopin Etude. It could have been 'Yes, We Have No Bananas,' or Durante's 'Inka Dinka Doo.'"

She giggled. "I'm linked up with a classic, not a novelty number, and that bodes well for you, brother. I don't know how I would have reacted the other way around."

He laughed nervously.

"Tell me," she said, putting her hand on his. "Are you in the book?"

"Book?"

"The phone book."

"Yes, why?"

"I want to call you. Maybe we can go out on a date...or something."

"I always thought the guy makes the move."

"And this Chopin thing wasn't a move? Subtle, and totally out of the blue, but...effective, I'd say."

"No...honestly..."

"I know, I'm toying with you," she said. "But listen up, my friend. There is a new revolution brewing out there. Women's Liberation. We're not going to be standing on the sidelines anymore. We're going to be calling the shots. You wait and see, and it's just around the corner."

"But," he said, "you're going with Liam Crosby. I thought... What I did was innocent—"

She cut him off. "Soon to be disengaged. I've had enough of him. I will be a free woman. Let me tell you something: his mother is a first-class butt-insky. She must think I'm an idiot. 'It'd be nice if ya did this... I'd be nice if ya did that,'" she mimicked in a passable Irish brogue, "And telling him what to do for me like a recipe—I've had it with that sow!"

"Well," Dee said, "isn't that so with mothers? No girl will ever be good enough for their boy."

She frowned. "Didn't we touch on this on the way to the el?"

He remembered and felt foolish. "Mea culpa," he said with downcast eyes.

She stared at him a bit too long. "I forgive you," she finally said.

"I'm glad you said that. I thought I was going to have to give you the order for my Last Meal."

She put her finger on his nose. "Had you going there."

"Tell me, Bea," he asked, "why are you dropping him? Is it just the mother thing?"

"No," she said, shaking her head. "I've been going with him since I was thirteen. My parents are friendly with his because I strongly suspect his father is a member of the IRA, and my folks are simpatico with that cause. But aside from that, he's just too much the artiste! All we do is go to museums, galleries, and art shows…and we hold hands. He's like a curator giving me a tour and conducting class-explaining and speculating on the psychological subtleties and nuances of the works and what ecstasy or trauma suggests this or that brushstroke—I've had it!"

"So if you wanted a course on Art Appreciation, you'd have taken one."

"Exactly," she said. "And," she continued, her voice lowering to just above a whisper, pointing to herself, "that's just it." She paused and then said, "I'm a work of art! I want to be gazed at and admired! I want concentrated and interpretive attention given to me!" She looked at him sternly. "So there!" She abruptly sat back in her seat.

He was a bit shocked and stayed silent for a while, allowing her to cool down. "Bea," he said, getting her attention.

She looked up at him. "Yes?"

"Why me?"

Her face softened, and her dimple creased as she smiled. "Because I like you. Because you make me laugh. Because you're very…very interesting." Her smile widened. "And because I find you absolutely delicious."

He was taken aback by her statement. "I never thought of myself as an appetizer."

"I am going to go home and listen to the record as I reread your poem to me. And"—she winked at him—"you're no appetizer. You're the main course, baby. And I can't wait to eat you up." She then got up and left.

He leaned back in his seat. He didn't know what she meant by that. All he knew was that he was going to have to take a breather before he got up.

3
CHAPTER

Dee Felico landed his first job on Wall Street by accident.

Jack Irving, a retired partner from Barlow Brothers, and a very dear friend of Dee's father, offered Dee a summer internship. His own son, who had actually been slated for the position, reneged on it in lieu of a backpacking travel fest through Europe with his girlfriend.

Dee needed the job. His father had died the year before, and his mother, a widow at forty-three, had to suddenly take on the responsibilities and workings for a four-family house. Funds were in an echo chamber, and the job would certainly help the kitty.

He was scheduled to start two days after graduation. His appointed time was 9:00 a.m. He walked in at 7:30 a.m.

He was processed very courteously, overhearing quips from the security men of, "nice," and "wouldn't have expected this from a kid his age."

He was then brought to Jerry Parcher, the Head Cashier, in a secured floor, guarded by uniformed officers packing firearms, where negotiable securities as well as cash traded hands. It was known simply as "The Cage."

Jerry Parcher, barrel-chested, six foot four, looked more like a butcher than a Wall Street executive. He stuck out a hand as large as a catcher's mitt and said, "So you're Jack's friend. Welcome aboard." He gave Dee the once-over and said, "You'll do. Come." Dee had to double time just to keep pace with Parcher as they went to the Bond Interest Department.

When they got there, Dee saw two old men nattily dressed.

"Kid, you'll be working with these guys. The guy behind the desk is Pete McKelvey, and the other is Stanley Conn."

Both men shook Dee's hand.

"Pete," Parcher said. "This is the new kid, Jack's friend. He's already been printed, processed and pictured."

McKelvey looked at him with eyes Grumbacher paints might have modeled as cerulean blue. "Does he have a pulse?"

"Go easy on him. He's brand new."

Stan Conn said, "The only thing Pete's easy on is the ice in his Scotch."

"He's all yours," Parcher said. He turned around and scooted back to his office shouting to Dee, "How's Jack?" just as he turned the corner, not waiting for an answer.

Pete McKelvey got up from behind this desk. He was very thin and had his straight gray hair slicked back, the part close to the middle. His mustache was as sleek as Errol Flynn's, and a Chesterfield cigarette dangled from his lips. He stood next to Dee and, with a sweep of the hand, as if presenting him to an audience, said to Stanley Conn, "Did you ever see anything like this before? Especially from Jack Irving?"

Stanley, the bags of his eyes shaking with the motion of his head, muttering, "Never. I reiterate—never. And," he continued, "I know Jack a longtime."

Pete addressed Dee, "Did Jack ever speak to you of tradition, custom...culture?"

"No," Dee said. "I just said yes when he offered me the job, and that's it. And here I am."

Both men stared at each other and simultaneously sighed.

Stanley, still seated, turned his chair around and looked at Dee's shoes. "You have a pair of brown shoes?"

"Pardon?" Dee said, confused.

"The man asked if you had a pair of brown shoes," Pete said. "That's not such a tough question for a college boy, is it?"

"Yes. I have brown shoes. Loafers. Penny loafers."

"No, no, no, no, no." Pete cringed, smacking his brow with the palm of his hand. "Wing tips!"

Dee was shocked at the outburst. He slowly said, "I don't think so." He was beginning to feel uncomfortable.

"'I don't think so'?" Pete mimicked. "You either know or you don't. Speculation is on the eleventh floor. That's trading. We're on thirteen. We're operations. We only speak in facts."

Dee began to feel a nervous tremor in his stomach as a bead of sweat slithered down his back. "No. I do not have a pair of brown wing-tipped shoes."

"Good," Stanley said. "Finally, a declarative sentence. I am over-joyed. Now, we can, at least, begin."

Pete looked Dee straight in the eye. "Listen carefully. Wall Street, and particularly this firm, has a tradition. We wear brown shoes, primarily wing tips. We wear them with blue suits, black suits, checkered suits, any color suits, and, if need be, bathing suits. In fact, I don't even own a pair of black shoes. Now, you, coming in here dressed like that…if you were in the Army, you'd be considered out of uniform and probably get gigged."

Dee, very nervous now, could not come up with any response other than, "I'm sorry, I didn't know. Nobody told me."

There was a long pause as Pete looked over at Stanley.

"Well," Stanley said, "we will take that up with Jack next when he has the occasion to visit us. But, as of now, you need a pair of wing-tipped brown shoes—tie shoes, that is—or else…"

Pete followed through with Stanley's thought, "You can't work here. It's as simple as that. And that's a fact!"

Dee was flabbergasted. He was totally stymied. His mouth felt dry and coppery.

"We want you to go out a get a pair of those shoes now. Once you do that, we can start. So don't dawdle. Get going," Pete said, turning and heading back to his desk to continue his work. Stanley was already on the telephone.

As Pete lit up another Chesterfield, Dee said, "Mr. McKelvey. I don't have the money for that now."

"What a kettle of fish!" Pete exploded, crushing the cigarette he just lighted. "We're not starting on the right foot today, college boy!"

"I don't have the money on me. I mean it. I have carfare, some lunch money, and five bucks in my sock—that's it."

"In your sock?" Pete eased out a small smirk. It was an idea that went back to his youth.

"My grandfather always told me to keep a five spot in my sock, just in case…you know, for an emergency."

"Now that," Pete said, turning around and putting his hand on Dee's shoulder, "is a wise man. Hope some of him rubs off on you."

"I don't know what to do."

Stanley slammed the phone down. "Son of a bitch!"

"What?" Pete asked.

"Rocco screwed up the margin instructions on that flower bond trade," Stanley said, running toward the head runner's window. "Joe! Don't send out the treasury deliver to Shearson! Rocco's sending new instructions! Margin department hock-up!" When Stanley came back, he said, "Well?"

"We gotta help the college boy out."

The two old men looked at each other in silent communication, pursed their lips, and shook their heads.

"Well. Only one thing we can do. Bail this uninformed, wet-behind-the-ears, college boy out." Stanley then turned to Dee. "Son. You're in a bind. But we know how to fix things. Now you listen to Pete. And you follow his instructions to the tee. We don't do this for everybody. I mean, seeing as you are Jack's friend and all. You just do what Pete says."

Pete said, "Get out of the building and walk up Wall to Broadway. Cross and get in front of Trinity Church. Make a left a few steps till you hit Rector Street and walk down. Trinity Graveyard will be on your right. When you're almost at the end of the graveyard, cross Rector—that's the South side of the street, college boy. You'll see a shoe store there that has a sign in the window that says, 'Final Sale This Week—Going Out of Business.' That sign's been there since the '29 Crash. Go in and ask for Mumbles. Tell him Pete sent you and that you need a good pair of brown wing tip, tie shoes that are comfortable. No two-tone jobbies, or else I send you right back—and make the hell sure they're comfortable. We don't want you limping around here all day trying to break them in. He'll try to sell you something else. You won't understand him. He has a cleft palate and he sounds like he has a mouth full of mashed potatoes. That's why we call him Mumbles. Just be firm. Get a bill and tell him we'll send a runner down with payment later. We'll take it out of petty cash. Don't worry, sonny, we won't bag your first paycheck for a refund. Consider it your welcome wagon."

"Th-th-thanks," Dee stuttered.

"With that stammer, you'll get along fine with Mumbles. Now, what the hell are you waiting around for?" Stanley barked. "Beat it! You heard the man. You got a lot to learn and the market's opening in a couple minutes."

Dee quickly bolted down the corridor toward the elevators.

4
CHAPTER

True to her word, she called him a week after graduation. They centered sights on a Saturday get-together in the city.

He picked her up at her apartment and met her parents, a rather stately, older couple.

She wore a white halter top, a St. Joseph's medal nestled in the hint of a cleavage, yellow hot pants, and candy-striped tennis shoes. He wore jeans, sneakers, a short sleeve white button-down sports shirt with a blue-and-white paisley kerchief around his neck. He was also developing a mustache, neatly trimmed, and already clearly defined.

"What time does Bea have to be home?"

Her mother looked at her father. "How cute. She has no curfew. Whatever you deem appropriate. Now go"—she shooed with her hand—"you have a full day ahead of you. Dee, have fun. M's, enjoy."

They went into the elevator that opened directly into the apartment. Dee had never encountered this before.

"'M's'?"

"I'll tell you about that later," she said. "I do like the kerchief. Very different. Very European."

He said, "Had to dress up a bit. Going into the city."

"I wore lipstick," she countered.

Her hair was strewn back tightly into a ponytail. Her facial structure accommodated that severe style beautifully.

"And the new sprouting, the mustache, very intriguing. I see why the old librarian said you resembled Gilbert Roland. Just like *Beneath the 12-Mile Reef.* He even wore a kerchief as I recall."

"Yes," Dee said, "and a wristband."

"Well," she puffed. "Now I know what to tell Santa." She wet her finger with her tongue and traced it over his mustache, then sucked on the finger, pulling it out with a smack. "Let me try it. To see if it tickles." She then kissed him, moving her head quickly back and forth gently while their lips were together.

The elevator reached the bottom and the door opened. He was a bit stunned by what she had done. "Well?"

"Couldn't get a good read," she said.

"Well, we have plenty of day for confirmation." He tried to be suave but was slightly embarrassed.

She suppressed a smile, raising her left eyebrow, her dimple accentuating. "Wipe your lips. Tell-tale signs of lipstick. We have a lot of gawkers in this neighborhood. Wouldn't want to send out the wrong impression." She winked at him and then they began to walk to the Flushing Line el.

They got off at Times Square. And when they emerged from the underground into the sour smell of morning, she said, "Must be low tide on the Ganges."

"No. Definitely an aftershave promotion," he quickly retorted.

They both laughed, their hands occasionally brushing against each other as they strolled on what Bea dubbed "The Hardened Artery." "And why, Mr. Felico, did you bring me to this neck of the woods?"

"Always like to catch a glimpse of the hangover's aftermath from Friday night, and then proceed to points east." There weren't many people on the street, but enough to navigate from corner to corner so as not to bump into a wayward drunk or sidestep a sleeping bum in a doorway.

"I thought you were going to take me to an exploitation film, as an eye-opener." She looked up at him in expectation.

He stopped dead. "An exploitation film?"

"Yes. One of those porno flicks. I don't exactly see *Singin' in the Rain* on any of these marquees."

"Now, why would I ever take you into a scratch house to see one of those triple X-rated features?"

She shrugged her shoulders. "Research?"

"I ain't no millionaire, sweetie. At five bucks a pop? For research, I'd rather take you to the 42nd Street Library and pour over the *Kama Sutra*. At least it's free, and we won't be sitting next to old goats in raincoats."

"Dee. There won't be any live action. We'd have to use our imaginations."

"I have a great imagination. Besides, if we can find some art theater that's showing a Fred Astaire film for a buck and a half apiece, that'd be right up my alley."

"Fred Astaire?" She suddenly did a quick tap step and twirled into a finale stance. It was at that moment that he realized what beautiful legs she had. "Now you're talking!"

They walked east on 42nd Street. "We're going to a much more civilized area."

"There are just as many cat houses in Sutton Place as are in Hell's Kitchen. Chief difference is furniture. Sutton has contemporary. Hell's Kitchen has the old workbench, and the end product is still the same; a spastic release and a lot of howling and barking at the moon, day or night."

"Now, how the hell do you know that?" he said.

"I read the *Village Voice*, Spunky."

He shook his head and sighed. When they crossed Sixth Avenue, she clasped his hand. It was a bit cold and clammy. "Let's beeline it!" he said. The light was red and they ran across the street, dodging the oncoming cars. His hand warmed up, and he relaxed. He was thrilled he was with her, and he felt the feeling was mutual.

There was no destination in mind. They just walked and spoke incessantly. If there was an odd sight, or a peculiarity to behold, they viewed it almost peripherally. They wound up at UN Plaza, sat on a bench, and spoke about their lives. She spoke at length about her dancing and swimming, her penchant for vegetables, and aversion toward red meat, which played a vengeance on her insides; her desire to read everything, experience everything, and live a life of wonder. She spoke hesitatingly, picking out the words as if translating a legal document from a foreign language, about her parents: the products of foster care in New York, and they, being Communists in their youths, meeting in Spain during the Civil War—he, a member of the Abraham Lincoln Brigade, and she, a nurse and an ambulance driver—and the dissolution of their affiliation with the Party when Khrushchev denounced Stalin for his lies, crimes, and reign of terror on his own people. She thanked God both her parents had maintained assumed names while Party members so the FBI was never able to clearly identify them to dog or blacklist them as with many of their fellow comrades. Her father became a math teacher at the Rhodes School in Manhattan, and her mother took a position managing the labs at Brooklyn Tech High School having first ended her nursing career at Bellevue because the heavy schedule infringed on the time needed on what she wanted to do for society. Both were committed social reformers, social activists, and social humanists. They were very liberal, Democrats hoping to make the world a better place to live in.

Bea's voice was halting, almost sultry to the ear, closer to an apology than a confession, and when she stopped speaking, she looked at him with trepidation, her mouth at rest, a slight sigh coming from her, and he saw her lips naturally part, a glint of her top teeth showing, and he was stricken with how beautiful she was. How he had never seen this before, he couldn't fathom.

"Will this put a damper on things?" Her eyes were glassy.

"No," was all he could say. He put his hand on hers.

"You'll—"

He answered before she asked, "I won't say a word to anybody. Ever."

She blinked several times, and her lips tightened. She was breaking on her emotions. "I've never told this to anybody before."

"Liam never knew?"

That seemed to break her anxiety.

"Liam was in his own world. Probably on one of the rings at Saturn much of the time. Too much of an effete, too esoteric. I tell you, honestly, if he was a fervent religious, I think he'd be a mystic," she said. After a long pause, she said, "I feel like a piano's been lifted off my shoulders."

"I hope it was a Steinway. That's the only make I deal with." He got up off the bench. "Let's go down by the water. Let's wave to the people on the Circle Line and see if anyone waves back."

"I love that idea. Let's," she said.

He put his arm around her waist as she did to him and momentarily put her head on his shoulder almost as a gesture of thanks as they strolled to the East River.

When the Circle Line came, they waved frantically. No one waved back. However, the boat did blast its horn once, perhaps as a signal to the oncoming tug pushing a barge. "Must be a bunch of New Yorkers on that vessel today. I bet they're shocked into paralysis by the fact they live on an island."

"I suppose you're right," she said as they walked hand in hand uptown.

Between 56th and 57th Streets, they made a right and walked into Sutton Place Park. No one was there. When Dee passed the bronze statue of the wild boar, he kissed his hand and patted the boar's snout.

"Why'd you do that?" Bea asked.

"Just making sure I don't get hit by a meteorite today."

"Are you Catholic?"

"Why?"

"Because," Bea explained, "I've read that Catholics shouldn't be superstitious."

"It's just a gesture, Bea. Don't read too much into it. However, I do walk under ladders for your information."

They sat down at a bench and watched the river traffic and listened to the drone of the Queensboro Bridge's grated roadway and the FDR Drive below. They didn't speak for a time. Nor did they hold hands. It was a crystal day, warm with an occasional cool breeze.

Suddenly Dee smiled. "You hear the pitch of the bridge traffic?"

"Hmmm?" Her mind was focused elsewhere.

"I just love the sounds of the city. You know, that's a wavering E-flat with some semi tones, hear it?"

She got up and walked in front of him, facing him, her arms holding the railing behind her. She had not heard a thing he said.

"You want to know why my mom calls me M's?" And before he could answer, she declared, "I'll tell you."

He was thrown by this. He had forgotten all about it. He looked up at her. He saw that she was very pensive.

"Well," she declared," it means M and M. And not the candy slogan." Her face was very serious. "It means mistake and miracle."

"I don't understand," he said.

"I," she softly said very slowly, her eyes downcast, "was a mistake. My parents got careless, and I am the result of that carelessness. My parents never wanted to have children. Coming from foster care, they both were adamant about not bringing a child into such a crazy world as ours. My mother was thirty-seven years old when I was conceived, and when Mom found out, I was," she cleared her throat, "one pinprick away from oblivion."

"What!" Dee was utterly flabbergasted. "You mean she wanted to abort you?"

"Yes. She was and is a firm abortion advocate, and being a nurse, she knew who'd do it discreetly—no back-alley stuff. But before she put the feelers out, she spoke to her foster mom, whom she adored, and bounced it off her. She was dying of cancer at the time; in fact, I'm named after her, and she, also an advocate, said it was Mom's ultimate decision, but whatever she chose to do, she'd love her no matter what. Mom slept on it, and somehow… I dunno, reversed her stance, and…"—she gave a finale pose—"ta-da—here I am, the miracle." Her eyes were watery.

Dee couldn't believe what he had just heard. "And your dad?"

"He went along for the ride." Bea looked straight at Dee and muttered, "He always goes along for the ride. Supports her efforts totally."

Dee was incredulous. "I don't know what to say, Bea." She was hovering over him like a panther. "And your mom told you all this?"

"Yes."

"I mean, isn't a mom…Where's nurturing?"

"Well," she blurted, in a bit of a defensive tone. "What do you expect? Considering where they came from! I'm good with it though. That's what really matters. She was honest with me—honest to a

33

fault. And I respect that. And, Dee, what you've got to understand is this: they're very different people."

"And they love you?" he asked.

Her face seemed to relax, and then lightened. "Without question. They would do anything for me." And then she smiled. "Within reason."

"My goodness." He stammered a bit, "How…how do you feel, I mean, about all this?"

"I feel I'm the luckiest person on this planet. And I'm here to do something. Don't know yet just what, but something."

"Something big?"

"Maybe not…big, that is, but something nevertheless."

He was silent and very confused. "Come," he said. "Sit next to me." It was all he could say.

She sat next to him, and he put his arm around her. She snuggled in. "I really like you, Bea. No matter what you've said, no matter what you've confided." She looked up at him, and he then kissed her and hugged her. He didn't know whether he felt happy or sorry for her.

She pulled away gently. "It doesn't tickle, the mustache."

"I'm glad," he said.

"I like you too, baby." She kissed him this time, rather passionately. She then rubbed her nose against his. "You smell delicious."

"Old Spice…and horse sweat," he blurted, surprised at the smidgen of wit he uttered.

She nervously giggled. They then sat for a while and enjoyed the sounds of the city and being close together. Suddenly, she grasped his head and sucked on the very tip of his nose, giving it an audible smack upon release, and then a quick lick as a cat would the last droplet of milk.

"Now, what was that all about?" he said, rubbing his nose.

"You've got a hot nose, baby. I gotta cool it down somehow." She got up. "Let's go to the Magic Pan for crepes. My treat. I'm famished." She took him by the hand and began skipping. He held her back. "Don't you know how to skip?"

He paused, almost embarrassed. "I do."

"Let's then, just to the street. Then we'll walk. Okay?"

He smiled and began to skip to the start of the park. He then held her hand and walked toward Third Avenue.

They ate sumptuously.

He insisted that she order for him—and she did with the relish a grande dame would do for her young hired male escort—since he had no idea what a crepe was. He ate his portion with his usual gusto and kept his banter to a minimum secured from exposing his ignorance, for he felt that, sometimes, things were better left in the blind.

When the check came, she snatched it up like a hockey player executing a slap shot. "I said it was my treat!" It sounded more like a command than a statement. He pulled has hand back lest it be severed.

It went against his grain, this female revolution, this women's lib, or whatever she wanted to call it. But he knew one thing. No matter what it was, he was not going to carpet the day's forthcoming events with barbed wire. He was going to oil up his neck muscles and practice the nod of "yes." He did, however, as a gentleman, offer to leave the tip, but she would have no part of it. So he left it alone.

She suggested they traipse up to the Monkey House in the Central Park Zoo for comic relief barring any stench that would have them don gas masks. He was more inclined to take her downtown and show her where he worked, possibly winding up at Battery Park. His normal instinct was to protest, but since the declamatory insistence at paying the tab put him in new territory, he resorted to what he did with his mother, a single parent, with a steel-trapped mind and constitution. He was quite familiar with this breed of cat, and he knew from firsthand experience when it was best to keep one's mouth shut and go along for the ride. Perhaps, he thought, he had some things in common with Bea's father.

They sauntered up toward the park, she in seemingly verbal perpetual motion concerning her upcoming entry into college, her free ride to St. John's University, her self-directed tour of the campus long before official orientation, the workload, the twelve credits of Theology and fifteen credits of Philosophy as part of the core, and the wonder of the vast library and the bookstore. She told of leaping on unsuspecting professors who were just on campus for other matters asking a ton of questions regarding the culture, the course work, and what was expected of a freshman. Many of them, she mentioned, were so stunned by her exuberance that they gave her succinct pointers and pathways to take with great joy. She walked away from the experience, her feet hardly touching the ground, totally enraptured, and with enough data to probably conduct the orientation herself. She also stopped by the gym, viewed the pool, and chatted with the swimming coach. He invited her to come by at her convenience to test the waters and gave her an application to join the swim team.

"I'm so excited about this new journey in my life," she said. "The theology courses, and god! Fifteen credits of Philosophy. I can't wait to delve into those ideas. I'm so fascinated by it all, especially philosophy and how it's involved in religion."

"Bea," he asked, "do you want to be a nun?"

She put her fists on her hips. "Dee. Just because I'm interested in mountain climbing doesn't mean I'm hankering to scale Everest. Come on, what's the matter with you?"

"I mean all this talk about religion, I just don't understand it. Your parents were Commies—they were atheists—"

"And still are," she interrupted.

"I'm… I'm lost…"

"I'll explain. I am Catholic. I became a Catholic of my own volition. A priest in my parish baptized and confirmed me in the faith. I took the course. And I did the work. My mother was the one who said that I should have some kind of a firm foundation. They had Communism. It was their faith, their religion. And then it was violated so much so that everything they did in the name of that cause was bitterly stained. They were let down. Hoodwinked. They were lost. And they're still not over it. They took up social causes now as social humanists to try to remedy the wrongs of society and plow ahead. But I must say they're doing it on weakened backs and broken hearts. Dee, she told me it was devastating for both of them. Their betrayal has never been forgiven. It was an ultimate betrayal. Just think: they were living a grand lie for a good portion of their lives. It was Mom that said I had to find something to truly believe in—believe in with my heart and soul. There were too many people in the world who were floundering. She couldn't give me any direction. She just said that she opened me to the world and it was to be my decision because it was my life. So I searched, and I found the Catholic Church, and, funny thing, it came to me by chance. I was in the religion section in the Strand Bookstore, and a person—I don't for the life of me even remember what they looked like, if it was a man or a woman—just picked out this book, handed it to me, and said, 'You'll find this fascinating. I'm sure this is just what the doctor ordered.' It was Merton's *Seven Storey Mountain*."

"Maybe that person was your guardian angel," Dee said.

A look of surprise came over her face. "You know. You might be right. I love that idea. But getting back to the Merton book, it intrigued me and kind of changed me. I seemed to understand this man, Merton. I forced myself to go to the local church, and a young priest took me under his wing. I was confused and probed him with a million questions. He was very open, never proselytized, always gave me books from his own library to read, and we talked endlessly, and then I made the move and commitment... I guess as Mom did on deciding to have me, and I converted. I converted from nothing into something. And when I told Mom and Dad, they did not exactly hire a brass band. They never thought I'd go that radical, but being old radicals themselves, I had their blood, and that they understood. Mom just hoped that some Dead Sea Scroll would never pop up finding Jesus to be a charlatan. Both my parents gave me their, for lack of a better term, 'blessing.' But had I registered as a Republican, they would have disowned me. So becoming a Catholic wasn't all that bad. The lesser of the two evils in their book."

He laughed. "Wow. That's some story. I'm speechless."

"Do you go to Mass?" She was very earnest.

"Not since Dad died." He looked down and sighed.

"I understand. You don't have an answer. But sometimes it's a question we must seek, not an answer." She touched his arm. "Come with me to Mass tomorrow morning. I go at seven-thirty in my parish. It's quiet, just a few holy rollers, and the homily is usually wonderful. Short, no singing, we'll be out thirty-five to forty minutes.

That I *guarantee*. And they give Communion under both species."
She was very excited about that.

He suddenly saw himself reverently putting his lips on the same
spot she did on the chalice to take a sip of wine. It was a very sexy
thought and it then fleetingly vanished. He was silent and put his
hands in his pockets. "Let me mull on it."

"Fair enough."

"And I am very happy that you are happy about college. I am
too. In a sense you're like Bogie, three drinks ahead of the rest of the
world.'"

She held his hand. "Let's check out the seals."

As they watched the seals frolic in seemingly mindless calisthen-
ics, he started to think deeply about Bea. He was enamored by her:
the beauty he missed as her classmate, which he still couldn't grasp;
that feisty, independent streak; the almost overly sensual warmth—
perhaps the fact his mother wasn't too keen on her, he didn't know,
but his insides told him there was a major fascination enveloping his
being about her. He felt like a moth dallying with a flame.

She would never be content like the seals, playing the same
game, protected from predators, and fed by a prompt schedule. If
she was ever caged, she'd be like the lioness—slinking back and forth,
eyeing distractedly the meal tickets that leered at her behind the bars,
beyond her reach causing her no fear or excitement, save for a wayward hand that might come within striking distance for a snatched
taste of human flesh.

He watched her as she gazed at the seals, smiling at their antics.
He thought her profile was cameo perfect—the skin, flawless in his
mind, and the lipstick, worn off a tad with all the talking and the
eating, the outline still red; he found that very attractive.

She turned to him. "Not enjoying the seals?"

"You look better."

She warmly reached out and touched his cheek. "You are a
sweetie pie."

"You said you saw the pool at St. John's?"

"Yes," she said. "Olympic size. Beautiful. I think I might try it
out next week."

"Maybe I'll join you. We can do some laps."

Her eyes brightened. "Want to race…fifteen laps?" She saw him back up. "Oh, sorry, too much for you?"

He couldn't believe the affront. "No. Fifteen laps is fine."

"You want to bet?"

"If I give you a five-lap lead?"

"No. We shotgun start together."

"What's the wager?"

She thought for a moment. "A Gene Kelly picture and a meal in Little Italy. Pasta is my heroin." She stuck out her pinky.

He locked it with his and shook. "Deal!" he sputtered out. "Bea. I'm taller than you. I have a longer reach."

She turned back to the seals. "I'll beat you anyway."

He wasn't going to speak anymore on their bet. "Are you going to join the swim team?"

She lowered her head, shook it, and then looked at him with a partial frown. "You ever see those ditzies? I don't know what you call them…gnats, mayflies on a lawn? They hover in a group, and then, all of a sudden, they move in unison to another area of the lawn?"

"Yes. I know what you mean."

"Well, I'm not one of those ditzies. I'm not a team player. I'm a solo act."

"But, Bea. I don't understand. We teamed up on that term paper."

Without hesitation, she said, "Come walk with me." They walked down a path surrounded by trees. "You've got to understand something. We melded two unique efforts into a cohesive union. Both papers on their own were great, mind you. We succeeded in combining it toward the common goal. That's not teamwork. That's meshed dialogue. A written conversation with a universal end point." She almost looked sternly at him. "Period."

He looked confused. "Well," he chuckled, "that sounds like pure double talk to me. Wouldn't you say that's intellectual gibberish?"

She expulsed, "Absolutely not!"

And just then, at that very moment, he felt a tap on his shoulder. Looking over, he saw a cylindrical wad of gray-green-yellowish half-solid ooze, about the size of a pierogi, of pigeon crap slowly sluicing down his shirt. He sighed and shook his head. "Jesus Christ."

She joyously clapped. "Ha! Even the heavenly hosts are against you! I am right after all! A sign from heaven."

He reached into his back pocket for a handkerchief not paying attention to her. She quickly went into the large bag she was lugging. "No. I have tissues. I'll be careful." She managed to take it off with the least amount of smearing and dumped it into a wire basket. She then led him to the nearby water fountain and washed it off with another tissue. She even put a bit of musk oil in it.

"Now I smell like you."

"Does this mean I have competition?" She chuckled. "You have to admit the timing could not have been better."

"I don't believe this. Being shit on by a pigeon. Now I know what the statues feel like. I wish you could grab that flying rat, hold him down so I could shit on him! That'd show 'im!"

She laughed. "When you said I was giving you double talk, gibberish, God commanded the pigeon to evacuate his bowels on you. That was God's hand, not chance. It happened too perfectly."

"Bea. On that note, I will pay you no mind. All I know is one thing: I won the Croix de Guerre on my first date with you."

She side-lipped. "Just think of what's to come."

"That's what I'm worrying about."

She put her arm through his. "Let's see Fifth Avenue." And they began slowly walking toward 59th Street.

They strolled their way to the park's entrance by the Plaza Hotel and sat on a bench to talk about old movies and jazz and sometimes commenting on the goings and comings of the people at the Plaza. Sometimes they just watched and muttered but gave no verbal editorials. They just enjoyed their company and relished what was left of the day.

"When's your birthday?"

He said, "December."

She seethed, "Shoot!" and slapped her hand on her knee.

He turned to her. "Shoot?" As she looked at him, he continued, "What's 'shoot'?"

"I'm disciplining myself not," she explained, "not to use bad language." She then took a deep breath. "I'm... I'm older...than you. I'm October 29th." She then stared straight at the Plaza.

He enthusiastically jested, "Do older woman have better hormones? Are they grateful?"

She smacked his arm playfully, clipping his question.

"I best be getting you home. I have some stuff to help Mon with tomorrow, and if the offer's still there, I'll... I'll come to church with you."

She was thrilled. "Oh. Wonderful!" She squeezed his hand. "Mind if I just pop in to St. Pat's? It's on the way."

"Sure. Let's go," he said getting up, offering her his hand. "You know, we can browse through Tiffany's if you like. It's on the way."

She looked at him sternly. "Dee. You may never in your life ever hear this from any other woman in the world. Baubles don't interest me. If I had a paper clip on my finger, it'd be the same as the Hope diamond. I'm funny that way."

He shrugged his shoulders, and when they went into the cathedral, she immediately took from her bag a lightweight shawl and put it over her bare shoulders. She then dipped her finger in the holy water font and blessed herself, making a modest genuflection. He blessed himself, forgetting to use the holy water. "Come," she said, moving quickly down to the left side of the cathedral slightly past the altar to the grotto to St. Joseph. "I just want to light a candle."

He smiled, a little uncomfortable.

She reached into her purse for some coins, but he quickly produced a dollar and gave it to her. "On me, Bea."

"Thanks," she said. "Doesn't work that way." She managed to fish out the coins and dropped it into the receptacle, hearing the clank of change as it hit bottom. She then lit a candle, snuffed out the punk in the sand dish, and kneeled, closing her eyes and prayed, her lips moving almost imperceptibly.

He watched her, a bit ill at ease, and then walked toward the back of the altar and peered down at the crypts housing the deceased archbishops of New York.

Lost in thought, he jumped when she touched his arm. "Sorry." She put her palm over her mouth. "I startled you. I'm finished. Thanks for letting me do this. It's important to me."

"That's okay." He didn't know what else to say. "Pray for the world's starving kids?"

"No. I thanked St. Joseph," she paused and then confessed, "… for bringing you into my life." Her eyes glowed.

He felt a flush come over him. "Why…why," he stammered, "St. Joseph?"

"Anyone who can breakfast with the Immaculate Conception and the Incarnation and not crack up is my kind of saint."

He didn't understand but said, "Oh. A solid sort. Hands down."

She looked deeply at him. "Yes. Hands down."

He took her home.

In the vestibule of the apartment house, she looked bewitching. She pressed her body firmly against his, his back butting up against the mailboxes, put her arms around his neck, and gave him a very long passionate kiss. "Thank you, baby. I had a delightful time." Again, she kissed him very passionately. "You'll call me?" she whispered in his ear. "I want to know you got home safely."

"Yes.

"Mass tomorrow?"

"Yes."

She smiled and he touched her dimple. She then turned, unlocked the front door, and walked into the house.

He deeply sighed and walked back to the el in a cadence, almost like a blues lick repeating itself, never wanting to end.

As he sat on the train going home, he fell into the spell of the day, revisiting it as one would reread a favorite poem—the turn of phrase, her smell, the meter and rhythm, her infectious laugh, the very poignancy, her touch—until he felt the atmospheric pressure change, the car lights going out, and the wheels now clanging muted on the steel tracks. He had missed his stop. He was in the tunnel heading back into the city.

He got off at Grand Central and doubled back making sure he got off at Bridge Plaza to take the Astoria train home.

The day was pure poetry, he thought. Even the pinpoint precision bombing of the pigeon only added to the verse. Yes, he thought, Wordsworth was right: "the spontaneous overflow of powerful emotions recollected in tranquility," now made perfect sense to him. The day with Bea was a perfect couplet. He'd have to share that with her.

When he got home, he called her and fibbed that there was a police action at the Woodside Station that delayed him. He spoke with her for two hours until his mother chimed in, "Hey! I'm not a shareholder of AT&T. Enough already!"

He told his mother that Bea had asked him to seven-thirty Mass and that he was going to go. "May the angels and saints preserve and protect us. She must be a modern-day Svengali. I'll be damned!" his mother said.

He slept well and had extraordinary dreams.

That summer was magical. They saw each other as often as possible. With long hours on his job and her irregular schedule, teaching tap and ballet to kids at the Dance Center, they always managed to set a little time to be together.

And every Sunday, whether tempest, drought, or alien invasion, she whisked him to Mass.

But toward the very end of the summer, right before college, they became lovers. Her mother insisted that she get on "The Pill" because she didn't want any surprise packages that might cause interference with her mission at trying to save the world. Bea complied with her demand without hesitation.

5
CHAPTER

When Dee came back from the shoe store wearing brown wing tips, both Stanley and Pete stood up and ushered Dee to his desk as if he was a UN dignitary.

Pete addressed him with authority. "Son. Today you are going to learn bonds. Inside and out. We'll take you step by step. Don't just try to get it. Just get it! We'll know if you don't, 'cause you'll flub. We're going to drum it into you. You can ask the same question a thousand times. We're used to dealing with the severely retarded. We just want you to get it right at the first crack."

"You see," Stan chimed in," we don't want no mistakes. We're a staff of two. And we have a shitload to do just to get things done on time. We don't need no snafus to add to our workload."

"I'll do the best I can," Dee said, feeling boxed in.

"The best you can leaves plenty room for error," Pete said. "We need it letter-perfect. That's all. Savvy?"

"Loud and clear, sir," Dee said.

Both men smiled. "Now you're talkin', preparatory college boy," Stanley said.

"Stan," Pete said, "I'll start the kid out. You take over if I have to get on the pipe." Pete then picked out a coupon bond from the large metal cabinet on casters. He then pointed out and defined everything on it. Within five minutes, Dee's head was swimming in odd terms—dated date, payment date, records date, indenture, purpose, long and short coupons, due bill, trading flat—until he thought he was trying to memorize the periodic table of elements from another galaxy.

"Pete, you're throwing a lot at me."

"You got it?"

"There's a lot…"

"You got a photographic memory?"

"No," Dee said.

"What a kettle of fish!" Pete spat out. "Then, why in the hell ain't you writing this down! How'd you expect to make the grade in school, college boy? By your looks?"

Dee was agitated. Not even a half hour into his first job and he not only felt a total failure but, with the smirking peer of some of the other clerks, a jerk as well. He grabbed a pen and pad, got his composure back, and said, "I apologize. Got my pad and pen. Ready to go."

"Okay. We begin again. Show me that you got more than cottage cheese between the ears."

Dee felt slighted. "Can I make a stat of the certificate and write my notes on that stat?"

"Now, I like what I hear. Gaw'head. Use that machine there where I can see you."

Pete's comment seemed a bit strange to him. "Pete. I'm not going to steal it."

"Not you, kid. Sometimes there's a distraction and a bond winds up unattended on the machine, and then it winds up in the garbage. Unsuspecting, mind you. There's a lot of drafts around here called carelessness. Something like that happens, and holy hell! We got a headache that'd sink a battleship!"

Dee took the stat and came right back with the bond. "I'm going to put notes on it, read it over at lunch and on the subway going home tonight."

"No, you're not," Pete said. "That doesn't leave this office."

"Pete. It's just a photostat."

"Yeah. And you lose it on the subway and we're in some fix. Plenty of counterfeiters out there. I'll show you some bad stuff we got in the vault. Some," he said, kissing his fingers like a master chef, "a beauty to behold. Wish I had those sorts in my cellar with a printing press doing ten spots…and others. Jesus, Helen Keller could even spot it."

"Pete," Stan shouted. Pete looked up. "You're on the pipe!"

Pete McKelvey went to his desk and picked up the telephone and, after a moment, spilled out a stream of profanities that almost boarded on the poetic. His tone was that of a rabid dog.

Stanley said to Dee in awe of Pete's verbal blitz, "Pay attention here. This is how you clip coupons on bonds."

He showed Dee the "Coupon Clipper," a small T-square with sharpened edges and how to fill out the coupon envelopes for the bank deposit. "Groupings of ten, paper clip, same bond only, and groups of fifty, rubber band. Then put the envelope in the shoebox in the same order you took it out of the cabinet in. Clip them one at a time. Make sure you don't snip off the price, the payment date, or the signature on the bottom."

Dee did the first five bonds under Stan's supervision. Peter covered the phone receiver, looking at Dee. "And?"

Stan verified with a nod that Dee had passed muster without a mishap.

"Now, de-couponize those bonds, college boy. You're on your own. I'll spot check," Pete said, two funnels of smoke billowing from his nostrils as he lit up another cigarette.

About a half hour into the coupon clipping, which was rather dull work, Pete hollered, slamming his phone down, "Hey, college boy!" Dee quickly looked up, a bit of boredom in his eyes. "Go to the chute. It's right by Parcher's office. Margin's sending me two flower bond instructions. One is a million two to Hutton and the other is seven fifty to Bache. Got to make those deliveries now. Stan's getting the bonds. Hurry, and bring me what you done. Lemme check 'em."

Dee brought Pete the box of coupons and then scooted around the bend to gather the delivery instruction Pete requested. The chute was a hole in the ceiling, and attached to it was a plexiglass structure so that when the fanfold instructions were dropped from the fourteenth floor, it wouldn't scatter on the floor. It fell into a heavy-duty wire basket. Dee fished out the two instructions and ran back to Pete only to see his face beet-red, a blue vein bulging on his forehead. He was holding up three fingers of his right hand and arrow pointing to it with his left shouting, "Hey, college preparatory boy! And we can't count this high!"

Dee felt as if his throat had been swabbed out with sand. He couldn't swallow, and pain seized his gut.

"Give Stan the instructions and get your keister over here!"

Dee dropped off the instructions with Stan and stood next to Pete. He prayed that the shaking in his legs didn't show through the suit pants.

"Six coupons. Two issues. And you failed to segregate them. Just because the color of the bond, the coupon, and the maturity date is the same doesn't mean it's the same bond! They're both dormitory authorities. One is CCNY and the other Brooklyn College. Are they the same place? Are they the same school? That's like saying New York and California are the same—God forbid." He glanced at Dee as he shook his head. "Your attention to detail stinks! If you was a brain surgeon, a lot a patients would be in the cemetery." Pete sighed. "Plus, look how you clipped these three! You clipped three-quarters of the coupon leaving the remaining quarter on the corpus—that's mutilation! You're not supposed to clip them in a group! You clip 'em one at a time. Didn't you see this when you counted them?" Pete didn't wait for an answer. "Now I have to get them validated! A waste of time, that's what you caused me. Just sit, sit the hell down. Gotta fix up these torn coupons with scotch tape and get Parcher to sign the validation stamp I have to affix to 'em!"

When Pete returned from Jerry Parcher's office, he said to Dee, "Jerry already has writer's cramp. He don't need no more bullshit signin' to do! He's not a happy boy—and this don't help his ulcer any. Now! You come with me!"

Dee was scared. He got up and followed Pete into the conference room.

When they both got in, Pete slammed the door shut. "Sit down and don't even make one peep!"

Dee sat in a chair, his ice-cold, wet hands in his lap, his stomach bubbling, and his heart pounding like a timpani roll. He hoped he wasn't going to throw up.

Pete's face looked ghoulish. It was like something out of a B-grade horror movie. "This firm brought you on board in good faith. Jack vouched for you, and I—mind you, yes, it was me—I accepted his word that you were a smart kid and a good egg. You are supposed to be an asset to me." He then lit up a cigarette, side-spitting out a flake of tobacco. "You're not even a liability." He stared straight into Dee's eyes. "You're a fuck-up!"

Dee had never been spoken to before in such a manner. He uttered a quivering, "Please…"

Pete slammed his palm on the table so hard that Dee shook in his seat, startled, and the ashtray's squelched butts and ashes scattered all over the table. "Shut up! I said not a peep! And, goddamnit, I mean it!"

At that point Dee resigned himself to the fact that he was going to be executed. He simply couldn't understand why this "bond sin" that he committed was so grave.

But he surrendered to his fate. He had made a tragic mistake. Unknowingly. He thought of jumping out the thirteenth-floor window. Forty Wall Street was an old building, and the windows still could be opened. That would solve his problem, he thought.

Being fired was so shameful and embarrassing, especially on the very first day of his first job, and before noon, no less, and then having to go home and tell his mother, and Pete informing Jack Irving. That, and that alone, would be worse than death. If he didn't kill himself, he'd have to live the rest of his life with that label, "fuck-up," branded on his soul. He didn't have the nature to just fluff it off. His conscience was speckled with too much scruple. He'd have to slug out each day knowing that that was what he was. And he could never run away from it. Even to some remote area in China. There'd always be someone who would know and then tell others. He truly would have to kill himself. Perhaps step off the subway platform—that would do it, and it would seem to the onlookers that he just slipped…it wasn't his fault. It would be…quick, a sudden pain, and…over.

Pete seemed to have simmered down. His face finally took on the look of a human being, and the blue bulge in his forehead dissipated. There was a lot of commotion outside. Dee heard the yelling.

But the parties out on the floor knew never to interrupt Pete while he was in the conference room. Even if there was an enemy invasion.

"Now," he said, taking a long drag on his cigarette, "if I had my way, I'd boot you the hell out of here. You're like a third tit—fucking useless. But"—as he puffed out smoke rings—"because of my deep regard and long association with Jack Irving, I'm going to give you a chance to wipe the slate clean. Mind you, I'm very reluctant to do this. You've already screwed up my day. But it's come to my attention, through Jerry Parker, that we are missing a very important, very crucial tool to our organization. It's something the bond desk needs, and I, especially, need. It's called a bond stretcher."

"Can I write that down?" Dee timidly asked.

Pete frowned. "You could remember that." His tone was very sarcastic.

"Every," he continued, "member firm is given one by the Exchange, and yearly we have to return it for updates. It gives us the status of outstanding issues, calculates accrued interest on irregular payers like medium-term notes, and earmarks defunct issues, amongst a load of other things. Now, if we lose it, we lose our membership with the Exchange, and once a client hears about that…"— Pete shook his head and made a slitting-one's-throat gesture with his finger—"might as well try to find a job in civil service. And who the hell wants to be a motorman on the subway?"

"What does it look like?" Dee asked, his composure slowly coming back.

"It's about twelve inches by six inches, so it's not something you'd put in your pocket. It was last known to be with Vance Barlow. Go see him. If he doesn't have it, maybe…he'll put you in the direction it might be. Also, wolf down a sandwich for lunch. Take only twenty minutes. I'll okay it on your time card. You'll get the OT. Don't worry 'bout that. You need all the time you can get your hands on. And no dawdling around. Barlow's on the seventh floor."

They sat facing each other. Dee didn't say a word. He was afraid to.

"What the hell," Pete yelled, "you gaping at! Get the hell out of here and find it!"

Dee ran out of the office and went to the bathroom. He relieved himself and dry-heaved, the bile like acid in his throat. He then slurped some water out of the sink, washed his hands and face to at least look somewhat presentable to the senior partner of the firm, ran to the elevator, and pushed the down button.

Dee got off at the seventh floor. He was calming down. What he walked into looked like a grand library in a Fifth Avenue mansion. It was mahogany paneled with rows upon rows of American first editions in mint dust jackets behind glass. He smiled as he peered at them, wishing to hold them. Or even better, to smell them. He loved the musty aroma of old books. Some of the authors he had read. Some were new to him.

Walking past the books, there was a large sitting room with plush chairs, a couch, and a fireplace that looked real. He had never seen one in an office building before. This was a perfect place, he thought, for business…or…a dalliance.

Toward the end of the corridor, a very attractive receptionist greeted him. "Mr. Felico?"

"Yes," he said, a bit taken by the fact that she knew his name. "Mr. Barlow is expecting you. Mr. McKelvey called on your behalf. Go right in."

When he walked in Vance Barlow's office, feeling a bit like some sort of royalty, he saw a heavyset man with white hair parted slightly to the left of the middle, slicked back with a ruddy complexion speaking on the phone. He waved him in and motioned for him to sit down. Barlow covered the mouthpiece of the phone and said, "Be with you in a sec."

Dee nodded in acknowledgment and scanned the room. It wasn't, he thought, terribly regal for a senior partner. What did catch his eye was a poled, full size American flag and Marine Corps flag flanking the U-shaped desk Barlow was sitting behind.

On one wall were two black-and-white photographs. One was of a boy and a man dressed in riding boots, jodhpurs, and leather flying caps standing next to a biplane. The man was smiling. The boy looked scared.

The other photograph was a ceremonial decoration shot. President Franklin Roosevelt was pinning a medal on a very gaunt-looking marine. Alongside the marine were two Marine Corps officers who Dee recognized immediately.

"Well," Barlow signed. "Sorry about that." He got up and walked around his desk, his hand extended. "You're Dee Felico. Jack told me a lot about you. I'm Vance Barlow."

They shook hands. Dee was grateful his hand was not palm-sweaty and cold any longer. Barlow placed his hand on the boy's shoulder and eased him back into the chair. "Glad you're on board with us. There's a lot to learn here. Maybe something might meet your fancy."

"Thank you," Dee said, not realizing that his eyes wandered over to the photographs.

Barlow noticed the eye shift and smiled. "A lot of people get intrigued with those photos." Barlow then turned and looked at them. "That one is of my father and me as a little boy. He loved to fly. In fact, he was in the Lafayette Escadrille during the First World War. As you can see, I was scared stiff. I still white-knuckle it on planes, particularly on takeoffs and landings. No window seat for me. I always wanted that in my office." He then sighed. "The other one...well, my dad insisted on me putting it here. It's—"

Dee suddenly interrupted, "You were a commando."

Barlow, a bit surprised, looked at Dee. "Why did you say that?"

Dee pointed to the older marine officer. "That's Evans Carlson. And the officer next to him is James Roosevelt, the president's son. You were in the Raider Battalion."

"Young man," Barlow said, "I am impressed. Are you a military history buff?"

"No. I know a lot about commandos." He stared at the photo and then slowly turned to Barlow. "You see, my dad was one too."

"Really?"

Dee nodded.

"What branch of service?"

"Army. He worked for Colonel Donovan."

Barlow sat back in his chair and whistled in surprise. "Wow." After a long pause, he said, "OSS. May I ask where? Or is that still classified."

"Greece," Dee said. "And he was also in the Greek Civil War for a short time. He resigned his commission and went back to teaching at Columbia."

"Why?"

"He found it repugnant to fight against the very partisans who saved his life and helped him fight against the Nazis. He couldn't stomach that. He simply left and never regretted it."

"I see. A man of high principle. Someone certainly to emulate."

They remained silent for a minute until Barlow changed the conversation. "Jack tells me you're going to Queens College."

"Yes. I am. Don't know yet what I want to do."

"Welcome to the club," Barlow laughed. "I'm still trying to figure that out for myself too."

"Mr. Barlow," Dee said, looking at his wristwatch, "Mr. McKelvey sent me down here to see if you have the bond stretcher."

Barlow's face suddenly ridged with concern. "The bond stretcher?" He stood up "You mean they can't find it?"

"No. He said you had it."

"Maybe a week ago." His brows furrowed. "I gave it back… wait! I think I sent it over to Bill Welsch. He's our head floor trader at the Exchange. Yes. He has it. Go there. I'll call him to alert security that you're on your way. I'll inform McKelvey."

Dee got up. Barlow shook his hand. "Call me the second you find it. I can't emphasize this enough." He gave him his business card. "My private number. I always pick that one up myself. I don't like not knowing where it is. Pete told you about how vital a tool it is and its importance?"

"Yes, sir. Mr. McKelvey told me all about it."

"Okay. You know the gravity of the issue. Looks like you're on a commando mission."

Dee said, "I won't let you down," as he ran out of the office.

Barlow yelled as Dee ran to the elevators. "Make sure you have your company badge! They need to see that ID!"

"I have it!" he yelled back as he stepped into the elevator.

When Dee hit the lobby, he bolted out of the building running across Wall Street, careened around the main doors of Morgan Guaranty, and zipped across Broad Street to the Exchange's entrance.

He was met by a floor clerk garbed in a light blue jacket with the firm's name stitched over the pocket and a large picture ID badge hanging around his neck.

"You Felico?"

"Yeah," Dee sputtered.

"Just get your badge out. I got you signed in. Gotta show the guard," the clerk spoke like a machine-gun report.

After Dee showed the guard the badge, he said, "Where to?"

"Just follow me. It's like a football game play in action. Just dodge the moving bodies and don't, for Christ's sake, stand still. Someone will bowl you over."

"Okay," Dee said, excitement all around him in the financial arena. There was heavy action happening all around him. "I'll hug your ass." He followed the clerk like a caboose on a runaway train until he reached the Barlow Brothers' booth. There he met a bald man with half-glasses who had the eyes of a wolf. His face was cringed with annoyance. "You the kid Vance called about?" There was a din of yells and shouts, scurrying bodies, and flying paper tickets.

"What?" Dee could hardly hear him with the ringing of phones and shouts all around him.

"You Felico?"

"Yes."

The man looked as if he was going to snap Dee's head off. "Focus on me. Not the noise. And turn up your ears! I canvassed my guys. No one here has the bond stretcher! Hear?"

"Yes, I hear you. Any idea where it might be?"

"You better goddamn well find it!" He turned overhearing a clerk on the phone taking an order, pivoted, eyeing one of his trader's at one of the posts, and hand signaled, calling out to the clerk behind him, "Thirty thousand at seven-eight! And work the order!" Then he turned back to Dee. "I'm Bill Welsch. We had the stretcher, but one of my guys insists that Herman Schindler, head of Margin, has it.

Why him? Beats me. He's a human calculating machine. But anyway, that's the only lead we got. He's on the fourteenth floor. One of my clerks will tell him you're on the way. See him! We can't afford to have that thing misplaced. You better get going. Find your way out?"

Dee shook his head, wrote Herman Schindler's name on a buy ticket, and ran out the same way he came in.

As it was getting close to lunchtime, Dee, rather than jogging back to the office, angled up to Broadway and went into Wolfe's Deli to order a ham and cheese sandwich and a Coke. It didn't take much time. He was ahead of the lunchtime blitz.

When he got back to the office, he dropped his lunch on his desk as Pete inquired, "So?"

"Nothing yet. I was told to see Mr. Schindler."

"Herman Schindler?" Pete's face screwed up as if he was sucking on a lemon. "Every time I hear that name I get the horrors."

Dee took the stairs rather than the elevator to the fourteenth floor. A margin clerk was walking by when he opened the door and he asked where Schindler's office was. The clerk's arms went up, pointing to a very large glass-walled corner office overlooking Chase Manhattan Plaza, and uttered, almost with disdain, "There," and walked off.

Before Dee got into Schindler's office, an elderly secretary with bluish-white hair permed like a honeycomb said, "Mr. Felico, Mr. Schindler advised me you were coming. He will see you momentarily." Dee noted that Schindler was filing his nails, a waste basket squeezed between his knees catching the filings.

"Kindly," the secretary said, "wipe your shoes on that welcome mat. Mr. Schindler has a strong aversion for people tracking filth onto his carpet."

"Yes, ma'am," Dee said and thoroughly scuffed his soles on the mat in front on Schindler's office as Schindler scrutinized the effort.

Once Dee finished, he said, "Is this okay?" showing her his cleaned soles.

She pursed her lips, squinting, and said, "Indeed. You may go in."

He thanked her and walked into the office.

"Mr. Felico," Schindler said in a booming voice. "Many thanks for following my protocol. Please, please. Come, come, come and sit here in front of my desk so we can talk."

Everything Dee saw in Schindler's office was immaculate. All things within were placed in such a way as to make it comfortably pleasing to the eye. The office even smelled fresh. Schindler was impeccably dressed and groomed. His smile was genuine, but his teeth appeared to be a bit too perfect, a tad too large. It reminded Dee of the smile a ventriloquist's dummy would have.

Dee shook hands with Schindler and sat down.

"Yes, Jack's friend, you do keep good company. Jack…a wonderful person and an extraordinary arbitrageur, but firstly, I must… I must," he said, tapping his chest, "explain my penchant for this wiping-of-shoe-soles procedure." He stood up and, with a sweep of his arm, said, "All this…all this… I, and I alone, put together. I decorated this office at great expense from my own resources, and I might add, personal inconvenience. I do have oodles of other things I'm involved with. But once done, it was perfect—*tres magnifique*. And then," his voice growing loud and stern, "some bumbling galoot moron, some cretin from the runner's cage, traipsed in here unbeknownst to me or even Ms. Tittleberg, my secretary, who was lunching at the time, having first stepped in a horsefly's haven of canine essence; his good luck, and my bad, and tracked up my carpet with such dreck, such desecration, that I, upon viewing it, almost went into a fit of apoplexy. Thank the good Lord that I come from good stock and have a hearty constitution. That, and that alone, saved the firm a worker's compensation issue had I landed in the ER of Beekman Hospital. I had a colleague with me at the time. I was so appalled, so embarrassed. It took a week to properly fumigate the office. The effluvia that wafted off that carpet… I can only compare it to a slit-trench. So"—he put up his arms—"you can readily see why I had to adopt this protocol."

"Yes," Dee interjected, "to alleviate any future occurrences of this nature from ever happening again."

"Absolutely," Schindler said with relish. He sat down appearing a bit exhausted. He observed Dee as if he was bidding for him at an auction. "Now, young man, what can I do for you?"

"I was told by Mr. Welsch that you, or one of your staff, might have the bond stretcher."

Schindler immediately said, "I have no need for it, save, perhaps to double-check on a default issue, but that would be once in a blue moon. And as for calculating, I do it, as does my staff, by hand. Keeps the mind agile, and you needn't worry if the electric goes out." He chuckled a little. "My adage has always been that if paper and pencil were good enough for Charles Steinmetz, it's good enough for me."

Dee had no idea who Charles Steinmetz was. He just politely sat and said nothing.

"However," Schindler continued, "if by the off chance one of my staff has it, I'll call them out on it. Come." He got up and walked out of his office. He pulled from his suit pocket a police whistle and blew it loudly. Everyone stopped work. Those on the phone put the call on hold. "Gentlemen! Listen up! Mr. Felico is seeking the bond stretcher. If any of you have it or know of its whereabouts, please come forward." No one moved. Schindler scanned the floor and then turned to Dee. "I'm afraid we cannot help." He then addressed his staff. "You may continue with your work. Thank you."

"Mr. Schindler," Dee said, a little exasperated. "I have to find it. Both Mr. Barlow and Mr. McKelvey placed their faith in me. Can you give me some direction? Please?"

Schindler thought for a moment. "Possibly Donnie Martino in the Purchase and Sales department. That's the twelfth floor. Go there. You'll find it. Of that, I have no doubt. A pleasure." He shook Dee's hand, went back into his office, and, with a feather duster he secured from under his desk, dusted the chair Dee had been sitting on. He then took an aerosol can out of his desk drawer and sprayed the area thoroughly as Dee walked away.

Since it was already well into the lunch hour, Dee thought it best to stop off at his desk, eat his sandwich and have his Coke, and maybe have the remaining ten minutes of his twenty minutes chow down to take a mental pause. He felt like he was plowing a wheat field with a manual mower.

Pete was away from his desk when he got to the area. He opened the brown bag, unwrapped his ham and cheese on white, and opened his Coke. He chomped on his first bite just as Pete stormed by. "Find it, college boy?"

Dee shook his head since his mouth was full.

"Then what in blazes are you doing here! C'mon, get the hell outta here and look!" Pete pushed on his chair. "Get up, get up, get up!"

Dee spat out his half-chewed sandwich into the garbage can. "You told me," he said, wiping his mouth, "to take twenty minutes. I'm not even here a minute."

"Yes! But not here! On the fly! Eat while you look! You can't do this job sitting on your ass! What do you think this is, a Country Club? Get going!"

Dee's stomach tightened. His appetite was totally gone. "Okay, okay, okay," he muttered in disgust, packing the rest of his sandwich and putting it back in the bag.

Dee heard him say as he walked toward the elevators, "You know, we got a business to run here, and the clock's always ticking!"

Dee's stomach was still undergoing volcanic activity when he reached the P and S department. What he saw there was more pandemonium, chaos, and outright hostility than he witnessed on the floor of the Exchange. Clerks were hollering on the phones confirming trades, cursing over late trade corrections, and passing long computer sheets to each other with seemingly monosyllabic instructions.

In a small paper-strewn glass-walled office, Dee saw Donnie Martino, his name stenciled on the door, the *M* of the last name slightly off from the other letters, screaming at a man standing before him. Martino was so loud he was overpowering the din of the department. Dee felt you could have heard him in Jersey City. The man taking the abuse looked like he was embalmed. Martino was shaking a phone at him with what looked like the intent to kill.

An older man, a midget standing no more than a yard tall, approached Dee. "You the kid, Felico, Jack's friend?" To Dee, he looked like a fireplug with feet.

Dee laughed, a bit shocked at the size of the man. "Everybody seems to know who I am."

"With the washwomen and the rumor mill on full blast, there's little that we miss around here. I'm Vito Dimone."

They shook hands.

"Am I going to witness a murder here?" Dee asked.

Vito let out a high-pitched laugh. "Kid, he's just warming up. But it shouldn't be long now. I know his antics."

Just as Dee figured that Martino was going to hit the guy with the phone, he turned and slammed it back on the cradle with such force that he broke it. "That's the fourth one this quarter," Vito said, shaking his head. "Telephone guys ain't going to be happy."

Martino opened the door and threw the guy out of his office saying, "Now get back to work! And if I catch you rolling your eyes, I'll fire you faster than the speed of light."

Vito walked into Martino's office and disconnected the phone. "You get the bottle of hooch for the phone guy this time." He stuck his thumb in Dee's direction. "The kid, Jack's friend, wants to see you."

Martino's teeth were crooked. He had the head the size of a St. Bernard and a flattened nose that had been the receiving end of some major disagreements. "Okay. Come on in, sonny." His voice modulated to an ear-pleasing timbre, quite a switch from his howl moments before. He picked up a huge computer run from a chair and said, "Sit." Dee sat down but adjusted himself quickly since the right armrest needed a good tightening. "What's up?"

"Mr. McKelvey and Mr. Barlow are asking me to find the bond stretcher. Do you have it?"

Martino frowned momentarily in thought. "Stretch!" he cried out. Vito sauntered in.

Dee found that moniker very untoward, but Vito was not offended by it.

"What do you want?" Vito asked.

"The bond stretcher. Did I have it?"

"What am I, your personal secretary? Of course you had it!" Vito saw the confusion in Martino's eyes. "You also had a couple of marriages too that went sour. Remember that? And you're still wearing a wedding band. So what do you want from me?"

Martino sneered at him. "Where'd I put it?"

"Donnie. I'm not clairvoyant. In this office…if they could ever pay a person enough to clean it up—they'd probably find Amelia Earhart. So don't ask me stupid questions."

"Jesus Christ, Vito! Forget Barlow. Pete McKelvey's the one on the hunt! And dealing with him when his Irish is up is like having a rectal exam by a porcupine."

Dee couldn't believe that Martino, this tough-looking guy, was afraid of Pete McKelvey. Vito said, "So what's the game plan?"

"I'll check my office. I'll tell the guys outside." He hiked his pants over his ample belly and rushed out of the office. "Guys!" Martino yelled. "I need to have the department policed for the bond stretcher. Every drawer, cabinet, under the stacks of runs, under the desks—all over! No one does his own desk! Switch! No foul-ups are acceptable. You guys on the phones, alternate the calls. If we come up clean, and I happen to find it buried here, someone's ass will not only be in a sling, I'll see to it that no fucking Christmas bonus will be handed out!" He stood with hands on his hips. "Now snap to it!"

As the P and S personnel rummaged for the bond stretcher, Martino said, "Vito! Take the kid into the archives room. No stone unturned. And don't forget the shitter too. I've found some runs on that window sill. I'll do my office."

The archives room was a preliminary storage area of boxed brokerage records awaiting pickup to a warehouse in Brooklyn where they would lay in wait for seven years by law before being incinerated. The room was managed by a meticulously dressed man doing the New York Sunday *Times* crossword puzzle in ink called Mr. Martin. The room was perfectly stacked and labeled. It had the feel of a museum exhibit.

It was not in the archives room nor in the men's room, as Mr. Martin noted. It took well over two hours for Martino and his crew to end the search. The department looked the most ordered it did in years, but the bond stretcher was still a missing issue.

Vito asked Mr. Martin, "You think Lenny might have it in the Vault?"

"Not in a million years," Mr. Martin quipped, "but I'd check with Mr. Deegan in Fixed Income Trading. The odds are greater there than anywhere else. And"—he cleared his throat—"I only bet on sure things."

"Mr. Martin," Dee asked, "to cover all bases, do you think I should try the vault just to play it safe?"

"You can follow your heart. But my money would be on Mr. Deegan."

Dee looked at Vito for direction.

"I'd take Mr. Martin's suggestion seriously."

Martino rushed into the archives room. "I gave the department the white glove, but sorry, Sonny. No dice with the stretcher. Check with Deegan down in bond trading, eleventh floor."

That ended the case for Dee. He thanked the guys and then ran to the stairwell, taking the stairs four at a clip and almost taking a tumble in the process. The butterflies in his stomach were no longer flying in formation. It was more like a World War One dogfight.

It was a little past the top of the hour of four when he got to the trading room. Startled that it was empty save two traders manning the desk, he saw the entire staff in a large glass-walled conference room. Dee ran to the desk of an older woman just outside the conference room. "I have to see Mr. Deegan," Dee spat out.

She raised an eyebrow looking at him like he was a plate of cold eggs. "He's in a meeting, young man. Clearly, you can see that, young man."

"Which one is he?"

She sighed. "He's the gentleman holding court. It is the monthly strategy meeting."

Dee saw a large man with his bow tie undone, hanging from his open collar, gesticulating with his right hand. He was holding his glasses. "I have to talk to him. I don't have much time. It's extremely important."

"You are welcome to wait until the meeting is over," she said, perusing an issue of *Cosmopolitan*.

"How long do you think it'll be?"

"Depends. Sometimes they order in supper. It can go on for a few hours."

"I can't wait that long!" Dee snapped.

She turned and glowered at him. "Watch your tone, young man! What's it about?"

"Excuse me, ma'am, but it's about something that Mr. McKelvey needs."

She frowned. "Pete McKelvey is not a partner. He can wait." And just as Dee was going to interject, she continued, "However, I will see if Mr. Deegan can accommodate you. This, young man, is very unorthodox. Let me see what I can do."

It was getting late, and he was beginning to feel his legs shake and his face burn as if it was splashed with acid. The older lady, whose nameplate he finally spied, stating Elsie Levine, Executive Secretary, went to the glass, and tapped on it. Deegan looked up and ordered one of the traders to open the door at the far end.

Elsie walked to where Deegan was sitting and she spoke to him briefly. He put on his glasses and momentarily peered at Dee. He seemed annoyed at the interruption and, after a brief exchange, sent Elsie Levine back out.

"He'll see you when the meeting's over—should be fifteen, maybe twenty more minutes—but I must warn you, he does have a habit of pontificating, and punctuality is not his forte."

Dee thanked her and sat down by her desk checking his wristwatch incessantly, his right leg bouncing up and down quickly, creating a vibration that had Elsie Levine's ashtray doing a high-pitched trill.

At five minutes to five, with the meeting showing no signs of breaking up, Dee jumped up and pounded on the glass window with his fist and then tried to open the locked door. Someone unlocked it from inside and Dee flew in, yelling, "I'm sorry, but—"

Deegan blared, "Who the hell do you think you are barging in to my meeting! Elsie! Call security!"

Dee shouted, his voice strained and quivering, "I'm here by orders of Mr. McKelvey and Mr. Barlow to find the bond stretcher!"

Deegan shot up so fast his back legs pushed his chair crashing against the wall.

"The bond stretcher! You can't find the bond stretcher!?" He scanned the room. "Any you guys have it!"

The entire meeting room responded in the negative. "Jesus Christ! We have a big fuckin' problem!" Deegan rushed to Dee. "Come with me! We've got to tell Barlow!" He grabbed Dee by the arm tightly. "Now!" They both ran to the elevators. "Why the hell didn't—forget it."

"Mr. D-D-Deegan," Dee was stammering. He didn't know what to say. He was totally spooked.

They got to the seventh floor and jogged to Barlow's office, passing up his secretary. Deegan was the first in. Vance Barlow was just putting on his suit jacket, calling it a day.

"Vance. We can't find the bond stretcher!"

Barlow leered at Dee. "What!" He pointed his index finger at Dee. "I told you—"

Dee was practically crying. "Mr. Barlow, I went everywhere—even the men's room was searched by P and S. I saw everybody…"—and then he clenched his stomach—"I'm going to be sick…"

Barlow rushed behind his desk for a trash can and made it back just as Dee violently retched and dry-heaved a watery bile. Deegan held his brow as the spasms came. After it subsided, Barlow said softly, "Dee, Dee, easy, easy…calm down."

Dee, tears dripping down his cheeks, ashamed, embarrassed, and totally defeated, tried to apologize with a coughed-up, "I'm sorry. I tried… I tried…"

"Take a breath," Deegan said in a soothingly calm voice. "Take a breath, Dee, one breath at a time." He was rubbing his back and shoulder. "Come on, son, calm down."

Vance Barlow was squatting in front of Dee. "Sit on the couch." They both eased him on the couch, Dee's hands holding his head. "Listen to me. Please. Listen to me."

Dee looked at Vance Barlow through tear-blurred eyes.

"Dee," Barlow said slowly, "there is no bond stretcher."

Dee blinked, confusion wrinkling his face, not understanding.

Deegan sat next to him, his arm over Dee's shoulder. "Son, there is no bond stretcher. There never was a bond stretcher. This was a test to see what you are made of. This was your initiation."

Vance chimed in, "And you passed with flying colors. You stuck it out to the very end. Took the responsibility and accepted it. Pete McKelvey did this to me when I was your age, and my father owned the business. When I couldn't find it, I thought I was going to be the cause of my father jumping out of a window. This test tells us more about you than you can put on a resume or have a guy like Jack sell us your worth. I am very proud of you and I am delighted to officially welcome you on board."

"I ditto that," Deegan said, smiling.

"If you ever join a frat in college and have Hell Night or Hell Week, it'll be a piece a cake compared to this. Come on, Dee. Go into my bathroom here and freshen up. Then say good night to Pete and Stan, punch out, get a good night's sleep. We have a boatload of work for you to do tomorrow." Both Deegan and Barlow shook his hand.

Dee nervously laughed. "I can't believe this…"

When Dee had finished, both Deegan and Barlow walked him to the elevators. "See you in the morning."

Dee gave them both a mock salute with his index finger. "I'll be here bright and early."

When Dee got back up to his desk, both Pete and Stan were standing, looking at him sternly. Dee picked up the bag containing his untouched lunch and hurled it at Pete. It bounced off his shoulder. "If my parents didn't bring me up properly, I'd kick the shit out of both of you old fossils!"

Stan and Pete laughed loudly. "Welcome on board, college boy. Sorry. Welcome on board, Dee."

"Catch you in the a.m.," Stan said as Dee left to punch out and go home.

Pete turned to Stan. "What say we go down to Harry's for a pop?"

Stan cringed. "I wouldn't drink with you if you was the last guy on Earth."

"I'm buying."

Stan smiled. "Why, that's different."

6
CHAPTER

That one particular summer, Benny Goodman's Orchestra played a concert in Central Park. They came prepared with knapsacks stuffed with blankets, pillows, snacks, and a bottle of wine. They set up shop a little off from the thick of the crowd, which was mostly of the World War Two and Korean War generation, for a bit of privacy. Dee opened the wine and gulped down several glasses as Bea opened up a bag of chips and a can of soda since she did not like the taste of wine. It was a brutally hot, still, asphalt-melting twilight as only New York could brew with a humidity that bathed the body with a sluicing stickiness. The only thing that brought them out was the King of Swing. And the music was just as hot.

And when they began to play the original arrangements, many in the crowd couldn't contain themselves and started to dance. Many danced as they did as teenagers who cut class to see Goodman at the Paramount. Shirts and pants dampened with sweat and brows beaded and dripped but smiles glowed, and forgotten steps suddenly came back a bit stiffer and weighted due to thickening waists and unoiled knees but always on beat, always on cue. Dee and Bea even went up and did the Lindy. Bea embellished on her steps unobtrusively so as not to upstage Dee's lead. And so impressed were some of the folks around them that they stopped, circled them, and clapped in beat with Goodman's drummer. At one point, close to the stage, Dee and Bea breaking into a unified time-step before spinning back into the standard jitterbug moves, Goodman eyed them and gave them a gracious approval nod with his clarinet, his mouth curled upward as he played which one might take as a smile.

When the song came to its rousting end, the throng around them cheered and applauded, some shouting, "Your parents taught you well! Just like when we were kids!"

Thrilled and a little winded from the fast dance, they walked back to their spot, sweeping their brows with wet hands. Dee was simply parched and, when he got back to their spot, quaffed the rest of the wine, its cold tartness relieving the dryness in his throat. He grabbed some chips from the bag and chomped on them ravenously. He then plopped down next to Bea. "Now I know what it feels like to be a loin-chop on the grill."

"It's brutal," Bea said, "but boy, that music's great."

Dee stuffed some bubble gum in his mouth to cleanse his breath and mask the aroma of wine. He knew, at some point, he was going to kiss her and didn't want to impose on her anything she wasn't too keen on. He popped in a couple more Bazooka bubble gum cubes into his mouth just for safe measure.

She reclined on the blanket, her head on the pillow, her hair away from her face, seeking the slightest bit of breeze that might, by chance, come. Her face, due to the sweat, was a sheen and seemed to glow, her mouth parting slightly, as she took small wisps of breath in the jungle-like heat, and then she closed her eyes. He gazed at her in adoration.

When she opened her eyes, they were languid, provocative slits. She smiled ever so slightly. He spat out his gum.

And as she peered into his eyes, she saw a certain strangeness that she didn't understand. "What is it, Dee?" she whispered.

"Don't move."

She tightened, alarmed. "An insect? A spider?"

His face was pale. "The gum landed in your hair."

"What!"

"God, I'm so sorry. I just…"

She tried to jump up, but he held her down. "Don't move. That jostle threw another wisp of your hair into the gum." He closed his eyes momentarily, a pain deep in his stomach. A mat of hair was already in the pink gooey mass. "See if you can calm down. I have an idea."

"Calm down! I have no compact with me. I can't see it! I'm going to explode!"

"Do you have a Kleenex so I can just squeeze it together to contain it?"

"My bag, my bag!" She was shivering. "In my bag!"

He rummaged through her large bag feeling many things but not feeling tissues.

"In the pouch!" she implored. "In the pouch!"

He frantically said, "The pouch?" He froze. What he viewed was a bag with multiple zippers and buttoned compartments. He was stopped dead as if he was trying to defuse a bomb. "The pouch?"

"Just gimme the bag! Gimme the bag, gimme the bag!"

He gave her the bag, and she found it instantly, holding herself as stiff as a plank, only her arms negotiating the issue. She gave him the tissue packet and threw the bag aside.

He took out several tissues and covered the pink wad of gum. Then he took out his keys and picked out his nail clipper and began to carefully sever the hairs around the thick ooze of sticky gum.

"Please, please, please, be careful." Her eyes were closed and she was trembling.

When he was finished with his operation, he handed her the tissue clumped on a wad of her hair. She threw it on the ground.

"Looks okay to me. I was extremely careful." Then he looked at her more closely. "Well, maybe if you sort of brush it this way a little, a little differently…"

She jumped up. "What! Brush it differently! That means both sides are not in sync. You ruined my hair! I have to go to the hairdresser and have it evened out! You idiot! I can scream!"

He got up also and almost lost his balance. "No. Bea. All you have to do is brush it one-two-three. No one will notice."

"No one will notice?! I will notice! One-two-three?! I don't brush my hair one-two-three! It takes time! You idiot, asshole! One-two-three! Never one-two-three! You idiot! I never do my hair one-two-three! There is no one-two-three with hair!" She was livid.

Goodman was playing the ballad, "Moonglow." Dee said, "Bea, calm down. Listen to the music. 'Moonglow.' One of your favorites.

C'mon. Let's dance. A slow one. It'll bring you back to Earth! Settle you down."

"Settle down?! I feel like I'm going to have a stroke!" She touched her hair, trying to ascertain the damage. She stared at him and took a deep breath. "I am so angry at you I can... I feel," her fists tightening and her eyes, razor shards, "like punching you right in the mouth!"

His emotions were totally jumbled. The heat, the wine, and the excitement put him in a somewhat giddy state. The phrase "punch you in the mouth," made him chuckle. Somehow he saw odd humor in the whole scene, and, for a reason he could not figure out, she did not see the same humor. He stated, "Well, if you want to punch me in the mouth, you go right ahead." He then smiled. "Just make sure you do it with your lips."

He never saw it coming.

She rocketed a wallop on him like a truck piston shooting out of the hood. It caught him right under his left eye, snapped his neck, and made him stagger until he tripped on his own feet and landed on a patch of dirt like a bag of cement.

She grabbed her bag and stood over him seething. "Get up! Take me home! Now!"

The subway ride home was painfully silent. His head throbbed from the combination of wine and her clout. There was no hand holding. No hug. And no goodnight kiss. And he also had to figure out what to tell his mother what caused the blooming shiner under his eye.

7
CHAPTER

The hair incident caused a great schism.

Woman's hair, to Dee Felico, was as foreign as Einstein to the Hottentots.

His mother lectured him, "Female hair is high seriousness. If tampered with…," she continued, putting both hands on the side of her head, "purposefully, inadvertently, or even professionally supervised, my God. Let's say it could be like rearranging a country's borders on a whim. And that's," she spat out, "out and out war!"

"I can't believe—"

"Boy," she said, "you are a knucklehead. That shit about your black eye you gave me, falling on the el stairway banister… Does my face look that simple to you? You're more sure-footed than a pack mule." She sighed. "I hate the fact that she belted you. Especially her! But I'd say from what you told me, you sure deserved it. You're lucky she didn't do worse." She snorted. "Maybe that speaks well of her. We'll see."

"Mom. What should I do?"

"She has all the aces. Let it take its own course."

Dee was kept at bay and in dry dock. She did not take his calls. His letters, poems, simple songs, and gifts were returned. The flowers he sent were thrown out. He witnessed it himself, standing across the street from her apartment house as he saw the flower delivery man deliver it. After several minutes, he saw the flowers fly out of the window into the alley that separated the apartment houses. And once, when he got up the nerve and came unexpectedly to her apartment, her father intervened on the intercom: "She will call you when she's ready. Now is not the time. And please be kind enough not to come here unannounced."

It was a harsh blow. He had gotten along with her parents famously, and now he felt like a pariah. When he left the apartment, his emotions totally mugged, he glanced up at her window and saw someone peeking through the venetian blinds, and as he lifted his hand up to wave, it suddenly snapped shut.

He felt that something in him had died. And there was nothing left to be said. Words had no meaning, its richness and importance no longer there. Words now were just background noise.

He could not shake thinking about her and dreaming about her. And as odd as it seemed, he didn't even have a picture of her so he played the Chopin Etude to death until his mother said, "You either put a dumb mute in that Steinway or I'll chop off your fingers! That melody is beginning to drive me nuts!"

He fell into a depression. His grades started to slip. Nothing seemed to matter any longer. His grade advisor called him in and told him that if he didn't hit the books as was his wont, he would lose his scholarship. Dee told him the story. It had not been the first time the grade advisor heard such a thing, and he gave Dee a talking to: "You can drop out, pine forever, and become a ditch digger, or you can screw your head back on and get steamed up. And make sure that steam is channeled toward your studies. This is just a dip in the grand scheme of things, and dips have a way of straightening out. It just takes time. Dwell on the dip and you'll drown. Here"—he handed him a self-help book—"read this and do something useful. Now, get out of here. I've got more important things to do. I don't get paid a psychologist's salary."

He thanked the grade advisor and went to the library. He had always found solace at the library. He went up to the third floor and found a desk and chair in the corner of the building with a nice view of the campus. He read the book in a single sitting. It was not deep, but it was practical. And then he wrote a program for himself: Time Spent: on studies, on enjoyment reading, on listening to music, on swimming ten laps a day, on writing haikus, and on writing a weekly sonnet. He even threw in breathing exercises incorporated in doing nothing for one-half hour deliberately—his daydreaming time. He called Pete McKelvey and asked if they ever needed Saturday help; he'd be willing to give them a full day for whatever they needed. The following Saturday he was clipping coupons. He overfilled his dance card, and at day's end, his sleep was soothingly calm and dreamless. Yet she popped into his mind every day, fleetingly, but every day nonetheless. Somehow his heart was her dance floor.

He was halfway into his daydreaming exercise at home, sitting in the rocking chair next to the window overlooking the air shaft, a cup of coffee staying warm on the metal cover of the cast iron radiator, the valve spitting a little as the steam heat came up, when the phone rang.

"Hiya, baby." It hit him like touching a live wire.

It was the better part of three months since he had heard from her.

"Bea?" It was all he could say.

"Baby. I'm in a fix. I'm all tangled up and I can't seem to unravel it. I really need your help."

"What is it…what…is the problem?" Dee said.

"Can you come over?" It was Bea's old voice. He was concerned. There was almost a tremor in the way she said it. She was nervous, he thought, and then felt that she was in trouble.

"Now?"

"Yes. Please."

The "please" edged him off the rocker. "I'll leave now. Figure forty-five minutes," he said.

"Oh. Thank you so much. Thank you. I'll be waiting." She then hung up.

He put on a warm jacket. The November cold had a neat bite to it. He then rushed out of the house first leaving his mother a note.

Miracles do happen once in a while.

He rushed to the el and caught the outgoing subway just before it departed and managed to transfer at Queens Plaza for the Flushing train just as it pulled in. He got off at her stop and sprinted the six blocks. The whole journey took him a little over a half hour, which was record time.

"Dee?" He heard the metallic distortion of her voice on the intercom when he pushed the bell.

"It's me," he replied as she buzzed him in.

When he opened the door into the apartment, his mouth opened like a broken letter box. Beatrice Sharpe was butt-ass naked, totally wrapped in cellophane.

"Help, help," she lampooned in her best damsel in distress voice. "Free me from my bonds. Untie me." Her smile could have melted the Ross Ice Shelf.

He went over and kissed her. And then as he looked at her face, her hair was cheek length rather than shoulder length, and it gave her a cuteness he had never witnessed before.

He removed the cellophane from her body, and she led him into her bedroom where they made love with an intensity that bordered on the savage.

They were exhausted and resting after their lovemaking, holding hands under the sheets, almost breathing in unison.

"You know, Dee, I am so content, so happy, so at peace here with you in my room; my books, my library all around us, surrounded by ideas and tales and stories—everything that I love." She didn't look at him but glanced at the bookshelves and said, "This is the closest I've ever been to God. Not in church. Not in deep prayer, but here, with you and my stacks of friends."

He did not know what to say. He just squeezed her hand.

He looked up at the shelves, a jumble of haphazardly stacked tomes, some with paper bookmarks in them, others opened to the page she was reading at the time. There were both hardcover and softcover books neither set up by author or subject. St. Augustine's *Confessions* was leaning against *The Story of O*, some stacked Merton and Dorothy Day's autobiography. Copleston's multivolume *History of Philosophy* was interspersed with *Black Opium*, Hemingway's *Death in the Afternoon*, and *The Collected Poems of Robert Service*, as well as the diaries of Anais Nin.

It was a rich, eclectic, and motley collection. He thought it said a lot about her, and he was trying to find out what that was. It was complicated. And he wondered if she was trying to find it out as well herself.

"Those Emily Hahn books you got me, *Congo Solo*, when she was with the pygmies, and the one when she became an opium addict, or when, as a POW, she smacked that Jap intelligence officer in the face—what a wonderful writer and character, that wandering adventurer. Where'd you get them again?"

"Mendoza Book Shop on Ann Street. The owner adores your taste. I'll bring you there one day. He's dying to meet you," Dee said. He noticed the Congo book next to St. John of the Cross's *Dark Night of the Soul* and *Bawdy Ballads and Lusty Lyrics*.

And in the corner of the shelf was her little grotto: fractured statues of the Holy Family that she garbage-picked scattered around a can and glued back with whatever pieces she found. St. Joseph's head was missing in the back; the Madonna's face was partially chiseled by time and neglect. The rosary was broken, the crucifix, coal black. And between them all was a little votive candle in a shot glass marked "Ole."

"I'm sorry I hit you," she said.

He turned to her. "I deserved it."

"I love my hair now," she said, shaking her head back and forth. "I had to get it cut, but the girl cut a bit too much, and I had to let it grow in a little. Now it's perfect. She leaned her shoulder against his. "Sometimes I'm not good with change. I had to give it time. I'm sorry about that too."

He patted the top of her hand under the sheets.

"Where do you see us fifteen years from now?"

She didn't look at him. "Fifteen years?" She leaned back on the pillow. "Fifteen minutes from now...probably a nice shower. But fifteen years? Oh, there's so much to do, so much to see, so much to experience."

He was quiet for a while. "What's on your 'to do' list?"

"So many things, so many things. I'd love a tour of the sewers of Paris and see those white fresh water dolphins in the upper Yangtze. I'd love to bag me a leopard in Kenya." She started to get a little excited and sat up, covering herself with the sheet. "And scuba in those vertical caves in the Caribbean, those blue holes, see a bullfight, and the silversword plant on Haleakala, and kiss the worn foot of St. Joseph going into the Vatican…so much, so much—and the reading! Want to read libraries and experience, experience all sorts of things." She sighed, turning to him. "And you?"

He was silent, thinking. "I really don't have a list."

"But there must be something."

He paused. "You know," he said, smiling, "there is a little thing—it's not much—it's something that I've always been hankering to do."

"Tell me." She was enthused.

"You know those big John McAllister tugboats? I'd like to go on one for a day. Tow some oil barges through the Gowanus or the Kill Van Kull, or dump some old subway cars off the Jersey Coast on those railroad car floats—sort of see the New York waterways from the water rather than the land."

She edged away from him unlocking his hand. She looked at him as if brussels sprouts were growing out of his head. "What?"

"What do you mean? I don't understand."

"That's so blue collar," she said and folded her arms, then whispered, "I don't believe you."

He didn't know whether to pout or get angry. He held his emotions.

A moment later, aware that she had pricked his little bubble, she said, "I was just thinking…perhaps…" She knew she was rambling. "I was thinking, maybe if it was a little more exotic… But if it's what you like, it's what you like. I suppose, well, let's just forget about it."

They lay there for a couple of minutes saying nothing.

Dee perked up from feeling slighted when Bea asked, "Dee, can you do me a favor?"

"If I can," he said

"Remember Bernie Paulson?"

He turned to her. At that moment he had no recollection.

She said, "Bernadette Paulson. I introduced you to her at the Dance Center. We share lunch, swap lies, and tap steps when we teach the kids. She's a real sweetie pie. Sometimes she comes to brush up on her steps and I help her." She then waited expectantly, a small smile on her face. "Remember?"

"You mean the voluptuous redhead with the Kewpie doll face and the Betty Boop voice?"

She side-glanced him.

"What? Not accurate?"

Bea fired back, "Too accurate, dearie."

He laughed. "Do I detect—"

"No," she jumped in. "I was just taken in a little by your lurid description. The appropriate response to my question should have been, 'Yes, I know who you mean.' That would have sufficed, but let's get on with it."

"Your move," he said as he put his arms behind his head.

"Well. She got a nice role in the production of *Dames Over the Waves*. I'm so happy for her. She has so much talent. And get this: because of several tap steps in her routine I taught her, she put together two songs—ad lib stuff from the guys in the pit—as a thank-you. Really, really good stuff. I have the tape recording. And the very best part is," she then paused for effect, "she blackmailed the director to give me an audition."

He sat up, shocked. "Wow! Are you kidding me! An audition for a Broadway musical! Unbelievable! And you're going to do the two numbers she put together? What are they?"

"'Happy Feet' and 'When the Sun Sets Down South.'"

"Great pieces. When is it?"

"Next Thursday. I was hoping you could come with me. I'm really nervous, and…"

Dee said, "Shit! I have my Dostoyevsky lecture that day for my seminar course. I'm doing my paper on 'Notes from Underground.' What time is the audition?"

"Ten on the dot. I'd like to get there early to stretch, warm up, and I do have two costumes…" She waited expectantly.

"Lecture's at two thirty." He started to shake his head. "I'll never make it back in time. Even if I cabbed it, traffic…in New York…the bookies wouldn't even give odds on it."

"So you won't go with me?"

"If I can somehow get the lecture notes… I just…just don't know." He put his hands on his head.

"Please?" Bea said.

"Bea, don't do this to me."

"Pretty please?" she wooed, batting her eyes with humor in her heart.

He ran his fingers through his hair. "If I could just get a hold of the notes, and… Maybe I can call the professor."

"Pretty please with ice cream on top?" She stared at him with mock coyness.

He looked at her and stroked his mustache with his index finger and thumb three times and said, "Pretty please with something a lot better than ice cream on top."

Her face drained out the humor for a second, then she flung off the sheets and straddled him.

"Bea! What the hell are you doing? What are you doing?" He was totally thrown off guard by her action.

"Shhh," she purred. "Just close your eyes. Close your eyes, baby."

He did what he was told. He felt her breath warm against his face. And then he screamed in pain.

She had bitten him on the nose.

He jumped out of the bed naked, holding his nose, "Are you crazy! What the fuck are you doing! You bit me!" He was squeezing his nose, his voice gurgling high-pitched and nasal. He was enraged but more frightened she was going to attack him. She already had given him a black eye.

She pointed her finger at him. "Don't you ever proposition me again!"

"Proposition you? Are you nuts?" his hand squeezing his nose, still in pain.

"'Pretty please with something a little better with ice cream on top'? I'd call that a proposition!" she flared back.

He looked at his hand. "I'm bleeding! I'm bleeding. You stupid jerk, I just wanted you to say it! Not do anything! Just say it! You jerk!"

She gasped. "Oh my god! I misconstrued. Oh, baby." She got out of bed and ran to him. "I'm so, so sorry."

"Misconstrued! Misconstrued! At this rate, being with you… I'm going to be misconstrued right out of this fucking world!" He squeezed his nose again, some blood oozing through his fingers, his voice, still high-pitched, nasal, and with a gurgle. It started to make her laugh.

"Let me see it," she said, trying to suppress her laugh.

He cowered, but he took his hand down. She touched it tenderly. "No puncture. I think the pressure just caused it." She stroked it. "The teeth marks will subside."

"Teeth marks!" He hopped back from her, squeezing his nose again. "Ohhh!" Again, the sound of his voice started to really make her lose it. She doubled up laughing.

"What the fuck are you laughing at, you idiot!"

"Your voice, that voice…" She was having a hard time breathing. "Sounds like…sounds like Clyde McCoy's trumpet playing the 'Sugar Blues' with the wah-wah mute." She couldn't contain herself. Tears dribbled down her cheeks, her laugh soundless, hysterical. She had a hard time coming up for air.

"First you give me a shiner and then you bite my nose off! Goddamnit! I'm bleeding! And teeth marks on my nose! Ohhh."

She held him, her face on his back, laughing, and said, "Come, Dee, let's shower. It'll be okay. I'm so, so sorry. Let's get going." Every few words were between hearty guffaws. "My parents will be coming home soon, and I told them they'd never find us in flagrante delicto."

"What!" he screamed. "They know!"

Her laugh welled up to the point that she couldn't catch her breath, and tears free flowed out of her eyes. "They've"—she was doubling over with laughter—"they've known since the first time. I told them. We're together over a year."

"You told them! How could I face—ohhh!"

"Dee. They said you're so good for me. They love you. Besides, nothing will ever be said. They're different. They're a different kind of people." She took his hand away from his nose. "Yes," she said, inspecting it, "it'll be all right." She took some tissues from her nightstand to wipe up the blood. "Let's give it a little peroxide and wash up. It'll burn like hell, but it'll be fine." She put her arm around him and led him like a puppy into the bathroom.

Somehow she knew he was going to escort her to the audition.

8
CHAPTER

Bernadette Paulson met them at the side door of the Bowery Bay Theatre by Chambers Street, Downtown.

"Come, come in, it's cold out there," Bernadette said.

Bea hugged and kissed her, smiling, exuberant, "Bernie, I'm so excited."

"Keep the excitement for the performance. You have all the stuff?" Bernadette asked.

Bea turned. "Dee has everything. You remember Bernie?" It was more of a statement introduction than a question.

Bernadette, her lower jaw edged out and radiated her mouth into a cute smile as she looked at Dee. Her brown eyes were like bonbons. "Yes," Dee said, extending his hand. Bernadette hugged him. Her perfume was enamoring.

She said, "I'm so happy for both of you. All is set. It took some doing, but it paid off. The bill of goods was bought."

"You're sure it's okay with him?" Bea asked.

Bernadette said, "I did my job. Now, knock 'em dead."

Bea was as giddy as a child at her first recital. "I have to stretch. I'll get into sweats. I have the costumes. I'll be ready to go at nine."

"Dee," Bernadette said, "have you heard the songs yet? The guys in the pit really put together some good stuff on the fly."

"No," Dee said, removing his knapsack that held Bea's sweats, costumes, and tape recordings of the audition songs. "I'm really bulled-up for this. I know the songs but never heard the renditions."

He handed the knapsack to Bernadette. "Bea, I'll show you where to change and I'll introduce you to Neal, the director-choreographer. Be with you in a few, Dee. Save a front-row seat for me. Make yourself at home. There's a coffee pot brewing somewhere," Bernadette said as she escorted Bea to the dressing room. Dee took off his coat and beret and found a seat center stage in the Off-Broadway theater.

Bernadette came back and sat next to Dee when she left Bea, having first introduced her to Neal.

"Coffee?"

"Already had my quota," he said. She was exquisitely attractive. Her eyes lowered on his face.

He felt a little uncomfortable. "What?"

"Hope you don't mind if I ask, but what happened to your nose?"

He sighed. It was not exactly a topic of conversation he wanted to engage in, but a tooth mark still showed, somewhat pink, but certainly visible up close, the resulting damage of Bea's misunderstanding. His mother was livid when she saw it, and he had all to do to keep her from calling Bea and dressing her down. "It's not a rawhide bone to gnaw at! What the hell is the matter with that woman! And what the hell is the matter with you!" his mother yelled, storming to the back bedroom with a bucket of wash to hang up on the line. "I give up!" was her last comment.

He said, "It disagreed with something that ate it."

Her laugh was a squeaky giggle but delightful. "Is that a pussy cat bite?"

He saw the playfulness in her eyes and decided to volley back. "A lynx, to be precise."

"Ohhh," she almost sang, gliding down her pitch. "I am told they are ferocious, but with the right approach, they can be trained and can become the most adorable of pets. I believe Mae West used to walk hers on Hollywood Boulevard in the thirties."

"I think it's best to leave them wild and untamed. Then you'll never get surprised if they turn on you."

"Does it still hurt?" she asked.

"If I blow my nose and touch it the wrong way, I'll go into a sneezing fit. And, yes, it does still hurt."

She actually showed concern on her face. And peering at it closely, her small mouth upturning at the corners, said, "Can I kiss it to make it better?"

Dee was beginning to love the banter. He played along and said, "Depends on what medical school you graduated from."

Without a moment she whispered, "Tufts."

"You're good. Very good." Her breath smelled of Pepsodent toothpaste. He laughed. "Okay, okay, Doctor, kindly proceed."

She held his cheeks and kissed the wounded area, and then, very gently, sucked the tip of his nose and gave it a lick. It was exactly what Bea had done to him on their first date. She then licked her fingers and rubbed the lipstick off his nose tenderly. "To remove any evidence," she said. "There." She leaned back to admire the finished product.

"I am told a lipstick stain and a date that will live in infamy could be considered one and the same. Thank you."

She laughed. "I like you, Dee Felico." She looked directly at him. Her eyes smoldered. "Is it better?"

"Much," he said. "By the way, is that a girl thing?"

"What?" she asked, confused.

"Kiss. Suck. Lick," was all that he said.

"Do I detect déjà vu?"

"Yes," he said. "Just different participants."

"Interesting." She smiled. "Imitation is the sincerest form of flattery. So, in short, the answer is yes. However, it must be…a noble nose…a Roman nose." She then delved into a Southern accent à la Tara in *Gone with the Wind*. "Or else…all is lost." She flourished her hand.

He laughed. "This conversation is so refreshing."

"I love it too," she said.

"I must ask…a personal question, all right?"

She raised her eyebrows. "Well, certainly, if it's the right question."

"What is that perfume you're wearing? It's delicious."

"Andiamo. By Borghese," she said.

"Thanks. I'll remember that."

"Please don't mind if I tell you," she said "Bea feels it's a bit too heavy for her. She's tried it already. Says it doesn't wear well on her. It is a bit costly."

"Thank you very much for looking out for me," he said.

She looked deeply into his eyes and slowly said, slightly above a whisper, "That has a nice sound to it."

Bea suddenly came on stage in sweat pants and shirt. She peered out, shading her eyes from the stage lights. "Getting along okay?"

"Famously," Bernadette said. "I've included Dee in our sharing…"

Bea, standing with arms on her hips, said, "There are some things that cannot be shared."

Dee became edgy and thrilled at the same time. To be the choice cut for two beautiful women was new to him. It was electric but dangerous, like feasting with panthers. "We share lunch and dance steps, why not Dee?" Bernadette said.

Bea stared at her. "Consider him my toothbrush."

Bernadette laughed loudly. She turned to Dee. "That's what I love about her."

He smiled, a little unsettled, looking at her. She was unusually beautiful. And if he was a player or a four-flusher, he would ask her out, but he was neither. Her blend of the theatrical and the real gave him pause. It made things for him hard to distinguish. He also felt very committed to Bea. There was love in his heart for Bea, but the thought of being with Bernadette seemed curiously fascinating. It was a scrumptious thought. It would be well worth his while to dredge that thought up if he had some bad moments down the road. What a pleasant thought, he considered, glancing at her.

A little before nine, Bernadette asked the sound man if the tape recording tested properly.

Neal sat next to Bernadette having been first introduced to Dee.

Bea came out on stage. Her outfit was quite simple: black short pants, a white ruffled shirt, black spaghetti suspenders, and a short black, silk kerchief. Her face was painted like a flapper on a *Vanity Fair* cover.

"Okay, Bea, whenever you want to give it the go," Neal shouted.

"Oh, boy," Dee sighed audibly.

Bernadette put her hand on his, leaned over, and whispered, "She's so beautiful."

He turned to her. "I'm so nervous."

She reassuringly squeezed his hand.

"I'm going to move over one seat if you don't mind. Depends on the music. Sometimes I like to conduct. Don't want to disturb you."

"How cute is that," she said.

"I also see the music. There's like a screen I see in front of me and I actually see the notes transcribed as it is played. It's kind of like reading a score as it's being written. It's something called synesthesia. I just don't want to disturb you."

Bernadette held her hand out to him and he touched it. She smiled at him but had no idea what he was talking about.

The music started up, the sound system right on the mark. A brief intro was played by the combo as Bea formed a sultry pose tapping her foot left to right keeping time with the beat. Then, when Bernie's voice came in with the formal introduction, charmingly declamatory, accompanied only by the strumming of an acoustic guitar, Bea rattled off a series of sixteenth note taps distinctively in a somewhat eccentric style, her hands and body moving with a controlled, delicate abandon, telling her story, building up to the refrain.

"'Happy feet. I've got those happy feet...,'" Bernadette sang as Bea started with a flat-footed hoofer's tap, athletic and aggressive.

Bernadette looked over at Dee. His face was almost trancelike, watching Bea, moving his hands and fingers as if he was actually playing the piano. He had never heard the recording before, yet his movements indicated that he was playing the piano part.

When Bernadette finished the refrain, an open trumpet came in playing jazz riffs on the theme as a clarinet wailed alongside with an obbligato in the upper register. It was a back-and-forth interplay. Bea's hips moved like a syncopated hula dancer, her eyes expressing the colored nuances of each instrument, especially when she did off-beat steps. Her hands, middle and ring fingers slightly bent, made flowing movements along with her shoulders and upper body, creating accents of excitement.

Some of the stage hands and members of the company stopped what they were doing and began watching. They were pulled in to her performance and were tapping their feet to the beat.

Bernadette looked quickly at Neal. His eyes were transfixed on Bea, bobbing his head to the music, finger snapping to the beat. He was more than enthused with her performance. She interjected, "Something else, huh?"

"This kid could dance," he said, not taking his eyes off Bea. "I've seen four, five styles so far, and stuff I've never seen. Damn. She's hot."

"Told ya," Bernadette quipped.

The brass and woodwind duel bowed in to a stride piano sixteen-bar sock chorus, a hard bass line with right-hand fireworks.

Dee, seeing the music before him, Bea dancing through the measures, mimed the notes with his hands, his lips tightly drawn but moving ever so slightly as if he was singing the improvisation close-mouthed. His left knee moved up and down with the beat as his right foot sought for the pedal that wasn't there.

Bernadette had never seen anything like this before. She felt that if she pushed Dee in front of the old upright piano on stage, he would be playing what she was hearing, note for note. She elbowed Neal and said, "He says he's seeing the notes as it's being played."

Neal nodded. "Yes. Some kind of neurological thing. I think Duke Ellington has it," he said, quickly returning to Bea's mesmerizing performance.

The piano passed the next chorus to a hot clarinet that issued out a leaping cadenza. A series of blue note arpeggios followed, staccato tongued as Bea spun with lightning speed and glided all over the stage alternating feet while machine gun tapping with the other like accentuating drum rolls. The stylized clarinet solo brought the song to a new level, and everyone watching felt the fire building. And just as the clarinet zipped in and out with short glissandos, Bea undulated her body to the dirty blare of a plunger-muted trumpet emanating buzz notes through the musical line and executing half-valve squeezes. She sashayed in a sexy gait, the rattling of her taps, seemingly produced elsewhere, as she sidled along, her body movements commanding the attention away from her feet. The trumpet's growls and lip trills accentuated every suggestion her body made.

Her tap dancing became more traditional and heated as the trumpet flutter tongued its last rip up to the combo that started to take the song home, Bernadette's voice one-noting the beginning of the last chorus.

Bea spun across the whole stage clicking her taps with clean fluidity, much like an ice skater building up to an Olympic competition's climax. And just as the combo articulated its joint ending, Bea leaped up twirling three times aloft, landing in a complete split facing the audience and recovering through the power in her legs to a finale stance, arms extended, right on the last beat.

Neal was already out of his seat. The rest of the participants applauded wildly. Bernadette seemed out of breath.

Bea smiled and bowed, accepting the applause, and yelled out, "Be back in a flash. I've got to change for the second dance." She then ran off the stage, shaking some hands on the way back to the dressing room.

Bernadette turned to Dee. "My god. How great was that?"

Dee smiled broadly. "Man! Those guys did some job on that song! And she said she was nervous. I thought I was going to have a heart attack several times watching her."

Neal touched Bernadette's shoulder. "Where the hell has she been? Wow!"

"And," Bernadette said, "you don't 'Wow' often."

"That's no flash act. That's the by-product of dedicated talent. I see what you mean, Bernie. Can't wait to see what else she has in store for us," Neal said.

"And she's a tough teacher too. She helped me with my stuff too. And I have the bunions to prove it," Bernadette said.

Dee sat back next to Bernadette.

"Dee," she said. "Are you in the *New England Journal of Medicine?*"

"No. It's just something that's a part of me. Funny. I thought everyone into music had it when I was younger. Isn't that a kick?"

"It's a wonderful gift."

"Only if you know how to read music. It also saves me a bundle. I don't have to buy sheet music," he said, laughing.

She kicked back her head with a guffaw. "Point well taken."

When Bea took the stage for the second time after the costume change, Dee knew that the dance was going to be different. She had exploded with virtuosity in the first one. This one, he felt, would be subtle.

She had on shorts and a top with shimmy tassels and a head band all in kelly green.

Members of the company quieted as she waited center stage, her eyes on the sound man waiting to give him his cue. Neal, hands clasped together, waited expectantly as Bernadette took a deep breath in awe of Bea's command of the stage.

She struck an alluring pose, and the sound man started the recording. The music started sassy, a bluesy bass line executed by the piano player's left hand, riding the beat. Painting the late-night mood, the smoky mood of heavy air, cigarette ends glowing like fire-flies, a clarinet and a soprano sax floated up in hugging harmony.

She moved her hips, her stance widening, her body moving like a vixen: sultry, suggesting—dangerous. Her taps slid on the wooden floor like wire brushes on a snare drum, her legs lolling, long sea-weeds in a pulsating current. It was seductive without the hint of vulgarity.

The moves she did with her body in response to the music became the conversation, became the solo; her taps, intricate and fluid, served more as an accompaniment. Using the entire stage, she became the wail of the horn, her body moving like a cobra's head in concert with the sax's hard vibrato; her hips, legs, and feet the percussion section. And then with a beguiling flourish, she started to dance a dark, lustrous rumba with an imaginary partner in her arms, her taps crackling a call, the echo response coming back from the specter that served as her companion. It was extraordinary. There was an almost audible gasp by the people watching.

Tapping out quick triplets in a twirl at her invisible lead's demand, Neal said, "If you let yourself go, really go, you can see who she's dancing with. This is really something. Oh, man. What a treat. I gotta hire this kid."

The song continued on void of brass. The woodwinds, color-fully exploring lushness and harmonies as only reeds can do, crossing each other's lines of flight like lamenting wolves vying for the moon's attention; her ghostly partner intimating his proposals; her body movements playing with the intentions like cigarette smoke curling upward, quivering in a thin white line on unknown currents, and then vanishing into the memory of a wanting heart.

The dance was pure romance, uncluttered by flesh and blood, pure as a genius's thought: undefined.

And as the blues ambled toward its closing chords, its cre-scendo seeking a torchy note, she removed herself from her shadow's embrace, her feet rattling and swishing now alone, the brief sadness ebbing, allowing her to complete herself as one.

The ending came without fanfare as a good blues would just leaving the hint of a chance to come, her very slow turn halting on the last beat. She closed gazing downward, her hands slightly upturned, still.

There was complete silence. People were still trying to under-stand what they had just witnessed. After a few seconds, Bea looked up and said, "I hope I didn't disappoint you."

An explosion of applause, hoots, laughter, and whistles went off like a cherry bomb.

Both Dee and Bernadette rushed to Bea to congratulate her on her performance. Bea hugged and kissed them both. "It was sterling," Dee said.

"A mind blower," Bernadette said, filtering through just as oth-ers stated their congratulatory noise and adulation.

"I'm spent and soaked. Gotta take a shower," Bea said.

Both Dee and Bernadette walked her to the dressing room holding her hands.

"Bea," Bernadette said. "Neal wants to see you after you're set-tled in. Take your time. All the stuff is there."

"It should have been filmed," Dee said. "It was spectacular. You should have seen yourself."

Bea had a bursting smile. "I'm so thrilled I was able to do it." She then slipped into the dressing room, turning back, saying, "See ya a bit later."

As Dee and Bernadette walked back to the stage, she caught his hand. He looked at her a little surprised. "While we're waiting for Bea, why don't we do something?"

"What did you have in mind?"

"You play piano. I sing."

"What song?"

"You know the old ones."

"I'm no anthology, but I'll give it a shot."

He sat at the old upright piano, played a few chords to see if it was in tune, and once satisfied gazed at her. She sat on the same bench he was on right next to him.

She seemed to muse a moment, composing herself. Looking at him soulfully, she began, a cappella, "'If you were the only boy in the world and I were the only girl...'"—her voice, a violin, the instrument closest to the human voice, colored by a mute, giving it a slight reed effect, playing nothing, his eyes read hers seeking no questions or answers, just beauty beheld. She slid up, singing, "'Nothing else would matter in the world today'"—the voice, the E-string, the rosin wafting off the bow in puffs as the horse hair caressed the string for its sound—"'We would go on loving in the same old way'"—his piano silent, his soul embracing her musically, lovingly; her brown eyes looking at him, looking in him, looking through him, burning a message, a feeling. "'A garden of Eden'"—his right hand sketching out single notes, the tones allowing him to compliment her. "'Just made for two...with nothing to mar our joy'"—incorporating plush chords, edging a slight crescendo, him following her design as she lingered on the last word, and with a stronger tone, aided the drama of her new phrase. "'I would say such wonderful things to you'"—his playing majestic, elegant, favoring her voice. "'There would be such wonderful things to do'"—his vision blurring, his eyes watering with tears, it happening so quickly, so unexpectedly, his father's rich baritone singing the same song to his mother, their love song, long forgotten. His eyes still hinged on hers, her voice, her love for him,

Bea's love, his father's, his mother's, and all those people who took him up to raise, their love all culled in the song. "'If you were the only boy in the world...'"—the tempo pulling back, leaving him alone; the overtones sailing off into infinity forever; her strong voice never wavering; his tears dribbling from his cheeks on to his hands and the piano keys, eliminating the tempo entirely on the parting phrase: "'And I were the only girl...'" The last note held beyond the music itself in a straight tone, ending with a gentle vibrato, his fingers completing the melody's final measures...alone.

When he took his hands off the keys, their eyes still fixed, he reached out and cried bitterly in her arms. She held him tightly stroking his hair and kissing it, confused.

Once he finally controlled his sobbing, he apologized to her and told her that it was his parents' love song and that his dad had died.

"Why didn't you stop me? We could have done something else. I feel so bad. I'm so, so sorry you were hurt. I would never hurt you..."

"Because...it was meant to be. Sometimes things like this just happen. Who'd have known you would have sung that song? And we did it so beautifully." He held her hands. "You see, it was kind of a prayer, and that was good."

She put her hand on his cheek. "Dee, you are such a beautiful person." She sighed deeply. "And, yes, we did make beautiful music together." She took her hand away from his cheek and smiled. "I hope we make music together again sometime."

All he could say was, "'Isn't it pretty to think so.'" He saw by her eyes that she did not understand his allusion. She obviously hadn't read Hemingway.

Bea suddenly arrived and noticed immediately that Dee's eyes were still red. "What happened?"

Before Dee could speak, Bernadette said, "He was playing piano, I was singing, and boom! He goes into a sneezing fit, fifteen, twenty in a row. I hope he isn't allergic to me."

Bea laughed. "Must be your perfume." She turned to Dee. "You okay, baby?" He nodded, as Bernadette, behind Bea, gave him a wink.

"So what'd Neal say?" Bernadette asked.

"Offered me a job," Bea said, in a matter-of-fact manner.

"Great!" both Dee and Bernadette expulsed.

"Well, not really…"

"What do you mean?" Bernadette said.

"I told him I wasn't interested. I wasn't looking for a job. All I ever wanted to do was audition for a Broadway musical, even if it's Off-Broadway. That's all. And he thought I was nuts. Bernie, how did you leave it with him? You know, he was kind of testy. I didn't like that."

"I just told him you've got to see this kid dance. I suppose he thought you were totally committed to musical theater. You just don't audition for a Broadway musical on a lark."

"Well, Bernie, you could have spelled it out for him," Bea declared.

"And if I did, we wouldn't be having this conversation now. What did he offer you?"

"A lot a possibilities—understudy, dance troupe replacement, choreographer assistant. Bernie, I'm going to school; this is full-time stuff. I'd even put up with the schlep, but it would have to be with flexible hours, or come in when I can, like the Dance Center. I have too many things to do. And then," she said in an angry tone, "he had the audacity to say I was wasting my talent—the nerve."

"I'm really sorry, Bea. We open in a few weeks. His brain is chock full of last-minute things. How did you leave it?"

"He just said, 'Take it or leave it.'"

Dee said, "At least you got your wish. And you did a damn good job."

Bernadette said, "I understand. But bear in mind, these opportunities don't come around every day."

Bea became a little irate. "This is not my life, and there will be other opportunities. I have to go," she said abruptly.

"I'm sorry," Bernadette said. "I was only trying to help."

"You said that already." Bea looked at Bernadette silently for a very long moment. Then she opened up her arms and hugged her, more out of courtesy than genuine affection. "Thanks, thanks for everything, Bernie. We'll miss you at the Dance Center. Break a leg."

Dee then went to Bernadette as Bea was gathering up the knapsack. "Good luck with the show. It was wonderful meeting you again." He shook her hand warmly. Bernadette's eyes showed a tinge of regret. She somehow knew that she would never see him again.

Dee said as they both went outside, "You didn't have to jump on her. She was only trying to help."

"What are you taking her part for? What are you sticking up for her for? You got eyes for her or something? You got a crush on her?"

"What's with you, Bea? You got what you wanted. Leave it alone."

"Wasting my talent! Besides what business is it of his? What business is it of anybody?"

"Give me the knapsack."

"No. I want to carry it. I have a pair of strong shoulders." She looked at her watch. "Look. Why don't you go grab an Express Bus? You could probably make the seminar with time to spare for a couple of dirty water dogs. I sort of... I... I just want to be by myself."

"Are you okay?"

"I want to be by myself. Go." When he kissed her goodbye, she seemed to push him away from her with her lips.

9
CHAPTER

The heat wave that Fourth of July weekend made Devil's Island seem like autumn in the Yukon. A garbage strike on top of it only added to the oppression. Tempers quivered like exposed nerve ends, and the rats, bolder than ever, attacked without provocation even during daylight hours.

Dee had been slated to work the weekend, including the Fourth, which was a Monday. He had told Bea he would be incommunicado for the weekend and that it wouldn't be worth her while to come down on the Fourth since he had no idea when he would be getting out.

The workload was momentous. They were working with compressed time. The clients had to be credited their interest no later than the fifth of the month. He had worked to midnight the night before and had grabbed a cab home and had gotten a good night's sleep.

Saturday was a ghost town on Wall Street.

He walked into the lobby at six thirty. There was no change in the air temperature. It was hovering around ninety. The wilted security guard, his shirt unbuttoned and his handkerchief draped around his neck, checked him off the list and said, "They're up there already. Came in at five."

Dee knew he was going to be busy. Not only did they have fifteen, six-drawer cabinets chock full of bonds to clip, but the market volatility generated a proliferation of manual adjustments on the last-minute purchases and sales that had to be made as well.

Dee walked in and was handed his cage badge by Sam Judson, the retired marine sergeant, who served as the security guard. He was in uniform with his cap on sweating profusely. Dee noticed he was packing additional weaponry. He had his normal sidearm as well as a shoulder holster holding a Colt .45. "Boy," Dee said, "looks like you're loaded for bear today. Expect to use those gats on the Fourth as a firework?"

"They are fireworks. And I'll use 'em if need be. And a good morning to you too, Dee Felico."

"And the top of the a.m. to you also, Mr. Judson," Dee said, walking back into the Bond Interest department.

He smelled the coffee percolating as he rounded the bend and saw both Pete and Stan working in their skivvies and sleeveless T-shirts.

"AC on the blink or what?" Dee asked.

"They shut it off on the weekends to save money. The only one on is the one in the IBM room upstairs," Pete said, Chesterfield dangling from his lips.

The area had a gamey tang to it. Whatever soap Pete and Stan showered with and aftershave they splashed on before coming in had long worn off. What was permeating the air was exuding from them, pure old man. And like old dogs, they both smelled bad. The cigarette smoke and coffee aroma didn't help much.

"Should I put on a fan?"

Stan shot up. "No, no, no. All's we have are them big jobbies. They're caged P-40 props. They got only one speed: 'Taking Off.' We can't afford any coupons blowing around here and winding up in some air vent or something. And don't open no windows—creates a vacuum and sucks everything out. Everything's gotta be secured."

"Strip down, Dee, and put your trousers and shirt in the closet," Pete said, squelching out his cigarette in the small area left in the brass ashtray already overfilled with butts.

Dee put his lunch sandwich and cold fried chicken supper in the small fridge. He then poured Pete and Stan coffee and brought it to them. He took a cup for himself too. They all took it black. Dee sipped it. "Wow! This is really good. What brand you using today?"

"Eight O'clock. Plus, I put in some chicory and a pinch of salt. That gives it the bang, a hobo recipe from the Depression."

Dee went to his desk. "Anytime, Pete. I'm ready."

Pete got up and walked to Jerry Parcher's office to key in the code for the cage vault. He hit the number and heard the opening click. He went in and wheeled out the cabinet they were working on the night before. Dee helped Pete bring it close to his desk and continued where he left off. Pete then went back to his desk, lit up another cigarette, and continued making the adjustments on the IBM bond sheets that listed the client account numbers that were either newly bought or sold.

About ten minutes later, they heard a commotion through the runner's cage barred window, a separately secured area.

Suddenly three plainclothes men in suits and ties confronted them with machine guns pointed in their direction. Sam Judson was the last man running around the corner with both pistols drawn. Dee was so shocked he almost wet his pants.

Pete glared at the three men. "What the fuck are you doing here? And put them Tommy guns down! You want to scare the shit out of the kid!"

Dee had never seen a machine gun before. He instinctively put his hands up. They were still pointed in his direction. Stanley lit up his cigarette and said in disgust, "Jesus Christ." He then hocked up a wad of phlegm and spit it into the waste basket.

"McKelvey!" the lead plainclothes man barked.

"Delahanty. What the fuck are you doing here?"

"The alarm went off," he said. They all put down their weapons and secured them by putting the safeties on. Judson holstered both his pistols.

"I got the click," Pete said. "The vault opened."

"You get the 'green light,' buddy boy?" Delahanty said.

"That light sometimes works...sometimes doesn't. I got the click. That means it's okay. Now get the hell out of here. You're wasting my time." Pete flicked his hand as if shooing away flies.

"McKelvey," Delahanty said, "you have to let people know when the lights are on the fritz. That's what triggered this."

"Listen, smartass. I wrote a memo myself to Parcher last month and personally handed it to him. And"—Pete saw Delahanty about to say something—"just shut up...saw Parker hand it to Joe Glass. The head runner is supposed to take care of this. I did my bit. Glass fucked up, now you want me to wipe his ass too!" Pete was angry and got up and walked to Delahanty, the FBI agent.

When Delahanty saw Pete in his skivvies, he stepped back and laughed. "Aren't we a little early for trick or treat, or are you the new stripper for the Old Ladies Bridge Club?"

"Delahanty. Tommy gun or no Tommy gun, I'll crack you in the jaw!"

"Okay, okay, sorry," the FBI agent said. "Faulty wire's what caused it. That's all. We still have to report it. And Barlow will be fined. Don't forget. Costs money for our response. Man, that coffee smells good. Mind if we help ourselves?"

"You probably trumped this whole thing up to steal some of my java. Go ahead, help yourself, but put some cash on the table. You ain't getting my coffee for nothing."

The agents and Judson helped themselves. Delahanty threw down a five spot and left saying, "See ya, Pete."

Stanley looked at Pete seriously. "All right. Let's get going. And Pete, if I was you..."

"Can it, Stan," Pete said. "I'm going to rip Joe Glass's balls off the second he comes in on Tuesday."

"Pete. He's a real mean bastard when he's hung over, and you can bet your ass, after a three-day weekend, he'll be nursing a beaut."

"Yeah? Well, I'm meaner than a stepped-on Gila monster when I'm sober! Now, let's get cookin' on these coupons!"

By eight o'clock, after several phone calls, Pete was well into making his adjustments. Progress was going well for them. If they kept up this pace, they might only have to work half a day on the Fourth.

At eight thirty, Pete said in a soft voice, "Gentlemen. We have a situation."

The phrase and the manner in which it was said, courteous, almost apologetic, was very unsettling to Dee and Stan. This was out of character for Pete. He usually blared like a bullhorn. And then he said, "I have to bring something to your attention."

Stan turned to Dee very concerned and whispered, "We may have to call Beekman Hospital. I think he's having a stroke." Dee was stunned and frightened.

Stanley stood up and walked to Pete's desk. "Pete." He responded by just looking up at Stan, his eyes blank. "Pete," Stan said louder.

Pete then picked up his arm, closed his fist, and suddenly slammed it against his IBM sheets, yelling, "Goddamn son of a bitch!"

Stan immediately turned to Dee exhaling audibly, "He's okay."

"Got a call from Barlow. Seems we're getting some help today, a client's kid." He sneered a smile, "A friend of the Kennedys." He lit up another cigarette. "The kid's being forced by his old man to work today as some kind of punishment, came home late, got drunk—who knows. What a kettle of fish! 'Pete, I have a problem. Can you help me out?'" Pete mimicked Vance Barlow. "Help you out? Now I got the problem. And I checked; the old man has seventy million in position with us. And we got to put on our duds, else the kid might think it's a male whorehouse. And with the clothes on, we'll be ringin' wet in an hour. And now we have to teach him something? And we have to be on best behavior so he don't tell his old man this is a shithole. Goddamnit! I have a good mind to retire right now!" He banged his hand several more times on his desk.

"Okay. On with the clothes. The snotnose will be here at nine o'clock or thereabout," Pete said.

"Pete. He's got to be bonded and printed."

"I told that to Barlow. He called Judson to print him, but bonding? Stan, that's not our job. If anything happens, it's on Barlow's tab. His responsibility." Pete got up to put on his shirt and pants. The rest of them followed.

The blue blood decided to grace the place with his presence a little before ten. Pete had separately told Dee and Stan take ten-minute intervals on the thirty-fifth floor IBM room to cool off. With his planned schedule botched up, Pete foresaw them getting out on the

Fourth after the Macy's firework display on the Hudson. He was not happy.

Judson printed the boy and escorted him to Pete and Dee. It was Stan's turn to cool off.

The kid was redheaded with a face covered in acne. "I overslept." He yawned. He had an attitude. Dee saw Pete's eyes turn into muzzles. "Shit," the kid said, "it's hot as hell in this dump." He looked at Pete. "Why don't you kick on the air conditioner, old-timer? Trying to save a buck?"

Judson walked over to Pete and patted his damp back and, looking at the kid, said, "Building protocol. Not ours."

Dee had to give Pete credit. He seemed unmoved by the out-of-line comment, but knowing him, was sure a volcano was bubbling in his belly.

Judson eyed the kid and stepped very close to him infringing on the kid's personal space. "What?" the kid shot out.

"Be nice if you was a little respectful, sonny." Judson's scowl could back up a Mack truck.

Flustered, the kid muttered, "Sorry," his eyes lowered.

"Dee. You have him double-check your coupon count," Pete said. He knew Dee's work was perfect since day two. It was a harmless job and wouldn't cause any problems.

"S'matter? This guy can't count?" the kid chimed in.

"You got a name?" Pete asked.

"Joe McBride."

"Well, Joe. Your job is to check his count. If he makes an error, you bring it to his attention," Pete said, his voice in complete control.

When Stanley came down, introductions were made and work was continued.

For the remaining part of the morning, Joe McBride hit the "head" more times than an amoebic dysentery patient. He also, on five occasions, stated that Dee had miscounted, only to be proven wrong by Dee recounting it in front of him

At noon, Joe McBride got up and said, "I'm going to lunch."

"There's nothing opened here," Dee said.

"I'll find something," Joe said and walked out.

The three of them opened the lunches they brought in and ate while they worked.

"Pete," Dee said. "I've got to hand it to you. You should get a medal just for restraint, above and beyond."

Stanley laughed.

"I want to kill that pimpled shithead!" Pete bellowed.

Stanley was clipping the treasury coupons off million-dollar certificate denominations. The pile he had in front of him was at least six inches high. He did it with the dexterity and care of a heart surgeon. He showed Dee a thirty-thousand-dollar coupon. "Lose one of these and it's like losing thirty g's in cash." He put each one in the appropriate envelope for deposit and put them in coupon and maturity date order in the shoebox that was on the window sill next to him.

A large metal box with two combination locks on it plus a lock that looked like it was used in the Tower of London housed the treasury securities. They were totally segregated from any other bonds.

It was close to two thirty when Joe McBride came back from lunch.

Pete, Dee viewed, kept his head down, busy with his adjustments. Dee knew that Pete had everything to do to maintain his composure. Stanley, oblivious to anything except his treasuries, was whittling down his pile of million-dollar certificates. And making good progress.

"Find a place to eat?" Dee queried. He figured he could get away with razzing him a little since they were close in age.

"Yeah," McBride said, sitting next to him.

"Where?" Dee then threw the mud pie. "Brazil?"

"Hey!" McBride shouted, obviously not used to being the brunt of some sarcasm.

"Two-and-a-half-hour lunch? You got a lot of catching up to do. Besides. Who the fuck do you think you are? King Shit?" He looked at him as a teacher would to an unruly student.

Pete, at that moment, looked up as if he had an epiphany. Stan chuckled silently.

"You know who my father is?" McBride said in a smart-alecky manner.

"Not interested. I only know who you are."

McBride stood up posturing. Both Stan and Pete stopped what they were doing and waited for the next move. "Do you know what I can do?" His eyes widened, somewhat wild looking, and dilated.

Dee stood up, his mouth turned down, staring at him. "I know what you can't do! You," Dee pointed his finger at him, almost touching McBride's nose. McBride edged back. "You can't do your fucking job!" Dee snorted on purpose. "Now, sit the fuck down and check my count!"

There was a pause. Then McBride slowly retreated and sat down, his face aflame. His acne glowed like hot coals. He resumed the count he had started before he went to lunch.

Dee felt good about himself. No blame could ever be placed on Pete or Stan. Dee was a part-timer going to college. If anything came of the stunted clash, Pete and Stan would surely stick up for him. Maybe even Vance Barlow, if it ever got to that level. *No matter*, he thought. *I just did what was in the best interests of the firm.*

Dee glanced at Pete and Stan. What he saw in their eyes were two old coots belting out Handel's "Hallelujah Chorus" like caroling birds.

Joe McBride was skittish in the afternoon hours. They never told him of the IBM room they frequented to cool off periodically. They just let him sweat like a convict on a chain gang. "Just 'oats' for his disposition," Pete said.

"Go get some paper towels from the bathroom, and quit sweating on the coupons!" Dee would bark when the desk was being sprinkled with his perspiration.

McBride, to Dee's annoyance, was also making more and more errors and was frequenting the head more than during the morning session. Dee detected a smell of burning leaves on his clothes when he returned from a somewhat long lavatory stay. He was probably taking a couple of tokes on a joint to get him through the remainder of the day. Pete and Stan would never have picked up on it sucking unfiltered cigarettes. Their sense of smell was just as shot as their taste buds.

Dee had a good mind to barge in the bathroom and catch him but decided against it. Only a few more hours, he thought, and he would be gone…forever.

It was Stanley's turn to cool off again. He put his remaining stack of bonds in a rubber band marked "To Do" and placed them in the metal box locking all three locks. He then put his ashtray, which was heavy enough to use as a door stop, on his handwritten cross-reference sheet. It served as his backup once the coupons were deposited in the event the bank had a miscount or a bad calculation. He then covered the box of coupons on the window sill and put a rubber band around it.

Several minutes after Stan left, McBride got up again. Dee thought nothing of it thinking he was heading for the men's room again, but instead he rushed to Stan's area and opened the window wide, saying, "Gotta get air."

The box of coupons on the sill flew out the window.

Dee screamed and rushed over to Stan's desk by the window. He grabbed McBride, pulled him away from the sill, and pushed him with all his might away from the desk. McBride tumbled over the treasury box and rolled against the wall. Dee climbed on the sill frantically looking out the window for the box of coupons.

Pete stepped over McBride, who was bleeding where he hit his head on the metal box and almost crawled out the window with Dee. "I don't see it, Pete!"

There was a large scaffold with a rooftop by the seventh floor where workers were sandblasting the brick work. The coupon box was not on the roof. They both scanned Chase Manhattan Plaza and saw nothing. There were no pedestrians or street traffic. They were grateful for that. "Hold my belt, Pete!" Dee stretched himself out as far as he could to search the area as much as he could. The scaffold obstructed his view toward the corner of Pine and William Streets.

Dee jumped down and ran to the corner of the office and opened the last window. "Pete!" he screamed. "I see it! It's across the street at the corner by the church. Goddamnit! It's by the sewer grate!

The cover is off and some of the envelopes are in the street!" Dee jumped down and ran for the elevators. He yelled at Judson, "Help Pete! The coupons fell out the window!"

"I'll go with you, Dee!" Judson said.

"I got it. Help Pete and the kid! The kid's bleeding! I got the coupons!" He hit the down button. It lit up. And then he kept punching the button like a Morse code operator, yelling, "C'mon! C'mon!" He was shaking.

The elevator finally came, which to him seemed like eternity-squared. He jumped in and hit down. He knew he had to run out of the Wall Street entrance since the Pine Street one was closed due to the sandblasting. Hitting the lobby, he raced out and turned left toward William Street. Once there, he made another left, deliberately running in the street to ward off any car that might drive through and blow the coupons about.

The envelopes strewn on the street he picked up first. One envelope was perched to go into the sewer but luckily became affixed on a gooey substance on the steel grate, halfway in. A nudge would have plopped it into the sewer. None of the envelopes had opened. They all housed coupons, which he saw through the glassine window.

Stan yelled from the thirteenth floor, "Is the number sequence okay?"

Dee looked up and held up his hand as he doubled-checked the sequence. All the coupons were there. His heart was beating like a hovering hummingbird's wings. He picked up the box as if it was a brittle holy relic. He covered the box and looked at the facade of the chapel of Our Lady of Victory. "Thank you, God, for saving the coupons." He instinctively blessed himself and went back up.

Dee handed the box to Stanley who thanked him and doubled-checked everything. The only thing missing was the rubber band. Everything was in place. McBride had a little cut on his forehead from the lock on the treasury box.

Pete was so elated that he pulled out a bottle of Scotch from his drawer stash. "We all deserve a shot. Maybe two."

Dee said as he downed the second shot, "Pete. How come you didn't throw McBride out the window?"

"Well," Pete said, nursing the drink, "Stan had just come down and wanted to do the same thing, but Judson had his hand on the Roscoe. I think he would have shot us both."

They all laughed. Then they stripped down and continued the work. Pete told Judson to patch the kid up and send him home early.

They worked diligently and caught up with the setback McBride had given them. Recovering the coupon without a mishap added fuel to their intensity.

They finished up ahead of time and left on the Fourth at four-thirty in the afternoon. Dee spent the remainder of the day with Bea but called it an early evening. He was going in to work the next day and was bushed. He got home in enough time to hear Jean Shepherd tell the story of "Ludlow Kissel and the Dago Bomb that Struck Back" on the radio. He fell asleep midway through the story, well before Macy's fired off great gleaming rockets and bombs bursting in air in celebration of the Fourth.

"Dee," Stan said the next morning when he came in, "take a slug of coffee. Barlow wants to see you."

Dee took several gulps just as Pete came back from Jerry Parcher's office. "Stan tell you?"

"On my way," Dee said, first stopping at the men's room to check his grooming. His stomach was tightening. He was a little upset that he was going alone. And when he arrived at the seventh floor, Barlow's secretary waved him in. "He's waiting."

Vance Barlow was sitting at his desk. His face was somber. "Dee. Sit down here." He pointed to a chair right in front of his desk. They would not be sitting together on his couch.

"Dee," Barlow said. "First I want to apologize for the mistake I made. A horrible loss, an embarrassment for the firm and for me personally was salvaged by your quick action. I, along with the rest of the partners, thank you most sincerely for what you did. This whole incident could have been avoided. And it was all my fault. I am sorry. And everything with the client is ironed out."

Dee was stunned.

Barlow handed him an envelope. "This is a little something on behalf of me—a token, if you will, of my appreciation."

Dee opened it up. It was a personal check payable to Dee Felico for five thousand dollars.

Dee looked up at Barlow unable to speak. Barlow smiled. "What Pete, Stan, and Judson told me…without your quick thinking, we could have had a very serious loss and a pile of legal problems. You saved our ass."

"I just thought I did what I was supposed to do," Dee said. "I don't know what to say."

"'Thank you' would be just fine." He got up from behind his desk." Now, go back upstairs. I'm sure Pete can find something for you to do." Barlow smiled and shook his hand, covering it with the other. "Many thanks."

"Thank you," Dee said. He wanted to say more but "Thanks so much" was all that would come out.

Dee returned to his desk and spouted, "Gentlemen, lunch today, your pick, my treat."

"Already covered you on that," Pete said. "I'm buying."

"The last time," Stan quipped, "he blew for lunch he was still in the Cavalry. Let's hope we don't get beans and hard tack."

"Nope," Pete said. "Put an order in for steaks—Delmonico's. Lunch will be in the conference room, a full hour, and I'll bring along the Scotch as a chaperone." He smiled and lit up a Chesterfield. "And, by the way, Joe Glass got himself reamed a new asshole, compliments of Vance Barlow. A fitting chaser for his hangover."

They laughed. "I feel like I'm on cloud ten," Dee said, savoring the moment. Everything had happened so fast. He felt in his pocket for the check to make sure he wasn't dreaming.

He couldn't wait to tell his mother.

10
CHAPTER

She was new to the game.

As an eager, ardent, and fledgling new member of the church, Beatrice Sharpe went to confession every week. She felt she needed a fresh slate, a new beginning. And, being a convert, delved into the ritual with a passion and enthusiasm a cradle-Catholic would sidestep as not only suspicious but pretentious.

She usually dragged Dee with her, much to his annoyance.

"But it's for your soul, your own good," she implored.

"I'm uncomfortable with it. Always have. Before, during, and after. It's intimidating," Dee said.

"That's ridiculous," she retorted, using her pet word when she couldn't comprehend a person's reasoning or feelings.

"When I was a little boy," Dee explained, "I asked my mom if I could stay home from school just to be with her and play. I wasn't sick. I was always up on my classwork. And my mom said yes. When I was in confession, I told that to the priest and he hollered at me so loudly, calling me a liar. I ran out of the confessional. My friends saw me and so did some of their mothers. It was humiliating! And I cried all the way home. Things like that just don't go away."

It did not seem to faze her. She merely quoted scripture, "'When I was a child I spoke like a child—'"

"Stop," Dee said, turning away from her.

She grabbed for his arm. "Dee," she said. "Maybe today you can tell that story to the priest, and he might be able to help sweep that grudge away." She widened her eyes awaiting his response. "What do you think?"

He knew she was well-intentioned, but he also knew he was being button-holed. If he didn't fall into her cadence, the rest of the day could become a series of interrogations and well-timed hen-pecking salvos. He relented with a sighing, "'Kay."

He left her seeking the shortest confessional line.

"Don't forget to examine your conscience," she called out to him.

"I have," he lied and walked off mumbling to himself. "My conscience is perpetually being examined. Sometimes by persons other than myself."

Thankfully the line he chose was that of Father Charley Schramm, a retired priest in the parish who was close to ninety and a bit deaf. Dee actually considered mentioning the horrid incident he went through as a boy but, upon reflection, thought it a bit too much for the old man.

When Dee went into the confessional, he still saw Bea standing in a line with a good number of older women. The line she was on was that of a new visiting priest, a Father Eli Saydah, from Lebanon. They had both seen him for several weeks during Mass. He fractured the English language, but he told humorous stories that fit the scripture readings in his homilies. Bea was enchanted with him. She even nudged Dee with her shoulder during one of his homilies, saying, "Isn't that accent sexy?" Dee could not believe what she said and frowned at her as she looked innocently at him. He let it go. She was unencumbered by protocol and was a free spirit.

When it was Dee's turn for confession, he let loose the usual laundry list of sins, both of omission and commission, adlibbing his way toward the stock penance Father Charley always gave: "Three Our Fathers, two Hail Marys, and a Glory Be." As with the roll of loaded dice, the expected penance hit the table. He came out of the confessional booth humbly with downcast eyes and hands clasped, for he knew he was in the sights of someone who occasionally had her thumb on a torpedo plunger. He slipped into a pew, kneeled, and mimicked as best he could his Act of Contrition.

In what he thought was a decent time spent in prayer, he got up from his kneeling position and gazed at her still on line. Sun rays shown in straight lines from the stained-glass windows and enveloped her and several other ladies. It made her hair glow. She was so beautiful, he thought. How very lucky he was to be with her. There were times, unbeknownst to her, that he just stared at her, not studying her features but apprehending and absorbing her exquisiteness. And, at other times, perhaps in conversation or just sitting and waiting for an ordered meal at a bistro, he would just reach out and brush back a single hair gracing her dimpled cheek and ever so softly touch her skin for no other reason than to feel she was truly real and not an apparition. She would smile at him, and warmth would cover his heart.

He saw now that she was alternating her weight from foot to foot to some internal beat. She appeared to be getting a bit pensive and restless, her turn coming up soon. He examined the faces of the women who left Father Saydah's confessional. None seemed to have the relaxed relief of knowing their sins had been forgiven and washed away. But then again, they were all older women and probably had shopping lists and housekeeping things plaguing their minds. One woman walked right out not taking a pew to reflectively say a prayer, her face showing the same annoyance one would have just missing a train.

Bea scanned the church. There were only a few people left. She spotted Dee, smiled close-lipped, and wiggled her index finger at him like a little girl. He winked at her as she strode into the confessional first putting on a little lace shawl over her head.

He moved to the last pew right outside the confessional to be close to her so that they could leave together quickly after she said a few prayers, unless she wanted to light a candle at St. Joseph's statue or the Madonna's.

After several minutes, Dee seemed to hear muffled, half-whispered voices, inaudible at first but increasing in volume where he could actually hear a word or phrase here and there. As it continued, Dee got the strange feeling an exchange was happening. Dee started to perceive that it wasn't going to end in warm whispers. Voices were increasing in timbre.

Bea's voice, still somewhat soft, was agitated, and when she was agitated, her speech pattern would increase in speed like a machine gun engaged in enfilading fire seemingly reporting words out on the inhale and exhale allowing no interjections, no give-and-take, no comeback retorts.

And then the priest said loudly, "*Silencio!*"

There was an ever so brief pause. Dee felt heat well up in his face. He was stunned. He couldn't swallow. Then Bea shot out, "Who the hell do you think you're talking to!" It was not a question.

"*Silencio!*" the priest bellowed. It was stentorian, almost operatic. The acoustics in the church wavered with its overtones. Everyone there centered sights on the outburst.

Bea rushed out of the confessional, slid open the curtained area where the priest sat, and confronted him face-to-face. "Who the hell do you think you are! You don't talk to me like that!"

"*Silencio!*" the priest barked out.

Bea took a step back, staring at him, with the controlled anger of a street fighter armed with brass knuckles and a broken bottle. She lashed out: "First of all: no American woman will take that paternalistic drivel you dish out! It's pure crap! Second of all, you're a chauvinist! The worst kind! Garbed in a black skirt and a white collar! Third of all, you know nothing of women! Read about Mary Magdalene. Read about Hagar. Read about Lot pimping his own daughters in the name of hospitality. Read about Ruth on the threshing room floor. Read about the woman at the well! Fourth of all, if you ever said to your own mother what you said to me, she'd give you twenty-five over the ass! Fifth of all, you call yourself a man who walks in the disciples' footsteps? They were no great shakes! They all ran away! Abandoned the Lord. The only people that stuck with Him to the end were the holy women at the foot of the cross. And St. John, who probably was a kid at the time!"

The few remaining people in the church, including Father Charley, stood transfixed. Father Saydah got out of the confessional and looked like he was going to have a stroke. No one recalled anything like this happening before.

Bea was shaking in fury. Dee was afraid to move. "Sixth of all, I'm writing a letter to the pastor! Seventh of all, I'm writing a letter to the bishop! Eighth of all, I'm writing a letter to the cardinal! Ninth of all, I'm writing a letter to the pope! And tenth of all, you're a disgrace to the cloth! Whoever gave you the faculty to hear confessions should be horse-whipped!"

Bea then turned to the remaining women on Father Saydah's line and said, "This man comes from a patriarchal country. And he's a male chauvinist! His thinking is from the Stone Age. Your role is to tend to the house, tend to the children, and tend to your husband's"—she shut her mouth and took a deep breath—"commands! Maybe in his country, these dopy ideas hold water, but not here! I feel sorry for all those women in Lebanon. Pets are probably held on a higher ground than women. They should have a revolution! If you still want to confess to this guy, go ahead. At least I warned you."

She glared at the priest. "And as for you, I'm through with you! I should smack your face!" She then turned to Dee, snapped her head, and said "Come. Let's get out of here." Dee quickly followed her and as they exited the church, she stopped dead in the church's vestibule. She then turned around and ran back in. Dee was behind her a step or two. She dipped her finger in holy water, blessed herself, genuflected, and ran back out.

On the sidewalk in front of the church, she let out a strained growl. Dee had never seen her this angry. Her frenzy was almost uncontrollable. The turmoil that raged in her was as violent as the Great Red Spot of Jupiter.

He put both hands on her shoulders trying to comfort her, to calm her down.

"Don't touch me!" she seethed. "Don't touch me!" She stamped her foot several times hard on the sidewalk.

"I'm trying to help you, Bea."

Tears dribbled down her cheeks. "Just take me to Carvel!"

He took her to Carvel pleading with her all the way because he knew ice cream was her mortal enemy. It would be as hostile as Custer's Last Stand.

She had three milkshakes and a banana split.

Dee simply couldn't figure why she tried to satiate one problem with another.

Fortunately for all parties, especially the NYC Transit Authority, Dee got her home to her mother right before her gastrointestinal tectonic plates shifted. He even hailed a cab for the last six blocks from the el station, Bea doubled over in extreme pain, crying that she was going to soil herself.

Her mother, upon seeing her, bolt to the bathroom when she opened the door, shook her head in frustration. "Thank you, honey," she said to Dee. "I don't even want to know what prompted this."

"I tried...," Dee began.

"That I know. But when she gets into one of those headstrong fits... God, it's worse than trying to reason with a drunk. I'm just glad you got her home."

Suddenly Bea yelled for her mother. It was the cry of a child.

"Should I stay?"

"No, Dee. I'll take care of her. She'll call you when the 'all clear' sounds. Get home safely, dear. I must tend to the wounded."

Dee left. He was very confused.

Walking to the station, hands in pockets, he knew he would have to attend Mass at her parish for the foreseeable future. His parish would be off limits for a long, long time.

11
CHAPTER

His mother and Bea already knew. They were all together when they found out.

The second person he told was Pete McKelvey.

"Pete. Can I see you in private?" Dee said.

Pete looked up from his desk, already cluttered with work he was scouring. He was upset and annoyed. It was a chronic condition with him. It was a busy time of the month as was every day in his life. "We got no secrets here. Blurt it out."

"I was drafted."

Pete looked at Dee, pushing back in his chair like he lost a big bet on the World Series due to a fluke play. He lit up a cigarette, a lit one already burning in his ashtray. Stan had immediately hung up the phone and turned to Dee. "Let's go in the conference room."

He eyed Stan. "Stan?"

"I'm with you," Stan said.

He then addressed some clerks around the conference room. "No interference. Period."

They sat down in the conference room. "You have your physical yet?"

"I'll be going down to Fort Hamilton."

Both men sat very quietly.

"No medical issues? I know your head is on straight," Stan asked.

"I don't think the bookies give me good odds. My lottery number was thirty-nine."

"Our Army days are in the history books, Dee. I was in the Eleventh Cavalry. Mexican Expeditionary Force. 1916. We were after

Pancho Villa. Stan was in New Guinea with an old-man division fighting the Japs in World War Two. Different wars, different attitudes. This Vietnam crap, I don't like one bit. We're just sending kids to the slaughter house. There's no ground being gained. It's a guerrilla war. Like our Revolution. That's why we won. Couldn't tell who the enemy was."

"What you gonna do?" Stan asked.

"Take the physical and the tests and see what my classification is. I have a student deferment. I hope the war ends before I graduate."

"That'd be a nice trick," Stan said. "Nixon's pulling the ropes. He's just like Johnson. I think he cut his teeth on Curtis LeMay's 'let's bomb the shit out of them' mentality. But I honestly hope for your sake it does happen as you say."

"If you have other thoughts, there is nothing to be ashamed of. This is not a declared war. It's not even a police action like Korea. And Stan and I know good people in Canada. We can, with their help, set you up. Richardson Securities. They're a correspondent of ours. They owe us. Plenty," Pete said.

"Then I'll never be able to come home. I don't want to be a fugitive."

Both men were silent.

Stan said, "You're in a bind. Take your chances. Not everybody winds up in the jungle. But if you do…get very acquainted with the .45. In close combat, it speaks better than any rifle, or whatever they're using today. Saved my ass in New Guinea on more than one occasion. Best to carry two of them for good measure."

Pete said, "How's your mother taking this?"

"She's a basket case."

Pete brushed his hand over his head. "I can imagine."

"My grandfather was in World War One, my dad, World War Two. Now it's my turn. I'm very scared. But if I wind up there, I'll do what I'm told and keep my mouth shut. Maybe…maybe…"

"No," Stan said. "You listen. Mind you, you listen, but you don't necessarily just do. You got to look out for yourself. Not everyone's out for your best interest—even if they say so."

"You're sole surviving son?" Pete asked.

"Yes," Dee said, "but it doesn't matter. I've already looked into it."

"Goddamnit!" Stan said. "Remember the Sullivans?"

Pete nodded.

"Five brothers all lost on the same ship. Tell that to their mother. Well, because of that, the service changed the rules, but they're just as screwed up as the IRS code—gotta be a half-assed Philadelphia lawyer to figger it out. Maybe because of your situation they won't throw you in the fire pit, but just because you're behind the lines doesn't mean you're not a target. A gook laundry boy could put a bomb under your cot when you're sleeping." Stan's face was reddening in frustration. "And, you know, I'll tell you something about the Army. And Pete could vouch. I don't have a tooth in my head. Got choppers. Upper and lower, full plates. Do you know I was ordered by a captain to see the dentist in boot camp? I told him my situation. Didn't want to hear it. And when I go to the dentist, an officer, mind you, he bawls the shit out of me. He thought I was doing it as a fucking joke. So. The Army can be brilliant or as half-assed as last night's broccoli fart."

They all laughed a little. The little levity helped.

"Will someone be with your mom while you're taking the physical? Cause if not, me and Stan will stay with her. We can distract her. We'll take the day. Barlow won't say 'Boo.' We'll come in on a Sunday to catch up," Pete said.

"My girlfriend will be with her."

"Two women," Stan said, "might cause more tears and upset. We can help if need be. Please let us know."

"I really appreciate this. Thank you. I got my notice to report for the physical, so I'm letting you know I won't be in that day. Just so happens I have that day off from school."

Pete took out his handkerchief and blew his nose. If Dee didn't know him better, it looked as if he had teared up, but he was always bleary-eyed—a direct result of the insomnia that plagued him and the Scotch that never seemed to work as a sleeping pill.

"You're going tomorrow?" Pete asked.

"Have to be there at eight o'clock," Dee said.

"Listen." Pete inched forward and went into his back pocket, taking out his wallet. "Here's a twenty. Ten from me and ten from Stan. You go home now. Take Mom out for a nice lunch or dinner. It's on us. And you get yourself a good night's sleep. You got a big day in store. And when you find out, you call me, hear?"

"Pete. I can't take this. And I can work today."

"'Nough said," Stan piped in. "Your mom needs you more than we do today. And the offer still holds, if you need us to be with her."

"But…"

"No 'buts,'" Pete said. "You're also getting paid for today and tomorrow. It's government business. It's like you being at the Fed on the firm's behalf bidding on an auction. Same thing, or, for that matter, like being on jury duty."

Dee was so touched he almost started to cry. He stuck out his hand. Both Stan and Pete shook it warmly. They also both put an arm around Dee's shoulder.

"Best of luck to you, and don't forget to call."

"I won't," Dee said and walked out of the conference room.

"Goddamnit," Stan muttered.

They both sat in silence for a while. Then Pete said, "Tomorrow morning I'm going to go across the street to Our Lady of Victory and light a candle for that boy."

"Last time you went in a church the organ broke," Stan said.

"I'll take my chances. Now, let's get back to work before we both start blubbering." They both got up and walked out, Pete mumbling, "What a kettle of fish."

Dee, courtesy of Stan and Pete, took his mother and Bea out for dinner.

His appetite wasn't there. He had an inward feel that it was like the Last Supper. And when his mother and Bea suggested Chinese, he said nothing. He let the symbolism drift away.

Upon completion of the meal, which he found tasteless, he cracked apart his fortune cookie. It said, "No fortune today. Try again next time."

Bea stayed over at the apartment, much to his mother's displeasure. His mother was civil and set her up in the living room with clean sheets, blankets, and pillow. She wanted to have the day to herself. She wanted to get through it in her own way. Dee talked her into letting Bea stay and be with her. He told her it made him feel much more comfortable than her being alone.

"I don't want to play nursemaid to some hysterical dame if it comes to that."

"And," Dee shot back, "what if you go off the deep end? I don't want you being alone." He didn't tell her that Stan and Pete extended themselves for the same position. It would have embarrassed her.

"I have strong feelings for her. She's there to help, not cause you agita."

She firmly felt that Bea did not have any place in the matter, but she did what her son requested.

"As you always say to me, get busy. There's a lot that has to be done. Make a plan. The both of you. And play it out. I have my work cut out for me," Dee said.

She nodded, hugged and kissed him, and cried.

Bea slept in the living room. He got up early, washed and dressed, and was on the subway at 6:00 a.m. having first hugged and kissed them both. He said he would call the second he was out. He bought the *New York Times* and *Daily News* for the hour-and-a-half ride to Brooklyn.

The girls went to early morning Mass and stayed for the novena. When they got to the apartment, the order of business was to spring clean the entire apartment top to bottom. They got into their work clothes, head bandanas, and had enough dust and polishing rags hanging from them that they could have been mistaken for Bedouins. They held floor brushes like pistols and soap, and floor cleaners like hand grenades. They communicated by eye contact and an occasional finger point. It was a perfect sign language only known to them.

Dee got off the train at the last stop, grabbed a coffee and donut from a breakfast wagon, and walked down to Fort Hamilton. The day was very blustery, and he hiked up his collar against the cold.

Stopping across the street from the fort under the approach roads to the Verrazano Bridge, he gazed at the Narrows. The water was choppy and feathered by white caps and some ice floes coming down from the Hudson. He daydreamed looking at the waters and wondered if he was able to hitch on to an ice floe, how many miles would he travel in to the Atlantic and how long would it take before it melted or broke apart. And when that thought drifted away, he viewed the bridge itself, its structure, its expanse, its symmetry with land and sea and sky, its mammoth beauty, and how the curvature of the Earth was taken into account in its planning. And he mused on those souls that were rumored to have fallen into the large vats of cement that grounded the towers that supported the span, and those that chose to end a life that, to them, was void of options or other alternatives…that long, long way down into a cauldron of sea mist, and spray and splatter.

"Hey! Dee!" His wayward thoughts were instantly broken.

He turned and saw a friend from the neighborhood. "Papa T. You too?"

"Yeah," Tony Belloque said. "Uncle Sam wants me too…and the corporation," patting a stomach forged by years of fried foods, ice cream, and, most recently, Carling's Black Label beer.

"Let's hope they have a Regimental Johnny on a Pony Team. You can serve as the pillar, as usual," Dee said laughing.

It struck Papa T funny also, but after that exchange, there was really not much to say other than wish each other good luck, which seemed to go without saying, save a "buck 'em up" pat on the back. They both walked through the entrance gate on to US Army government property. It was like walking on a carpet of hot coals in bare feet.

The second they headed for the line of inductees being identity proofed, they saw two Army medical personnel attending a long-haired man visibly shaking and vomiting yellow bile, his eyes rolling back into his head.

An older sergeant, seemingly unmoved, watched and said to the corporal checking the IDs, "Asshole's fucked up on flak juice. Yesterday was bad. Looks like today's gonna be shit."

"Welcome to Fort Hamilton, ladies," the corporal checking the induction notices and the IDs said.

"Why you calling us ladies?" Papa T asked. The corporal verified Dee's identification and peered up at Papa T.

"Because," the corporal said, "real men enlist."

"Thank you, ma'am," Papa T said with a smirk as he gave the corporal his paperwork.

"Where's the other ID?" the corporal asked.

"What other ID?" Papa T said, "I gave you everything I had."

The corporal barked, "For what's in that fuckin' gut of yours! That stomach's in a different time zone, asshole! Either you got a tumor or it's your parasite twin! My money's on parasite twin!"

The corporal looked at Dee who was waiting for Papa T. "You get inside, and you," he said, turning to Papa T, "step aside. I'll deal with you later. You're holding up the line." Dee went in and never saw Papa T at the physical or in the neighborhood again.

He was cordoned off with a group of twenty and issued a large clear plastic bag. Another corporal, his blouse and pants looking as if it was the top layer of starched and perfectly creased skin, said, "Ladies. If you are fucked up on any drug or any shit to that effect, don't worry. We will keep you here up to three days and purge that crap out of your system and then test you. You are temporarily government property, and Mommy and Daddy can't claim you. You are our property till we release you. Some of you will be okay. But some of you will have the ride of your life and then may be shipped off to Vietnam at the pleasure of the United States Army, compliments of President Nixon."

At that point, everyone was cold sober, and, to some extent, those who were dancing on the edge of their substance abuse too.

"Put everything in the plastic bags. I want you stripped to your shorts and socks only. The belongings in your bag are your responsibility. Anything gets lost, not the Army's fault—strictly yours."

A scrounge three down from Dee with long greasy hair and looking a bit zonked-out interrupted by blurting out, "What if I lose my virginity, General?"

He gazed around smiling, impressed with his own wit, seeking approval from the others.

The corporal came to him, nose to nose, and, without hesitation, responded, each word clipped and distinct, "We will hack off your dick, stuff it in your mouth, and sew up your lips." He made sure his spittle sprayed the hippie's face. "And then we'll test you for VD."

No one chuckled or laughed as the corporal scanned the line with a visceral stare.

The hippie, visibly shaken, uncontrollably broke wind like a baritone horn working the scale.

The corporal's face turned a harsh purple-red. "Don't you ever talk back to me like that again and stink up my corridor, you goddamn asshole!" He stood, arms akimbo. "Apologize, fuck-face! To me! And to this group!"

He pulled him out of the line to face the group. "Apologize! Tell them that your brains are in your ass since that seems to be where you communicate from! And beg for their and my forgiveness!"

He stuttered, "I'm sorry," tearfully shaking like he had been thrown in ice water. And then, he collapsed on the floor, totally blacked out, the net result of rushed adrenaline, spiked blood pressure, and the self-induced chemical additives he took that morning.

Several bent to help, but the corporal yelled, "No one move. Don't touch him." As he began to walk away, he barked, "Follow me!" and then screamed out, "Medic! Corridor three!"

The corporal led them into a classroom. There were already twenty men there. Each desk had a booklet and pencil next to it. What shocked Dee upon entering the classroom was the figure standing in front of the class.

He was a buck sergeant and so unusual-looking that if it was the turn of the century and he was in a sideshow, he could have been labeled as a different specie: seventy percent human and thirty percent bulldog. Dee made it his business not to stare but scanned the entire front of the room, glimpsing him without appearing to fix his sights on him directly.

Built like a refrigerator, he had steel bristled hair and a face totally out of kilter. It looked as if it had been blown up and put back together incorrectly. He had a smidgen of a nose and a salt-and-pepper mustache that seemed to be the only thing even on his visage. There was a large stucco burn scar on his neck. Something in his eyes perplexed Dee. There was a certain sadness in them as if he was in his body against his will.

After everyone was seated, he addressed the class in a raspy, almost metallic-sounding voice, uncomfortably pitched too high for a man of his girth. Several people smiled, but no one laughed or chuckled.

He read hesitatingly from the instruction pamphlet. "You will find a booklet on your desk. This is your apt…apt…aptitude test." His wire-framed glasses were specifically bent to accommodate his crooked face, and he constantly edged up the glasses with his thumb, his fingers widespread, which appeared as an inadvertent "Kiss My Ass" gesture. "Please answer all the (he pronounced it *thee*) questions with the number two pencil provided. If your pencil point breaks, raise your hand. I will sharpen it for you. You will begin when I say begin." He took out a stopwatch. "You have one hour for the test."

Everyone heard the pencil snap.

He looked up, taking off his glasses, as two pieces of pencil sailed through the air from the back of the room and bounced off his chest. The pieces landed at his feet. He bent down and picked them up saying, "Who done that?"

The culprit stood up. "I did." He had long hair and a well-groomed beard and mustache. He closely resembled the Protestant depiction of Jesus Christ.

"Advance," the sergeant said, "and be recognized."

The young man, showing no trepidation, obviously doing the deed as a legitimate protest rather than posturing, walked up to the sergeant.

"You broke government property intentionally."

"Indeed I did. And I don't care—"

The young man never finished his sentence. The sergeant punched him in the mouth with a fist the size of a ham hock. He landed on the floor, knocked out cold, blood streaming out of his mouth and nose. "Musta tripped on his shoelaces," the sergeant muttered before he opened the classroom door and yelled, "Medic! Room

302!" He then looked at the class, taking his seat, and said, "Once the mess is cleaned up, we'll begin." He then went into an olive drab briefcase and pulled out an *Archie* comic book.

Once the unconscious man was removed via two stretcher bearers along with his plastic bag and the blood cleaned up with enough bleach to open the sinus passages of all in the room, the test commenced with the sergeant sounding off, "Begin!" as he hit his stopwatch.

Dee breezed through the arithmetic and vocabulary. The analogies and more advanced math were a snap for him. He even snickered silently to himself in astonishment at its simplicity. He also felt pretty comfortable going through Section Three, which was tool identification and classification except when he came to the last two pages. There were tools shown that he had never seen before. He gave it his best guess figuring that the bulk of the test was already in his pocket.

The fourth section was identifying machinery and that stopped him cold. He knew what a lathe was, and a table saw, and a cylindrical grinder, but the other machinery drew a blank. He felt a little uneasy since he had five more pages to the section and not only did not know one item but couldn't even venture a logical guess on it. He was stumped. He dared not look at anyone's test around him. The repercussions of being caught did not sit well with him. He did not relish the thought of having his jaw wired and his nose reset. He just guessed and hoped his twenty percent odds worked in his favor.

The last section, Section Five, caused him to silently belch. He felt the heat of fear flush his face and his mouth suddenly turned dry. He was rapidly going downhill with each progressive section. He felt sick, for the section was ten pages of boxes and crates in unfolded and folded positions. The questions were geared to determine what unfolded position, once folded, would look like the box heading the example. It was something, he thought, that would be more applicable to a post office exam rather than an Army test.

Anxiety enveloped him, his heart racing. Was this to see if he had a geometric mind? Or was this deliberately set up to spiral him to garbage scraps because latrine diggers were in short supply? He guessed on every question praying that luck was on his side.

He finished the test with a half hour to spare. He then reread every question carefully as a double check. He marked those questions wrong he guessed at and those he logically thought were right as wrong also to fairly assess his situation. It did not look good. He closed the booklet and placed the pencil on top of it and waited the test time out.

He resigned himself to the fact that his future in the Army was to be ordered about by idiots to do stupid things.

The sergeant looked up from his comic book and said, "Two-minute warning. When I say stop, you will close your booklets immediately and put your pencils down and leave it on your desk."

Dee tried some deep breathing Zen exercises to calm himself down during the remaining time which, to him, seemed forever. He counted ten deep full breaths before a little bell sounded on the sergeant's stopwatch. By then, his temples were pounding. The exercise was a complete failure, as was his self-appraisal as a member of the Army that moment.

"All stop!" he said, standing and peering at the entire class to observe if his orders were being complied with properly. Satisfied, he continued. "Leave your test booklets and pencils on your desk. Pick up your belongings and file out by rows. Don't bunch up. One at a time. Back row is first and wait in line in the corridor. I will mark your tests and hand it to you when I call out your last name in the corridor."

They all filed out as ordered and stood in the corridor. It was drafty, and because of this, Dee had an urge to urinate. A corporal was awaiting them and shouted, "No leaning against the walls! Hold on to your bags! Do not put them on the floor! And no talking!"

The wait for the test results was interminable.

The sergeant emerged from the classroom a half hour later. It seemed to Dee that Army time had its own schedule. A time-sensitive issue could be immediate or endless depending who was running the detail.

He began to call out the names, many of which he mispronounced and had to resort to spelling them to hand them out to the proper parties. It took fifteen minutes, and in keeping with his luck that day, when he heard "Felico," it was the last test handed out.

Dee's bowels almost evacuated when he saw his test score. He held his sphincter muscle and bladder in check. He had received a 63. There was a Roman numeral III circled in red next to the score. He was currently pulling a 3.87 out of a 4.00 scale on his cumulative average in college and now he got a 63 on the Army test. His two-year hitch would probably have him hauling galvanized pails of piss and shit as a permanent latrine orderly.

Before the sergeant turned to return to the classroom, Dee said, very politely, "Excuse me, Sergeant."

The sergeant looked at him as if bean sprouts were growing out of his head since no one ever posed him a question. The sergeant just stared at him in response with his lopsided face.

"Can you kindly tell me what this Roman numeral III circled in red means?"

A small one-sided smile graced his face and, with a flourish of the hand upward, said, "Officer material. Good job, son." He patted Dee's back and walked back into the classroom.

"Okay, ladies," the corporal said. "Down the hall we go. First stairwell to the left. Go down two flights. Get out and go through the first doors you see in the corridor. Our medics are itching to give you your physicals. All the gloves are ungreased and the needles square-tipped. Move it!" They all broke into a trot, the corporal leading.

Getting into the large hall already packed with scores of men awaiting their turns for the various parts of the physicals, Dee understood the system. It was hurry up and anxiously wait.

A guy in front of Dee was breathing heavy and very agitated. He turned and faced Dee with eyes aglow and twitching. "Man. Feel my pulse, feel my pulse. It's going a hundred; it's going a million. Those horse amphetamines…feel my pulse."

Dee switched hands on the plastic bag and his test booklet and tried to feel the guy's wrist.

"No, man, no, man, the neck…my neck, feel it in my neck."

It was visibly throbbing. Dee felt it. "It feels like a drum roll."

Laughing, the guy said, "Thanks, man. A drum roll, a drum roll… I'm gonna have a heart attack and…beat it, a drum roll." He was ecstatic.

The corporal came up to him. He had not noticed Dee's exchange with him. "Shut up! No talking!"

"I'm gonna have a heart attack! Feel my pulse! It's like a drum roll!"

"No shit?" the corporal said. "A heart attack?" He smiled. "Well. First we test you and then you can have your heart attack. And if you kick off, we'll find us a bugler to blow you 'Taps,' but until such time—shut the fuck up!"

A topkick helping out who, by the hash marks running down his sleeve, looked like he was in World War Two said in a voice that would have jiggled the Richter scale as they all jumped, "You four follow me." He hand-tapped them. The potential heart attack victim was not one of them; however, Dee was.

They bypassed a long line of men.

He handed them a clear plastic cup and bellowed, "Piss in that fuckin' cup!" He then sat at a nearby desk with a jar full of litmus sticks.

Dee held the cup in one hand and his belongings in the other. It wasn't that Dee had balls or an attitude, but he ventured out a question. "Sir. I was told not to put my plastic bag on the floor. And to do what you want me to do, I need two hands."

"Now, that's pretty good reasoning. You'll probably do okay on the psychological test. Put your stuff down, all of you. If anyone gives you an issue, they'll have to answer to me. My pay grade is higher than all of 'em." He looked at the four of them. "Now piss in the fuckin' cup. Halfway. We don't want no spillage. That happens, you lick it up. And if you have a shy dick, go in the corner over there. Use one of the urinals down there," he said, pointing to a row of urinals queued up by lines of men, "to finish your business. You bring it to me when you're done. Gotta test the pH. I'll mind the bags. Go!"

Both Dee and a blond-haired guy walked to the side of the hall, which was a bit more private than the milling of throngs in the middle of the hall. Dee urinated like a burst dam, as did the blond guy; however, his plastic cup showed a shamrock green. Dee looked at him as they went toward the urinals to finish emptying their bladders. "That's some trick," Dee said.

"No trick," the blond guy said.

Returning to the topkick, the blond guy gave him his cup. The top said, "What the fuck is this? A joke?"

"No."

The top squinted, standing. "Let me see you do it again."

"I'll try." And with a bit of concentration, eyes closed, the blond guy managed to fill one-quarter of the cup with green urine.

The topkick's eyes widened. He called an orderly. "Wilson! Come!"

A man ran to him. "Yes, Top."

"What the fuck is this? Look at it."

The orderly looked at it and smelled it. "It's green piss."

"I know that, you fuckin' idiot! Ever seen shit like this before?"

The orderly frowned. "No. No. But I been told if you was really scared shit, you pee green."

"Get the fuck out of here!" The orderly ran back to his duty.

The topkick glared at the blond guy. "You scared?"

"Shitless," the blond guy said in earnest.

"What is this?"

"I can explain," the blond guy said.

The topkick snorted, "Talk!"

"I have a urinary tract infection, and my urologist gave me some pills. They look like blue M&M's. I'm to take them until the infection clears up. Just so happens to turn your piss green. I have a note and the pills."

"Git 'em."

The blond guy fished out the pills and the note and gave it to the top. He wrote everything down on the blond guy's paperwork.

When the four of them were done, the topkick sent them to a small curtained area for the hearing test.

Walking over, the blond guy said to Dee, "Do your best not to hit the button when you hear the sound."

"Thanks," Dee said. "Good luck. Thanks for the advice." He then kept quiet, the "no talking" ingrained in his head.

"Luck to you too, buddy. God bless," the blond guy said.

Dee went through the hearing test legitimately and next went to the psychological test.

It was a one-on-one with a doctor, or so the name plate said. The gist of it, Dee inferred from it, was to determine any anomalies in sexual orientation and aggressiveness. Dee felt that the conversation was going downhill when the doctor spoke at length about Dee's lack of exuberance and interest in competitive sports until it was mentioned that he worked part-time on Wall Street. That perked the doctor to ask, "How would you describe working on Wall Street?"

Dee said, straightforward, "It's the last of the Wild West shows."

Thinking it a rather odd remark, the doctor said, "Explain that. In depth."

"Well. It is a business. And that business is to make money. We don't make soup, and we don't build bridges. We just make things happen. It is structured. We do have rules and regulations, but we deal in situations more than anything else. You have to be part diplomat and part gunslinger to make it there. The objective is to do what's in the best interest of the firm and the client. We know how to put the train on the track and get it to go. We don't ask stupid questions and we never ask permission. We do and then we advise what we've done. Sometimes we make a mistake, but not very often. My boss, Pete McKelvey, always says, 'I don't care how hard or how long you have to work. I'm only interested in results.' And, I guess, that about sums it up."

"This Mr. McKelvey sounds like an interesting character."

"He was in the Army. The Cavalry, for that matter."

The doctor was a bit astonished. "The Cavalry? My God. Was he with the 26th on Bataan? That's the last Cavalry I'm aware of in World War Two."

"No. He was with Pershing and a Lieutenant George S. Patton—I'm sure you've heard of him—in the 1916 Mexican Expedition."

The doctor laughed. "The Poncho Villa chase. He's still working? How old is he?"

Dee frowned in thought. "Midseventies, I think. And if you don't mind my saying, he could probably run rings around some of the guys around here."

The doctor became stern-faced. "I don't doubt it." He then wrote extensively on Dee's paperwork. All information put on the inductee's paperwork was put in the same test booklet. It was classified and stamped "Eyes Only for Army Personnel." The doctor handed the booklet back to Dee. "Proceed with your physical."

He left the doctor and was escorted by a corporal to an area where they were taking blood samples. A large black enlisted man eyed Dee. "Put your stuff down and give me your paperwork. Sit down next to me."

After reviewing the paperwork, he said, "Both arms. Stretch out. Let's see those veins." Smacking his left arm near the elbow with swift blows, he smiled. "Beautiful." He looked at Dee. "Listen carefully. At the count of one, you tighten your fist. At the count of two, you throw it into the inner section of my right thigh. You fuckin' hit me in the balls and I'll deck you, and you'll be in a fuckin' rice paddy before your first morning shit. At the count of three, I take all the blood I need. You got that?"

"Yes, sir."

And as the commands came, Dee did what he was told to the letter. The third count produced much burning pain. Dee thought he heard an actual puncture sound as the needle entered his vein. He looked away, making no noise, save his left eyelid drooping a tad as he winced. The black orderly knew it hurt Dee. It didn't just slip in. He had to push it in with a bit of effort. The needle was certainly dulling.

He took the needed vials of blood and gave the needle to another orderly. "Sharpen this thing on the sidewalk. And don't forget to spit on it when you bring it back." The orderly took the syringe and handed him a fresh one from the canister of bubbling water. "Hold your arm up and press hard with this gauze."

The arm hurt, and Dee began to see a purple bruise mark forming. When the black orderly told him to put the arm down, he viewed it. He said, wiping it with a medicated alcohol solution before putting on a bandage, "Shit. Some broads would give their left tit for an eye shadow that color." He gleefully laughed. "Okay, bub. Take your stuff. Here's your paperwork. You're done here."

Dee got up and was then escorted to the last and most dehumanizing part of the physical.

A corporal led Dee and a line of others to an area in the middle of the hall. Other inductees were either standing in some line or milling about waiting to be ordered to stand in some specific line. This, Dee thought, was a meat factory. It was probably the same way cattle go through the steps in a slaughter house. Here they didn't prod you with pokers. Here they prodded you with words of fear and intimidation, hostility to shatter the sensibilities.

A black orderly said, "You five"—he crooked his index finger—"on me." Dee and the other four followed him. When he told them to line up, they each stood in front of a stationary gurney. "We will check you for hernias and also check your prostate."

A large black medic addressed them. He had on rubber gloves. "At the count of one, you will drop your plastic bags and your shorts. I will check for hernias. I may ask you to cough. Cough normal, not like someone with TB. After I check for hernias, this is what will come next. I will sound off the number two. You will spread your legs and put your elbows on the gurney. I will have you on your tippy toes. Of that, I have no doubt. My magic. Because I will put not one but two greased fingers in your anus. I always use two fingers because I am a firm believer in a second opinion." Dee did not, nor did the others, think that was funny. "I will check you to see if there are any enlarged prostates. And any of you fuckers farts in my face, I will have you personally sent, at the expense of the US government, to a spot in Southeast Asia where your talents could be utilized in eradicating the spread of Communism for the better interests of the United States."

Dee tried his utmost to relax, but he tightened and it hurt.

"Oh, girly? You was so tight I almost lost my glove in there. Now, take some tissues and clean yourself off. I don't wipe asses. Here's your paperwork. Put your clothes back on. You're done."

Dee took his paperwork and slowly put back on his clothes.

He was hungry and tired and frightened to death.

Once fully dressed, he stood on yet another line to officially exit the facility. An ill feeling surrounded his soul. It was the same fear one might have in a pitch-black area close to a stairwell going down. He was unsure of his footing. At the end of the terminal line was a series of doctors reviewing medical records and notes. They were the ones that stamped the final paperwork "Accepted" or "Unacceptable," depending on the final evaluation.

He resigned himself to his fate. He didn't bother praying for a miracle. A miracle, he knew, that day was not coming his way.

It took well over an hour before he stood before the captain that was to give him his sentence.

"Any medical records or notes for me to review?"

"No, sir," Dee said. "I'm unfortunately plagued with good health."

The captain showed no reaction to the remark.

"Are there any dispensations today?"

"Beg pardon?" the captain said.

"Any dispensations being granted today?"

"Well," he said, "if it was the pope's army, perhaps. Here? Not a fucking chance."

"I see," Dee said. "I suppose it's my turn to pay back the Army for helping me."

The captain found this to be a curious statement. "How so, son?"

"My grandfather was with the 77th in World War One, and Dad was in the OSS in Greece in World War Two. They are both dead. Mom is getting Social Security for me. And…the US Army is giving me a small stipend for my college books. Maybe this is the way…my way to pay back."

The captain frowned. "Well, son, that's a healthy way to look at it. Problem is, you were just born at the wrong time."

He stamped Dee's paperwork. Nothing materialized on the form. He then slammed it down with a force that made Dee flinch. It was clearly readable but very light. It said "Accepted." "No more fuckin' good stamp pads," the captain muttered. He handed Dee the paperwork but held it for a second before Dee could pull it from his fingers. "Good luck, son. Not everyone is sent into the jungle."

"Thank you," Dee said and walked out.

The paperwork stated that he had a 2-S student deferment, a temporary delay, until he graduated, at which point he was reclassified as 1-A, ready for immediate induction.

When he got outside, the sun was on its way to setting. The wind had died down. The air was crisp and the visibility crystal. The bridge was a pretty sight, aflame in orange tones from the sun's glow. He heard the traffic above. He was hungry.

He decided to eat something before he called his mother and then... Pete McKelvey.

The walk up toward the subway station did him good. It seemed to blow the tangles out of his head and eased down the coil spring in his belly that was about to snap. It was one thing to go through hell, but he had to smell the earth and view the beauty of the world before he went back to hell again.

He needed to eat. After a few blocks, he saw a place called the Twisted Dish Tavern. He went in and saw that it was a Blarney Stone setup. The smell of the food hit him immediately: hot roast beef. Virginia ham, knockwursts, homemade meatloaf, assorted vegetables, mingled with the dank and hopsie aroma of beer.

Over the bar was a moose head wearing a campaign hat looking down on five older gents nursing their drinks, talking to the bartender.

Dee pulled up a stool and sat down. The bartender noticed him, continued his chat until the punch line was executed, and then walked over. "What can I get ya, son?"

"Want to see my draft card?"

"You look old enough to me. And I run the show here."

"I'd like a large Rheingold draft and a knockwurst sandwich on rye. Sauerkraut and couple of them nice fried potatoes. With mustard, if you have."

"Righto," the bartender said. He gave Dee the beer first and put together his plate.

Dee took a sip, savored it, then wiped the foam off his mustache. He saw a sign to the right of the moose head. It read, "In God We Trust… All Others Pay Cash."

When the bartender came back and served him his plate, steaming hot, Dee said, "You get that saying up there from Jean Shepherd?"

"Nope," the bartender said. "Shep got it from me."

Astonished, Dee said, "No shit?"

"No shit," was the bartender's response. "Enjoy."

He then went back to his old regulars to swap another lie or tell another joke while he freshened their drinks.

With the first bite of the knockwurst sandwich, the juices squirted into his mouth. He was happy and content. There was a lot more than steam heat that gave warmth to the tavern.

He finished his plate and paid the bartender. "Another beer?"

Dee said, "I'm good. But I do have to say I really enjoyed the knockwurst. It was really great."

"Thanks," the bartender said, smiling. It was rare that he got compliments on the food.

"Got a pay phone here?"

The bartender pointed to the back. "To the left of the bathrooms. We have two booths. If ya need change, gimme a holler."

Dee nodded his head and got off the stool. He decided to call Pete McKelvey first. It would be short and sweet. The call to his mother would be rough. He fished in his pockets for change. He had a feeling he was going to have to feed the phone with his call to her.

12
CHAPTER

Dee's mother, Margo Felico, stood with fists placed on her hips. "Spic and Span. That's the ticket."

Bea smiled back. "Ready when you are."

Margo, viewing Bea minus makeup, fresh faced, a bright eagerness in the eyes, had to admit to herself that she was quite pretty—strike that, she thought: cute. That's more like it. The dimple and slight overbite fostered an unusual attractiveness along with the wide-spaced tawny eyes. It made her very photogenic, judging from the picture Dee had of her on his bedroom mirror. But the best part, according to her evaluation of her thus far, was that she was not a prima donna. She had a good attitude and a correct disposition, but there was something about her that troubled her, and what annoyed her the most was the fact that she couldn't put her finger on it.

By all appearances, Bea was deeply religious. They had gone to early morning Mass, the "Hunter's Mass" as Margo always put it, and she saw her follow all the steps throughout the service properly. She observed her steeped in prayer as she examined her conscience before Communion and actually had to gently elbow her so she wouldn't miss going up for the "Body and Blood."

This was not playacting. This was real. This was a girl in total devotion. Yet Margo still had a doubt in her mind. She thought, initially, it was a natural reaction, a typical mother's reaction to a girl in her son's life—any girl, it didn't matter. But it was more than that. It had something to do with Bea, and for the life of her, she had no idea what it was. It was much like a dog she had as a little girl who always growled at her uncle Gus. He was kind to the animal, never hurt it or raised his voice to it, never gave it cause for such a negative reaction, yet the dog, for whatever reason, simply did not like or take to him. Something instinctive spooked her dog. And, somehow, she was getting the same feeling. She would give it time, she thought. She was willing to see how the relationship would bloom. She didn't want to base it on the instincts of a dog, although she knew many people who did that. And they usually turned out to be right.

A lot was happening to Margo Felico that day. She felt like seaweed in a stormy surf. But the thing that irked her the most, that rattled her to the core, was the thing she was most noted for, her signature dish: spanakopita. It was part of her very fiber, her blood, her sinew. It classically defined her. It was lovingly made for holidays and special occasions, the secret recipe handed down to her by her maternal grandmother, Helen, her *yiayia*. And now it was being taken away from her by her son. Dee wanted Bea to make him her rendition of that sacred meal to be awaiting him when he got home from Fort Hamilton.

It was not the smartest move he ever made in his life, but he did like Bea's spanakopita and wanted, very much, his mother to experience it too.

When it was told to her, Margo flew into a rage. "This is absurd! This is a violation of my kitchen! No other spanakopita has ever been made in this kitchen other than mine! I will not have it! How can you do this to your mother!"

He tried to speak slowly and calmly, her pounding pace in the kitchen actually rattling a pot lid on the stove, "I just want you to taste it. This is no competition. Please understand."

"Understand?" She threw a drying towel on the sink. "Now I understand how the French felt when the Nazis marched into Paris! My kitchen…my kitchen will be occupied by a foreign power with no Greek blood in her! My stove, my oven, my pots and pans—my utensils! I'm relinquishing all my stuff! And you don't want me to be upset! And I have to understand! Is this the way you treat me?"

"Mom. Please. I just want you to taste it. It's different. That's all."

Her eyes smoldered. "Hers better?"

"Just…different, I said. Like hamburger cooked in a frying pan as opposed to cooking it on an outdoor grill. Just plain different."

"Hamburger is not spanakopita!" She snorted out a punch of air like a wounded bull. "Goddamnit! Sometimes I wonder about you!" She flayed about the stove but, finally, reluctantly, resigned to accept his request. She was not very happy. "Let her use the whole fucking kitchen! But I'm warning you! I'm not cleaning up any of her shit!"

She looked at him and then, after a little while, saw her boy smiling at her with deep love in his eyes; her little boy…the little boy she nursed, the little boy she played with, the little boy she helped with his homework, the little boy whose boo-boos she kissed. She took him in her arms and hugged him, tears forming in her eyes.

"Mom. Dealing with you is worse than dealing with Attila the Hun!"

She laughed her throaty laugh. "I know. I taught that bastard what rampaging is all about!"

He held her in his arms. "Promise me you'll behave."

It took her a long time to answer. Sighing, she said, "I'll bite my tongue before I say anything." She then looked up at him after a short time. "I just hope I have a tongue left when you come home."

Oddly enough, she seemed to get along with Bea during the cleaning binge. Little was said that wasn't related to the job. Margo was content with Bea's eye for detail and didn't have to repeat herself on any direction given. What lifted her a bit was the fact that Bea whisper-sang as she cleaned. It was a soft sound that came in single puffs only when applying heavy effort to some tough grime or straining to dust a hard-to-reach spot. *Maybe, Margo thought, she's like me and relishes cleaning, and her epitaph on her tombstone should read like mine: "She Died with a Dust Rag in Her Hand and a Smile on Her Face."*

"Should I do Dee's room? Or is it off limits?"

The first question was fine. The second question didn't sit well with Margo. "If you like. Excuse the sloppiness. It doesn't come from me."

Surveying the room full of books and papers, and music man-uscripts scrawled with snippets of notes scattered in any nook that would hold it on the overloaded bookcase, she found it terribly disordered, but delightfully so. There was a low, wide rocker and an opened typewriter on his single bed since he had no desk. The dresser was strewn with aftershave; combs; brushes; a coffee can half filled with change; and a large, chipped beer mug that held pencils, pens, clips of all sizes, and a letter opener. The mirror above the dresser was long and narrow. There was a snapshot of Bea squeezed into the corner bookended by a cut-out picture of Kim Novak and an exotically sultry snap of Ava Gardner when she was perhaps fourteen years old which he had probably ripped out of a library book. Bea chuckled, "Wow. I guess I'm in good company."

Margo harrumphed and then hummed. *That Ava Gardner and that Kim Novak—two first-class pipperinos. Yeah, sweetie, you're in some real good company.* She then shivered as if she had swallowed unsweetened cranberry juice.

At the end of his bed was a small but sturdy table that held an RCA Victor Victrola with a large horn jutting out right in front of the airshaft window.

"I've never seen one of these before. Only in books or magazines," Bea said.

"My husband's."

"And Dee's tranquilizer, right on the turntable." It was an old 78 rpm black lacquer record titled "If I Could Be with You One Hour Tonight." The faded HRS label said, "Bechet-Spanier Big Four 1940." "God, he told me so much about this."

The record had more scratches on it than a retired cue ball, and there were three distinctive pin-head sized paint droplets on it, pale green. Next to it was Dee's handwritten score of the arrangement. In his cryptic penmanship, Bea saw the instrumentation noted: Soprano Sax, Cornet, Guitar, String Bass. It was in a clear plastic folder.

"You read music?" Margo asked.

"No. But I've seen music scores before. I can read a choreographer's score though. They're sort of something like you'd see a football coach do on a play, but nothing like this."

Margo pointed out a lot of circles with Xs in the middle throughout the score. "Know what this is?"

She had no idea what the symbols meant and looked at Margo questioningly.

"The scratches."

Bea made a funny face. "The scratches? In the record?"

"Yes. He noted the scratches. Says it gives it complete and total authenticity."

"My god," Bea said, shaking her head.

"And," Margo exclaimed, "Get this: that's not all. See these three triangles with the circles on top?"

"Don't tell me," Bea said with a schoolteacher's knowing look. "The paint."

"Exactly. The paint spots. The paint spots that produce the three skips on the record."

Bea gave a big sigh. "Unbelievable." She then said, "You know, I can get the paint spots off—"

Margo jumped in. "Heaven forbid. He'd kill you. He says it adds a certain early modern, progressive style to the measure, unknown in 1940. Can you beat that?"

She laughed. "That's Dee. He's certainly different. That's why I love him."

It might have been said innocently, but it jolted Margo. She bit her tongue, refraining from comment.

"Think I should clean it?" Bea asked.

"I wouldn't. The grit and dust are probably what's holding it together."

Bea examined the record, and the record arm with the two silver dollars taped to it for weight. "I understand the scratches." She looked up at Margo. "That's no diamond needle…"

"A nail," Margo interjected.

"But," Bea continued, "where'd the paint come from?"

"My husband. God rest his soul." She quieted, somewhat dreamily, conjuring his face in her mind's eye. "A beautiful person, so loving, a scholar, a soldier…a painter? Wasn't his field. Felt it was a form of capital punishment. Only did it to save a buck. Preparation? Clean-up? You must understand. These were concepts unknown to his mind. Dee gets his sloppiness from him. I swear. If a cockroach was crawling on the wall, he'd paint right over it." She then looked directly at Bea. "Of course, the record was fully exposed when he did the room."

Bea chuckled then said, "Dee told me a lot about this record. Says it calms him down, relaxes the nerves."

"I know that to be true for him. Unfortunately, not for me. Yes. When he's in a funk, he reads the music he wrote as he plays the record. Sometimes he even conducts it. And he plays it, and he plays it—not once, not twice, a thousand times, and all I hear is that tinny sound, and all I want to do is throw that infernal machine out the window…and him with it." She heaved in exasperation.

"I guess it beats smoking pot."

She bit her tongue. "Well," Margo sniffed, "let's finish up," and walked out of the room.

The cleaning feat resulted in an apartment that would have glowingly passed white glove inspection by the Marine Corps.

The next business was Bea's solo flight in preparing and cooking the spanakopita.

After the Chinese meal Dee took them to the night before, compliments of Pete and Stan, Bea went shopping and purchased all the ingredients needed for the feast's making.

Bea made from scratch the phyllo dough. She used very hot tap water in the mixing and kneaded it with delicate hands. Working the rolling pin, she did it exceptionally well under Margo's observation and made the sheets the thickness of newspaper. Margo had never quite gotten it to that thinness and blew her nose needlessly, watching. Margo knew that working a seasoned rolling pin was an art. It required that right pressure on the dough and the correct arm movement and knowing exactly when enough was enough. What seemed to get Margo's goat was that Bea was not intimidated by her presence watching her like a panther ready to pounce. She was totally oblivious to her. Her mind was set, and only set, on the task at hand.

Bea did a formidable job on the dough. She put the sheets in plastic wrap and refrigerated them.

She then cleaned up everything with the same purpose and thoroughness she did earlier that morning when she helped with the apartment.

They finished cleaning around 2:00 p.m.

"Let me wash up. I'll start the spanakopita, if that's okay."

"I suppose so," Margo said. "You're making several batches. There'll be plenty for Dee when he comes home."

Bea took a quick shower and jumped into a comfortable, raggy housedress. Margo liked the unpretentiousness.

Bea then proceeded to combine the spinach, scallions, garlic, parsley, dill, oregano, the cheeses, eggs, salt and pepper, and pre-heated the oven. And after thoroughly mixing the filling gently, she tea-spooned out the mixture on to the phyllo dough she had taken out of the fridge and folded the dough carefully over into triangles. For a golden brown finishing color, she brushed the patties with some melted butter.

In the meantime, Margo showered. Everything in the bathroom was spotless after Bea had used it. She was very pleased. She was beginning to get comfortable with her presence in her home, and a mild form of fondness was developing. But the spanakopita had to be taste-tested, and a lot of very strong feelings were riding on that. She finished washing up quickly and also came out in a housedress.

Margo noticed Bea leaning against the small work station, standing by the stove.

"Sit," she said. "I'll get you a chair."

"I like to watch it," Bea said. "Every stove cooks differently. I just don't like to put things in the oven and walk away from it. I have to watch it."

Margo liked what she heard. She had a habit of doing that also. She then suddenly thought of Dee. The hard work during the day had distracted her.

"Bea?" she said, and then realized that it was the first time she had addressed her by name.

Bea looked at her inquiringly with a smile.

"Can I get you anything?"

"Water'll be fine."

"Ice?"

"Cold tap. New York has the best water in the world."

Margo filled up a large glass after letting the faucet run for a minute to get it very cold and handed it to her.

She drank the water in large gulps a little too quickly, two rivulets streaming out of the corners of her mouth down her neck, forking between her breasts. She patted her chest, a wet stain showing. "Ohhh. That was cold. Excuse me." She blushed, a little embarrassed. "I was really thirsty." She smiled.

Margo laughed and, at that moment, found her refreshing. But she was still very confused about her. "Don't worry. It'll dry."

"Shouldn't be long now." The cooking time was twenty to twenty-five minutes. Bea checked the patties through the oven window and giggled. "They look beautiful."

"Smells good too," Margo said.

Bea's internal egg timer went off in her head. She cooked by feel, smell, and observation, and occasionally, depending on the dish, by taste.

Bea then took the pot holders, opened the oven, and grabbed the sides of the tray, careful not to burn herself, but in her squatting position, she lost balance. Margo quickly steadied Bea's hands on the tray but in the process burned her right hand. No patties fell off the tray. They just bunched up on one side.

"I'm sorry. You're burned." Bea's voice was a nervous quiver.

"It's okay. Not the end of the world or the first time."

They put the tray down on the stove top and evened out the patties, allowing them to settle.

Bea rushed over to the freezer and cracked open an ice tray. And as she was about to hand Margo some cubes to put on the burn, saying, "I'm sorry," she saw Margo biting into one of the patties.

Bea stood expectantly, holding her breath, the ice still in her hand.

Margo seemed in thought, her eyes curiously unfocused. She muttered something in Greek.

Bea said nothing. She suddenly became frightened, her mouth going dry.

Margo looked solidly at Bea. "Bea. This is not good." She took another bite. "This is heavenly." Her eyes closed as she finished one. "This is exactly how my *yaiyai* Helen made them. I was never able to duplicate it. This is my grandma's spanakopita." She then spoke to Bea in Greek unknowingly and hugged her tightly, sobbing.

Bea's cheeks dribbled with tears too. The ice had melted in her hand.

Margo, after the hug, and being handed more ice by Bea for her hand, ate another one, savoring each bite in a state of quasi ecstasy, wetting her fingers with her tongue, picking up every flake of dough. She then told Bea stories of her grandmother with a lightness and joy that only good memories bring.

"How did you get this recipe?"

"A lady in our apartment building, Mrs. Vassilatos. She taught me. I couldn't write down anything. She measured everything by eye in one glass. She gave me a duplicate glass and just told me to watch. It took me a long time, but when she kissed me, I knew I passed the test. Rolling the dough to paper thinness was the hardest. That took me the longest to master."

"They are wonderful. And I have to hide the next batch under lock and key or else Dee will be out of luck." She smiled at Bea. "Now I see why he wanted me to experience your spanakopita. And did I give him a hard time."

"He never said a word to me." Bea saw a smile in Margo's eyes.

Bea made a total of four trays.

They both called it a day. It was busy with no time to think too much. They took some patties, opened some aluminum TV tables, and ate sumptuously in the living room with their feet up on ottomans.

"I really think this calls for a drink."

"Mrs. Felico. I don't drink," Bea said.

"Well, it's really not a drink-drink. It's ouzo—the nectar of the gods. I have a case down in the basement my father made before he died. We only give a taste on special occasions. And this, indeed, is definitely one. And, dearie, you can call me Margo. Let me get a bottle. I'll be back in a flash. If the phone rings, pick it up."

She was back with the bottle with no label on it in less than two minutes. Margo opened it and poured a portion into two ornate wine glasses she got from the china closet.

"You can have it with a little water. It'll give it a milky look. I, personally, like it neat."

Bea said, "I'll take it neat." Bea took the filled glass and smelled it. It had distinctive licorice aroma. She looked at Margo questioningly.

"It's like drinking liquid licorice."

"I love licorice!" Bea said excitedly.

They both toasted each other and quaffed it down. It was made well and had little harshness. Bea felt a volcano of heat rush up her neck and face. "Oh boy!" She said, "It's delicious, but my face feels I stuck it in the oven."

Her neck and cheeks were scarlet.

That's called Kefi, the Greek spirit. Now that you have it, it'll not happen anymore." She then filled Bea's glass as well as her own.

Bea smiled and said out loud. "Kefi. What a splendid word." She then took a sip of her drink. Margo was right. She obviously had the Greek spirit because it went down like warm velvet.

While sipping her third ouzo, Margo cleared her throat and said, "I've got a bone to pick with you. And now's as good a time as any to ask away."

Bea, taken off guard, took a mouthful of her drink. Her face was numb and flushed, and Margo's accusatory tone issued another wave of heat coming up to her face. She looked wide-eyed at Margo.

"You physically abused my son on two separate occasions. You gave him a black eye, of which I fully agree with you on. In fact, I would have broken his nose too. That was horrible what he did. But it's the biting thing. That really goes against my grain. I couldn't pry anything out of him about that other than some cockamamie bullshit that you guys were horsing around and things got out of hand." She looked squarely at Bea. "So what really gives?"

Bea felt like a pinned butterfly. She knew she couldn't tell the exact truth. That would pain Margo terribly. And she might even be accused of being a succubus. Their giving of themselves to each other was mutual and selfless. But a mother wouldn't understand that. Especially his mother. And told to her in her home. And, now, of all times, now that they were making a good connection. Bea felt that she had to tell the truth obliquely. She couldn't out and out lie. She had to hold herself together and make it a good, plausible performance, something to mull on, something to consider. And she began with, "I'm a good girl, you know."

Margo leaned back. "I never suggested—"

Bea's mind sprung up Cole Porter and she blurted out, "It was just one of those things."

Margo accepted the statement and dwelled on it. But Bea knew she couldn't leave it there.

Bea then continued, "We were smooching."

Margo giggled, almost like a teenager. She took another sip. She liked the word.

"And then," Bea said, "he got...a little—frisky."

"Frisky?" Margo said in a ringing tone as if she hadn't heard the word in years.

"I admit it was impulsive, but it ended what could have..."

Margo laughed. "I totally understand."

"And, please, please don't tell Dee. I'd be so embarrassed."

Margo toasted Bea, finishing her drink. "Our little secret." She then laughed to herself. "And just between us girls, I think his father invented the word *frisky*. Like father, like son." Her smile was genuine. "Would you care for another ouzo?"

And that ended everything.

Relaxing, her short verbal tap dance over, she said, "I would. Thank you."

After pouring Bea a glass as well as herself, she said, "Gotta hit the shuttle. Be back in a few." She walked, a bit unsteady toward the bathroom, brushing her shoulder against the arch between the rooms, audibly muttering, "Excuse me," which Bea found extremely funny and muffled her giggle with her palm.

Bea felt very light and content. She was happy, but then she suddenly thought of Dee and what he might be going through at the moment. Her thoughts were like snapping rubber bands. She couldn't dwell on anything. And then she saw Margo on wobbly footing carrying the Victrola, the horn sticking out in front of her like a character out of Dr. Seuss.

Immediately, Bea jumped up to help but lost balance and plopped right back down in the chair. "Mrs."—she started edging out of the chair more carefully and corrected herself—"Margo. Let me help you with that." She rushed over to help her negotiate the Victrola and horn appendage and placed it very carefully on the closed lid of the baby grand.

"I think we need a little music on the subject," Margo said, adjusting the horn of the Victrola and plugging it in with an extension cord. "Since you never heard this beforehand—it's very much a part of Dee—I figured you might as well hear what he hears."

"I'll never hear what he hears. He snaps his fingers and hums all the time, always hears music. But, yes, I would love to hear it." She then looked at Margo, terribly touched, as if she had given her a relic from the Lord's manger. "Oh, oh, Margo. That was so thoughtful of you," she said and impulsively kissed her on the cheek.

Margo's intent was more on blowing the dust off the Victrola and did not even respond to the kiss. Bea then helped blow the dust off as well. "We can always wipe it off the piano with a dust rag. But later," Margo said, the dust particles dancing in the setting sun's orange hues slipping through the angled venetian blinds.

She turned it on. A low-frequency hum emitted along with a burning electrical odor.

"I hope we're not going to start a fire," Bea said.

"No, honey. That's just the tubes warming up. I know when to start it. I have it down to the scent," Margo said.

Bea found that remark very funny and laughed loudly.

Margo picked up the record arm and the turntable spun with a shimmering whir, the label becoming a black-and-brown blur. The burning smell had dissipated. Margo took precaution by whiffing the air just to play it safe. The tiny nail serving as the needle slipped into the record groove. Several scratches were heard before the cornet introduction floated out of the horn with a smooth, tinny sound.

It was a pretty piece, scratches and three skips aside, Bea thought. Soft and very sweet sounding, it was a moderately paced fox trot with some sassy jazz riffs peppered in the right spots, but nothing, Bea felt, that was worthy of a thousand playbacks. To play it once, twice, perhaps even three times would have satisfied Bea for a good period of time. It was catchy enough for Bea to put together a soft shoe routine on it within minutes, but why Dee was so enraptured with it, she had no idea.

She speculated that since it was his father's record, there might be some nostalgic love bond in there, but other than that, his infatuation with it escaped her.

"Well," Margo said, "what'd ya think?"

"It's a nice song, not overdone. But... I can't..."

Margo chimed in, "Me neither. So you can see. Play it fifteen times in a row. That'd make anyone go apeshit."

"Play it one more time. I just thought of a step. Wanna show ya."

"Okay. Here we go." Margo then put the record on from the beginning.

Bea waited until the cornet intro was completed and then did a time step, which was followed by a shuffle to the right and then to the left. She then did a slow triple spin, almost losing her balance, and ended with a tight turn, her arms loosely extended. "See? Ooo. Got a little dizzy there," she said, stopping as the music continued.

Margo, the glow of the ouzo in her cheeks, said, "Let's dance the record out." And they did a foxtrot, Margo leading. They were in sync with the music although on shaky feet.

And then they heard the phone ring.

Margo released Bea and ran for the phone. She almost tripped on the saddle between the rooms but caught herself. Bea followed her into the dining room as Margo sat in the rocker next to the phone stand. Bea saw her holding back tears and quickly found a box of tissues. Margo's phrases were punctuated. She was holding back crying. She did not want to upset Dee.

"You told them? About what Dad did...and your grandfather?" There was a long stretch where Bea kept feeding her tissues to daub her eyes and nose. She intermittently muttered, "Okay," and, "I see." And then she said, "Yes. Yes. It was delicious, and so is she." After a pause, she implored, "Cab it, please? … Traffic? Oh god, it's rush hour. Yes…love you too. Wait."

She handed the phone to Bea. "Dee," was all she said and listened for a good minute. "She's fine, and we have good stuff here when you get home." Her "bye" was a breathy whisper because Margo began to break down. Bea quickly covered the mouthpiece and hung up the phone.

Margo's lip was quivering. She couldn't contain herself. "My baby, my baby." Bea rushed and hugged her. Margo was shivering uncontrollably as if she had a high fever. Her sobs were deep and heavy.

Once the initial crying jag was ebbing, she felt totally spent. She looked at Bea tenderly and said, "Thank you…for being here…with me." They hugged and kissed like a mother and daughter would.

"Take a deep breath, Margo. Try to calm down." Bea felt her face with a loving touch. "Maybe you should wash up? Huh?"

Margo said, "He's taking the subway, said he needs to sit. To cab it would take longer. He says he needs to sit."

"Needs to sit…," Bea said and simply closed her eyes.

"Imagine," Margo said, feeling a bit more in control. Her eyes were red. "Needs to sit."

They both shook their heads in puzzlement.

Margo washed up in the kitchen sink, saying, "Ah, thinks we needs ta sit! An' have 'notha fuckin' drink," with a rubbery tongue. Her emotions were in multi-collision.

Bea thought it very funny and laughed loudly. The relief was unexpected but greatly needed. Her laughter was hair trigger now. And she felt it was wonderful. "I'll get the glasses…and the likker-ish." Everything seemed very funny and light. She giggled delightedly.

They polished off the bottle, and Margo went back down the basement for another. Bea had no objection. It was just fermented liquid licorice, she thought. As Margo went to get another bottle, Bea, with the care of a mother moving a newborn from a changing table to a crib, hoisted up the Victrola from the baby grand and carried it from the living room to Dee's bedroom, leaning against the hallway wall for steadiness and placed the contraption, horn and all, precisely in its original resting place.

On the way back to the living room, she stopped off at the bathroom, saying out loud to herself, "Gotta winky-tink," and had a minor mishap. Upon completing her business and washing her hands, she rushed out of the bathroom, her large house dress blousing and caught the pocket on the doorknob, which pulled her back into the door, ripping the pocket.

This random act of carelessness became funnier for her than seeing someone doing a double gainer, slipping on a banana peel.

Bea laughed on her way back through the railroad apartment as Margo observed the naturally sexy gait Bea had withered to a measured, wide-based waddle. She walked like she had a pot between her legs and suction cups on her soles. Finding her chair, Bea plopped down, her legs back up on the ottoman.

They sat quietly in the living room for some time sipping their drinks seemingly without care as if on vacation. Margo, outwardly calm, was in hot-cold confusion concerning Dee. It was a nightmare as fresh as a smacked face. The ouzo was simmering the fire.

Bea was aware of Margo's issue, but things were beginning to get fuzzy with her. She was on a delicate edge between crying like an infant and laughing hysterically. She had never experienced such a frenzy of emotions. She felt terribly sorry for Margo and terribly sorry for herself and impulsively blurted to Margo, "I have a 'fession to make, Margo," emphatically adding, "I do."

"Whaaa?" Margo looked up at her, awakened from her circle of numbness, closing one eye for better focus.

"Confession... I have...to make," Bea said stiltedly. "I...a... I am," she began, formulating each word slowly as if translating from a different language on the spot, "terribly...terrible," swigging a slug of ouzo and completing her thought in a half-swallowing, half speaking gurgle, "jealous of your son... Dee... Felico." She then nodded her head as if answering herself. "I am."

"Jealous? I hear right?" Margo asked.

"Yesh," Bea slurred. And when it registered as to what she had just said, she started to giggle. Her laughter was as contagious as a yawn, which set off Margo as well.

They both took deep breaths. Their chests pained them from the laughing. Their faces were red and their eyes wet.

"So," Margo said, still breathing like she walked up a hill, "what ya mean, jealous?"

Exasperatedly, Bea said, "The man is by all accounts in good with the Lord."

Margo was certainly puzzled by that statement. "What?" she asked.

"And," Bea went on, her eyes widening, "he doesn't' even know it. He's graced. Definitely." She brought her hand up, waving, as if for emphasis, and for a moment paused, as if forgetting her thought. "Without question," she added as a final note.

"I don't," Margo said, taking a sip, "follow."

"He needs to sit. He has to sit—that's what he's doing on the train. You know that. Whether listening to that song, endlessly, or even alone. I've seen it…all by himself…without effort, like some contemplative or Buddhist monk perched on a block of ice in the Himalayas, working with great effort, intensely, diligently doing… nothing. Absolutely nothing! Nothing!" Her voice raised a bit. "And…he can do it for hours! And then"—taking her legs, the house dress opened to the crotch, off the ottoman, and sitting upright in the chair, her finger pointing—"walk away…totally refreshed, a new person, raring to go, like a cripple wading out of Lourdes's healing waters, completely cured."

Margo said, "I know what you mean. He is my son."

"I want that! I want that!" Bea stood up and leaned on the chair to steady herself, completely wound up. "For what I want to do…"

"Honestly, Bea," Margo said. "No reason to get your piss hot. Things come to deserving people at different times."

"I deserve it!" she jumped in. "I deserve it! I even pray for it. Sometimes I wonder: am I praying to the right God for the wrong reason or the wrong God for the right reason?" Her voice cracked, and she swallowed the remainder of her drink. "I just know one thing. I want that! Desperately! Why should he have it and not me!"

"Sometimes," Margo said, "you get things when you least expect it."

Bea spat out, "I least 'pect it now! I least expect it now!" Her eyes flared as she stamped her foot on the floor, slapping her hand hard against her bare leg, a red print of her hand, fingers and all, materializing on her white skin.

Jolted by the outburst and well into her cups but still a long way from Never-Never Land, Margo yelled back, "Don't you raise your voice at me! In my house! Who the hell do you think you are, you drunken twit!"

Bea instantly sat down, tears forming in her eyes, realizing she was out of control and horribly embarrassed, and muttered, "I'm so sorry. I…" She put her face in her hands and cried bitterly.

At that point Margo knew her instincts were right just like her dog was with her uncle Gus. There was something wrong with her, and not interested in psychology, cared little what her malady was. She just cared about Dee. It was not a good time to let her have a piece of her mind. That girl, that little girl was quivering on her chair like a baby in the cold. The better part of her felt sorry for her and that angered her. Her parents had brought her up to forgive and forget. That never quite sat well with her. Yes, Margo always forgave, never forgot, and, most of the times, got even. Margo felt totally sober now but completely exhausted.

She went to Bea and put her hand on her head. "You need to rest now. I'll get you some water. Put your feet up. All will be okay." She got her the water which Bea gulped down and almost immediately fell into a sound sleep. Margo covered her with an afghan and sat down next to her.

She was a pretty girl, Margo thought, but a pretty mess as well. She then closed her eyes, only to rest them.

Dee heard the sound in the hallway of the apartment house after he came through the front door vestibule. The sound was a distant buzzing, much like a wayward lumberjack sawing a tree down after everyone called it a day. Walking up the stairs, the sound got louder.

Opening the apartment door, and turning to the right, he saw a spectacle. His mother and Bea were stretched out on two overstuffed living room chairs, cuddled in afghans, mouths open, snoring in tandem on the inhale as well as the exhale.

A tang of licorice permeated the air, and he cringed looking at them. They were totally pie-eyed on his grandfather's ouzo, a libation that would flatline a weak heart as sure as a bullet. He knew it intimately. It went down well, took tension off the soul, but it snuck up on you and showed as much mercy as the Indians did to General Custer.

He yelled as loudly as he could, "Thanks so much for the wonderful welcome!"

Their eyes cracked open groggily. It took them more than a moment to process his presence, and they suddenly sprung up, bumping into each other. They fumbled and grabbed him like offensive players looking to make a tackle on a quarterback, almost knocking him over in the process.

They heard nothing, kissing and hugging him as he bellowed, "Jesus H. Christ! You two are three sheets to the wind! What the fuck is the matter with you! Mom! What did you do!" Their eyes spouted tears and their mouths issued wails of glee.

He finally pried them off, and he looked at them weaving like sailors on a rolling deck. "You're shitfaced! On grandpa's ouzo, no less! They use that stuff for Molotov cocktails! There's battery acid in that shit! You're going to wind up soft in the head!"

They looked at him as he spoke as children might when they are being reprimanded. Then they looked at each other and laughed hysterically, bending over, maintaining their upward stance by bracing their hands on their knees.

He had gone through a wrenching day and, looking at what he had before him, knew that his night was going to be a pip. Perhaps, he thought, this was a taste of what the Army was going to be like.

Both Bea and his mother wanted to serve him his banquet. Dee saw that they were in no condition to stand, let alone serve him dinner. Their arms and legs were so rubberized that if left to their own devices, they would do serious damage to themselves and possibly blow up the house.

Dee managed to sit them down to listen to his simplified version of what had happened that day as he toasted up the spanakopita himself.

They smiled at him like cartoon characters with Xs as eyes and he managed to pied piper them to the bathroom to wash up before bed. Once they finished, they were led to the bedrooms to cozy up and rest until he said he would call them for hors d'oeuvres and drinks to continue his saga at Fort Hamilton. He knew once they hit the pillow, it would be light's out until the bubbles of hangover welled up.

His mother hit the bed like a carpet rolling off a loading dock. Bea, however, gave him some lip about sleeping in his bed since she was set up in the living room already. He told her very slowly, stroking her hair, that since his bedroom was closer to the bathroom than the living room, if push came to shove, she would be able to make an emergency sprint to the can with no mishaps. She bought his logic and crashed into his bed.

He knew it was only a matter of time before the ouzo did its violence. Considering what they drank, and how much, the aftereffects would be of seismic proportion.

He got two buckets from under the kitchen sink and splashed in some water and placed it on the floor toward the head of their beds. He also strategically set up some night lights so that he could tend the wounded without kicking anything in haste.

He set up his bivouac on the rocking chair, carried into the kitchen for close proximity to the wounded. Along with wash rags, ice pack bags, tissues, warm fizzed-out Coke, a pot of coffee on the fire, and a sleeve of Uneeda biscuits within ready reach, he was set.

He took the quiet to call Bea's mother and explain the situation and stressed that any attempt to get her home by subway or cab would be like juggling nitroglycerin blindfolded. He promised to keep her apprised and would escort Bea home after the white flag was raised and reconstruction reinstated.

He then, with a sigh, put on an easy listening station on the transistor radio in the kitchen, popped a Piels Light Lager, polished off some more spanakopita patties, which he likened to manna from heaven, and awaited the Vesuvian eruptions that were embryonically percolating in their heads and bellies.

He had had a bad day. The night didn't look much better.

Dee called Pete McKelvey the next morning to alert him that his mother was in a bad way and that he couldn't leave her. Pete said, "Take the time you need. When all's well, we need you."

It took the better part of two and a half days before the semblance of normalcy brought the girls out of their twilight zone. Dee had wet-nursed them, cooked and cleaned their clothes, and only made small talk with them. All value judgments were parked on the side. Margo, having dealt with her father's ouzo in the past, came out of the calamity a little ahead of Bea. Though her headache felt like carpet bombing, she was blessed with a galvanized stomach so whatever went down, stayed down. Bee, however, in the throes of the pile driving assaults on her cranium, prayed for death to take her, with no care on whether her soul was accepted by heaven or hell. When she finally came around to actually walking on shuffling feet, she looked like she had the measles having dry-heaved so violently that it ruptured the delicate capillaries in her face.

Both ladies were embarrassed to the nth degree. Margo became Mrs. Felico once again, and Bea became a body, only spoken to within earshot, without name. Margo did call Bea's mother as a courtesy to apologize, which was accepted with total understanding because that was the type of person Mrs. Sharpe was. And to ease the awkwardness of the call, Mrs. Sharpe told Margo that she had a similar experience in her youth with a young man who introduced her to his grandfather's homemade Prohibition dandelion wine, three bottles of which put them into Bellevue to have their stomachs pumped, while the other bottles exploded in the old man's cellar as they were in recuperation.

Looking at the two ladies, whom he loved dearly with saddened eyes, reminded him of the zombies in *Night of the Living Dead*. He felt exhausted and disgusted.

He couldn't wait to start clipping coupons again.

13
CHAPTER

"Bring your trunks."

"What?" Dee said.

"Your bathing suit, dummy."

He gave her a wiry smile. "You mean…"

"I do." She laughed. "Yes. I challenged you a long time ago. And you let it drop. Now, there's no excuse. You're off…and we have time before the lecture in the chapel. So? There you go!" He felt like someone had snapped his suspenders on his back.

He remembered. It had been their first date and she challenged him to a fifteen-lap swimming race with no spotting.

Initially, he suspected it was the usual verbal foreplay a first date brings, the modest boasting, for impressions, the wiseass remarks to feel each other out, the bringing of bullshit to a higher level. But she actually meant it. And finally, after three odd years, she was setting a date in stone. True, he mulled, there were always excuses, all of them good and legitimate—that was before, but not now.

It gave him a funny feeling, a little nervous stomach flutter, like some stranger buttonholing him on an insignificant issue. But he was game and in good condition. He swam every day that he could since she booted him temporarily out of her life after the chewing gum catastrophe.

He accepted the challenge and said," Okay. Deal. But," he continued slyly, "what say we make it interesting?"

"You wouldn't be trying to sucker me into a wager, would you?"

"Who, me? Why, I've never been in a gambling den in my life."

"Yeah, right. What," she said, pointing a finger right at his nose, "did you have in mind?"

"Well," he paused, "nothing big. Just," he continued, making it up as he went, "something you could hang your hat on."

She thought for a moment. "You're on, buster." She stuck out her left pinkie and he locked it with his, securing the deal as she said, "Bet."

"Done," he shot out as if he booked a trade.

After a moment, Dee said, "Give any thought to what the wager should be?"

"Yep," she shot out.

"I know that look. And I'm getting a little worried."

"Deal: Shotgun start. No spotting. Fifteen laps. Loser buys, if by a fingernail or half a pool's length…," she then continued, smiling at him, "dinner at Delmonico's. With all the trimmings."

"What!"

"Hey! That's the booty! I'm working, you're working. We have some pennies in the cupboard jar. Shouldn't put anyone in the poorhouse. And if worse comes to worst, the loser can always wash dishes. Looks good on the resume."

"I feel like I've been had."

She laughed deliciously. "You have, baby. You have."

"You mean," he said, hoping he misconstrued, "now, let me get this straight. Are we talking about the Delmonico's on Beaver Street, around the corner from where I work?"

"Indubitably." She then walked over and kissed him. "My goodness. Another Einstein in the making. There's no end to your gray matter."

He waited for her by the gym on the campus. And being early, he took in the glory of the day. It was a cloudless sky. Spring had certainly crept in. There were some breezy snaps, a little too cold in the shade, but perfect for the sun-drenched frontage of the building he was standing on.

The year, 1970, thus far, had not been good to him. The Army induction and the escalation of the war with the invasion of Cambodia ended all hopes of him being eliminated from service.

And the recent Kent State killings only compounded the turmoil of a country turned upside down.

He tried to daydream while waiting, but the accidental meeting of an old stickball crony from the neighborhood still had him rattled.

He had been walking to the station when he bumped into Dwayne "The Duke" Dukeatelli. The Duke had returned from the jungles, a discharged jarhead, with a chemical dependency he was actively honing to quell his PTSD episodes. He mentioned to Dee, in passing, "Dee-Man. If you go over, do not, I repeat, do not go as an officer. The life expectancy of a second looie in the hot zone is six weeks, tops. Give or take a day."

Whether the Duke's statistics were government culled or a product of his own fried cogitations really didn't matter. The knife twist in Dee's belly felt the same.

Luckily, his anxiety eased when he saw Bea in the distance. She was wearing a midi dress. He always loved her in it because it accentuated her ass, but he never told her that. He always said it was a lovely change from the minis that all the girls were wearing at the time. It was much classier. And she accepted the compliment. She delighted his sensibilities when he saw her, and an inner warmth touched him like prayers bombarding his soul.

They were scheduled after their swimming match to a lecture in the chapel by a Jesuit on "Forgiveness." Bea desperately wanted to forgive his mother for getting her drunk and fracturing their newfound relationship. She was having great difficulty with it and jumped at the lecture posted in the school paper. She hoped she might be able to find some insight or approach to foster the happening.

Dee kept his distance on the issue. That day had been a day of jumbled emotions. It was a bad day for everyone.

Noticing him, she quickened her pace, lugging her heavy satchel of books. "Hiya, baby." She kissed him lightly on the lips. "Ready for the onslaught?"

"Lay on, McBea, and damned be the one who cries, Hold! Enough!"

"Think misquoting Shakespeare's gonna help ya?"

"No. I'll just place my faith in the stuff that dreams are made of."

"Now," she said, "you're beginning to make me sick."

"Good. Hope it gives me an edge."

She connected a wide swung open palm smack on his arm. "Inside, buster." She led him to the men's locker room. "Meet you on the front lines."

"Methinks we are going to partake in the breast stroke. Is I or ain't I right?" He held out his palms to her.

"If you're trying to psyche me out, it's not working. I'll be there before you." And then she coyly stared at him. "And this is the time to keep your hands to yourself."

He laughed as he ran into the locker room.

He found an empty locker and got on his suit quickly and then entered the pool area. She was already there, on the far side, chatting with seven V-shaped surfer hunks who were obviously members of the swim team. They, according to what Dee spotted, were ecstatic that she was there and, he figured, that each one would give an eye-tooth to have a date with her. Even though they were talking innocently, Dee felt a bit disconcerted. When she saw him, she waved him over. She introduced him to the team as, "This is Dee Felico." That was all she said, and that slighted him a little. Yet he was sure they all knew who he was in her life.

The fact that she was poolside before him led him to believe that she had her suit on before she entered the gym.

She looked exquisite in the gun-metal gray one-piece. It was cut high on the hip and two bloodred streaks of fabric rode up from thigh to armpit, making it look like a plum-line on a Destroyer. Her legs were not muscular as some dancers or swimmers but beautifully defined, much like Betty Grable or Marlene Dietrich, perfect, not a blemish or an ounce of fat.

Each hunk hugged and kissed her for luck. It should not have bothered him, but it did. She looked at him after their display of affection. He looked very lonely. She then went over to him, looked warmly into his eyes, put her arms around his neck, and gave him a long, passionate kiss. Pulling away gently, still looking deeply into his eyes, she whispered, "Good luck, baby." The hoots, catcalls, and whistles from the team members became peripheral noise compared to the quickened heartbeat he heard in his ears.

"Thanks," he said, touching her face.

He quickly shook himself out of his adoration mode for her and centered sights on the task at hand. He mentally noted that he had a greater reach, but he weighed more. His breath control was good, and he had been able to increase his endurance due to his recent activity with the Queens College water polo team.

His strategy was to sprint as quickly as he could for ten laps. He knew he couldn't do it for the full fifteen. He would have to then ease into a fast rhythm to conserve his strength. It would take a lot out of him, but he felt it would give him lead enough to overcome her catching up with him. He was a bit nervous when he looked at her as she took her position. She looked as cool as a lady taking a stroll down Fifth Avenue for no other reason than to get some air.

The team captain said, "Take your positions. I'll blow the starting whistle. Next time you hear it, it'll be the final lap."

They took their stances. Knees bent into a semicrouch, arms back, aimed to spring, and at the ready, both their eyes glowed with determination.

"Ready!"

Dee felt the beat when the captain said "Set," and he thrust himself out with all the strength he had when he heard the whistle blow. He was in the air for a second and hit the water cleanly, slicing it like the bow of a canoe going down the rapids and engaged in his very aggressive crawl. He overreached with each arm and pushed down, palm cupped toward his belly. His only resistance was his head, which came up briefly on the side when he took a breath on every fourth stroke.

He didn't spy her until he took his flip on the fifth lap. As he was coming up for the stroke, he saw her underwater just coming toward the pool wall. She was an eighth of a pool length behind him. He was applying all the power he could, yet she was closer than he had expected. He had to keep up his speed and dig deep for more, push himself harder because at ten laps he had to be a good half-pool length ahead of her to win. He began to quicken his kick and over-extended his arms, pulling back as much water as he could with each stroke. The ladder climbing technique, one of the water polo players called it. With his next flip, it began to work. He was edging further and further ahead of her.

At the tenth lap, he was in good position. He was half a pool length ahead of her. If he could maintain his pace, he was confident he would win. With every flip, he saw she was gaining on him, yet his comfort level was not upset. His arms were aching and his legs were beginning to jelly. He tempered his concentration keeping his chest high and maintaining balance.

On the thirteenth lap, they were neck and neck. He couldn't apply anymore power. He was on overdrive already. What astounded him was her breath control. She had very minimal head resistance. Her head was in the water for a full pool length before she took a breath. And when they were neck and neck, he gave her a fleeting look underwater. It almost appeared to him that instant that she was smiling at him and winked. He didn't know whether it was a mock or just the grimace of her effort.

They were fighting each other for lead on lap thirteen and the early part of lap fourteen, and then, as if she had a motor up her ass, she bolted forward. Her body naturally rotated, breaching slightly with each powerful stroke, her center of buoyancy totally balanced, her legs fluttering like a propeller. She was passing him with motion.

When he heard the final lap whistle blow, she was half a pool length ahead of him. He stopped dead in the water and watched her finish like a torpedo hitting an enemy ship. Once done, she hoisted herself out of the water and stood, legs parted, looking at him. She smiled, dove into the water before the swim team ran over to congratulate her, and swam right to Dee. He was winded and exhausted. She was as fresh as after an afternoon bath.

"You got me," he said.

She hugged him and kissed his cheek. "It was because of you that I won."

"Oh no it wasn't. I didn't take a fall for you. I gave it my all."

"No. Not that, it was what you once told me some time ago. I used that technique, and I really pulled it off. But I'll explain later. C'mon, baby. Let's shower and get dressed. We'll sit in the sun before the lecture."

She ripped off the rubber band holding her hair back and shook her head, the water spraying his face. "Hey! Watch it! You're getting me wet!" She giggled. He then hugged her.

They sat in the sun after their showers overlooking the track field.

Some students were just strolling around the oval while others played Frisbee. The sky was crystal save for a network of multicolored vapor trails that seemed like stitchwork on a quilt. Dee was drawn to it as an art lover might gaze at *Starry Night*.

They were both silent. Dee was enchanted by the heavens, and Bea watched the Frisbee players almost as an afterthought.

"Dee?"

"Hmmm?" he replied, still looking at the sky.

"Did you swim to music?"

Dee felt pulled back to Earth. He was so enjoying the spectacle in the sky. "Ahhh," he sighed. "No. I was doing a 'climbing the ladder' technique one of the water polo players suggested. Might have worked if I wasn't competing with a torpedo." Then he followed through with, "Were you?"

"Yes," she said with a burst of glee. "And you planted the seed. Remember that Louis Prima fast number you said might be a good lap workout?"

"You mean, 'Oh, Marie'?"

"That's the one. What I did was play it in my mind and relegated strokes and kicks to it. For the four-beat measure, I did a stroke and two kicks for the first three beats and then doubled up on the fourth beat. That gave me the propulsion! And it was all because of you."

"So," he said, "you're saying my efforts aided you in winning against me?"

"Exactly."

"What then is my commission?"

"A kiss on the cheek."

"Any room for negotiation?"

"Not here there is, you naughty boy."

He laughed. "Let's be honest. You have tremendous power in your legs and your breath control is astounding. Plus, you had a cheering section that wants, as I see it, a little more than your autograph."

"They want me on the team, in more ways than one, and do I," she coyly queried, "detect…?"

"Yes," was all that he said.

She quickly pecked him on his cheek. "Thank you, Dee Felico."

He then gazed back at the vapor trails merging in the upper atmosphere.

They were silent for quite some time. She moseyed close to him so that the side of her leg was touching his.

"Dee? Do you think your mother would go on a retreat with me?"

It was a very strange question to him, and he looked at her a bit confused. "A retreat?"

"Yes. After this lecture, the priest will pass out pamphlets regarding a retreat on forgiveness. I touched base with him already 'bout it. Think she might come with me? Oh, it's only a day, not an overnighter."

"Bea. I don't want to sound out of line, and believe me, I'm the last person who should be speaking for her, but I think you'd have a better chance of having a reunification of Germany than to have that happening."

She frowned, disappointment on her face. "Does she hate me that much?"

"Hate?" He shook his head. "Too harsh a word. Indifferent, embarrassed, ashamed—they all fit, and don't forget: she's a tough nut. If you were a Greek girl, there would be a way of making amends. I guess it's some kind of blood thing; they sort of have a half-assed ritual they go through to iron things out—old fashioned village courtesies, something like that."

"So I'm written off? She wants you to have a Greek girl?"

"In her heart of hearts, yes. But I am a different person, and this is not the old country. They are good people. They want the best for you, but often they think their 'best' is better than your 'best.' They're a clannish people and live in a subculture. I am not part of that and neither was my father. He went through a lot of guff with my grandfather after he pulled out of the Greek Civil War, and he was partially Greek." He looked at his watch. "Lecture should be starting in a little while."

"What should I do? This is eating me up. I can't live this way." She was getting upset.

He held her hand and patted it. "For now, leave it alone, let it rest. Sometimes things turn around from resting positions."

She hugged him and then kissed him on the lips. "What makes you so wonderful?"

He stared lovingly at her and said, "Wheaties?"

Stunned, she shook her head and then really had to laugh.

"Had to inject a little comic relief. The conversation was beginning to sound like something out of Eugene O'Neill. Now, let's hear what this priest has to say."

They both got up and, hand in hand, walked to the chapel.

14
CHAPTER

No one ever rubbed off on Pete McKelvey as Dee Felico did.

Over the years, as a kid hawking newspapers or delivering ice, or as a trooper in Army days, even with his breakthrough into the Wall Street community, had any one person touched him so deeply and sliced into his skin so totally as this young kid, Dee Felico.

It was almost against his nature to extend himself. He had no frame of reference. No one ever did anything for him. He clawed and fought his own way up on everything he did. He always went his own way and called his own shots. When he won, he kept the winnings, and when he lost, tended his wounds.

He was a confirmed bachelor and ministered to his mother after he mustered out of the Army when she became ill and took care of all her needs until she died. After that, work became his reason to be. He put in sixteen-hour days without effort and enjoyed listening to sports on the radio or watching a Knicks game when he got a television as he nursed a few nightcaps to ease his tension and lull himself to sleep.

The feeling he had toward Dee was new to him. He somehow felt compelled to help this young man advance his standing in the organization. He wanted to protect him and give him guidance and support. He felt the boy was gold and a tremendous asset to the firm.

What confused him most was why he felt this way. It wasn't a missed opportunity at being a father. He never wanted marriage or a family. It wasn't that. He didn't ask Stan's opinion or any of the other old-timers. He never would ask questions that personal of anyone.

That was for the gossip columnists. And he didn't want his balls in anyone's vest pocket because of loose lips.

He did, however, after much deliberation and reading too much of "Dear Abby," thought it had everything to do with his age. And when several nightcaps did not put him into a soothingly calm sleep one evening, he concluded that it had to be the advent of senility. That aggravated him so much that he showered, put his suit back on, and went back to the office at midnight.

He would occasionally browbeat a trader or salesman during a walk through the trading room to take Dee under their wing, but he always ran into the Berlin Wall. "Pete, no one here wants a back-of-fice shithead who can't make a declarative sentence without a 'fuck' in it to pony up with a sophisticated, Ivy League..."

"Gunslinger," Pete would fire back finishing their sentence for them. And ofttimes, as he would start to intimidate the trader and lace it into him, an eavesdropping colleague would butt in alerting Pete that he was needed upstairs on some urgent matter. It was their polite way of booting him off the floor.

The Berlin Wall between back office and front office, between operations and trading, was not only segregated by floor differences but by traditions as well. They didn't talk to each other except by phone, only if absolutely necessary. They didn't work well with each other if they worked with each other at all. It was said there was a language barrier between them and it had nothing to do with the *King's English* or profanity. They went to different watering holes after work and different parties during the holiday season. It was as if they were two different companies with two different agendas.

They worked around each other and, through tug-of-war efforts, somehow, got things done. And the only thing that breached the Berlin Wall was a memo war. When that happened, usually a senior partner became the arbitrator to settle the blaze, which always would reignite down the road by the department that got the bigger burn scar as justification for a poorly put-together compromise. Or purely on spite. Sometimes, a mustang might breach the wall for the good of the company, and if the profit was substantial enough on the contested issue, and properly allocated, might keep his testicles.

Pete McKelvey didn't have to breach the Berlin Wall. He could walk right through it any time he wanted to.

He had access to Vance Barlow. No one else had that deep personal bonding. Pete had been hired by Vance's father, as everyone in the firm knew, and had diapered Vance as a little boy on more than one occasion, which no one in the firm knew about except Pete and Vance.

"Gotta talk to you about Dee Felico," Pete said, skirting pleasantries and getting right down to business as was his wont.

Concern etched Barlow's face. "A problem?"

"No. No. Nothing like that," Pete said, sitting on the sofa. "The kid's gold. Always jumping in to help. Asks a million questions. I'd like to see him work on the desk. Comes in early. Stays late. He's smart, good with figures, aced out on them Institute of Finance courses. Be a good shot in the arm for the firm. He'd never write a bad ticket 'cause he knows what can go wrong if you do. What do you say?"

"I agree with you, Pete. But the problem is that if I place him, he'd be considered one of Barlow's Boys, and he might not be absorbed into their inner sanctum. You know how traders are—always looking over their shoulders." He took a sip of a large glass of ice water on his desk. "He has to resolve some ongoing problem they're facing. They have to request him. He has to be welcomed into their complement. If that happens, it's a go. I'll place him."

"What do you suggest?"

"We're going to open up a new department to trade Ginnie Mae pools. It's that new mortgage-backed government paper."

"Yes, yes. My pal at Mabon gave me stuff on it. Self-liquidating paper." Pete shook his head and smiled. "New security. New rules. Lot of bumps with this stuff. This is not plain vanilla. If we get a jump on this, we can set the standard regarding the ops-end of the equation."

"Try to do some of your magic, Pete."

"Thanks, Vance. I'll get right on it." He then shook Vance's hand.

Vance did not let go. "Let's do lunch one day. To catch up."

"When it's slow. I'll buzz ya."

"I promise I won't hold my breath." Vance laughed and let Pete loose. He wished to himself he would have Pete's energy when he was creeping in his seventies.

Pete McKelvey knew exactly who to talk to regarding the Ginnie Maes. He was going to talk to Zoltan Kiss, senior partner, Sales Bank Service department. If anyone knew what a client wanted, Zollie Kiss's name would be written all over it.

On personal matters, Pete didn't trust Zollie Kiss as far as he could throw the Woolworth Building. However, in business, he was a ruthless scalpel and a magician when it came to customer service excellence. An extremely handsome, white wavy haired six footer with dark eyes that brought out the mother in women, he modeled Pierre Cardin suits in *Gentleman's Quarterly* upon occasion as a lark, or so he said when someone poised the public relation's question. When the stated issue was released, he then bought the magazine in bulk and messengered them to his top accounts. Aside from being a shameless self promoter, Zollie Kiss was driven to any deal provided it gave him a good cut of the action.

He was a reformed drunk who found God and a trophy wife twenty years his junior at the AA meetings. His priest hosted the meetings. Being an ex-alcoholic himself, the priest shepherded Zollie not only to sobriety but to the altar as well.

The new wife was Brooklyn born and bred, an ex-fashion magazine editor who sported a self-taught Southern drawl along with a body like Raquel Welsh. Though Zollie declared that her mind was what captured him into the vortex of love, his business associates and clients knew better. He would always attend various industry functions and customer soirees with her linked on his arm, much to the delight of his cronies of finance as well as the lowlife portfolio managers, as a lure for a possible trade or joint venture. In whispered bars and boardrooms, she was known as Zollie's "Prop."

He was dry for ten years and hovered a tad north of fifty. The only drawback from his sobriety was a flash temper so violent that he kept several silk dress shirts in his office closet because when he lost it, he would rip the shirt right off his back like a raving lunatic.

Only once did he flip out when he was drinking. He caught his then wife coupling with two of the pool boys in their private cabana overlooking the tennis court on their estate. The shock was too much for him, and fortified by five or six double martinis, he drove her vintage red Porsche, the one she loved and purchased with her own money at auction, right into Long Island Sound. Even the best mechanics in Connecticut could not bring back to life what the salt water cancer did to the engine.

That event added just the right amount of sass and dirt to the cocktail party chatter that particularly dull summer in Cos Cob to ward off the ennui that always comes in those last days before Labor Day.

Pete liked Zollie when he was still a drunk. He had always been happy, mild-mannered, and a corny jokester, yet crackling when it came to his business acumen, which remained unaffected no matter how much he quaffed.

Now, he was sarcastic and had a tendency to proselytize. His conceit was high-toned with his reformation, and he firmly believed his every bowel movement should be cast in bronze and housed at the Smithsonian.

Pete McKelvey strolled into Zollie Kiss's office.

Zollie looked up, removed the Lucky Strike from his mouth, placed it in his ashtray, smiled, and said, "Ah... Pete McKelvey, my favorite curmudgeon." He raised his black eyebrows, a striking contrast to his cotton white hair. "I missed you at Mass this morning."

Pete snorted.

"What can I do for you, you old reprobate?" Zollie asked.

Pete sat in the chair in front of Zollie's desk. "Vance tells me we're getting into Ginnie Maes. I am familiar with the instrument. It's a bit complex, and since it's new, I think we should set the standard before others make a mess of it and make it impossible to get things done. My question: your players...what do they want? What do they expect? What would make them happy from your prospective...and that of the firm's?"

"Simple," Zollie said. "They want guaranteed delivery, and they want the certificate registered in their name at the time of delivery."

Pete frowned. "That's a tall order considering that they transfer in Washington, DC. There's no New York transfer agent. Could take close to a week to put in to their names, and…"—Pete lit up a Chesterfield— "if we buy the bond from a dealer or an issuer, they could fail to deliver to us, which can screw up the settlement date, which screws up the final monies." He shook his head. "What a kettle of fish."

"I'm stumped on this one too. But we have to figure out how to make this clean. We can't screw this up. I have a boatload of interest on this stuff. And I don't want to lose any business. Pete, the spreads on this can be three-quarters to two points a pop. And we're talking million-dollar blocks. No odd-lot shit. My players are committed to size—big size! That's grand slam territory any way you look at it."

Pete whistled. "That's hefty money." Pete mused for a moment. "Let me go to town on it. Got a couple of ideas." He got up. "When do we start trading this shit?"

"Tomorrow," Zollie said. "Glad you stopped by. I was going to touch base with you. You beat me to it."

"Tomorrow!" Pete barked angrily. "Does Barlow know?"

Zollie picked up the phone. "Just about to tell him."

"And when the fuck were you going to let me know?"

"Peter," Zollie said mildly. "You know how it is. You can't do business sitting on your ass. Everything's under control now that it's in your capable hands." Pete knew it was useless to argue. It was a typical Zollie Kiss, kiss-off non-answer. "Oh, Peter?" Zollie said.

Pete looked at him squarely.

"Shall I save you a seat at early morning Mass tomorrow?"

Pete snarled. "No! I'll be at my shrine. I get divine revelations at my desk." He threw the remnants of his lit cigarette on Zollie's carpeted floor in disgust and walked out.

Zollie jumped up and picked up the butt before it burned a hole in the carpet. "What the hell's the matter with you, Pete?"

"You fuckin' tell me!" Pete side-lipped, not turning around as he stormed out of Zollie's office.

Pete marched past Dee's desk toward the conference room and bellowed, his hand raised and waving in the direction he was walking, "Dee! On me! Grab a pad and pencil!"

Pete explained to Dee what was needed and told him to call anyone he thought might be able to give some color or advice, and to do it discretely. He told him to call Ginnie Mae in Washington regarding timing on transfers.

"You have to put together a business plan, a proposal. I want to review it when you complete it. We have to bounce it off Jerry Parcher. As head cashier, he's gotta know the score on this. And I want you to present it to Zollie Kiss. Three p.m. on the dot."

Dee was flabbergasted. "Pete. I can't do this. I'm not qualified."

"Horseshit! Nobody's qualified. It's new." His voice became scruffy. "You understand the problem?"

Dee shook his head.

"Then un-problem it!"

"Okay." Dee was unsettled and apprehensive. "But why me?"

Pete's stare could have melted the barrel of a howitzer. "Because!" was his emphatic explanation. He then got up and walked out.

Dee felt very alone in the conference room. He had no idea what to do. He did know that he needed fresh air; he needed to unclutter his head. He had plenty of time before deadline, but that was little relief. He was just an unsuspecting soul that was abruptly thrown into a vat of quicksand. He walked out of the conference room.

"Where you going?" Pete charged, covering his phone mouthpiece.

"Taking a walk. Need some air. Helps me think."

"Just make sure you don't get hit by a bus." Pete then continued with his phone call.

Dee put on his suit jacket, placed his hands deep in his trouser pockets, and strolled to the elevators.

He went out the Pine Street entrance. The morning rush was over. Pedestrian traffic was light. Some runners passed him on their way to make their deliveries. Dee started to walk up to Broadway as two suited men passed him, one muttering a little too loudly about an interview gone sour.

When he reached Broadway, he made a left and crossed the street and entered Trinity Church. He slipped into an empty pew in the front. Only a handful of people were there scattered about. He felt very comfortable and secure in an empty church. He didn't have the same feel of presence and warmth that Bea needed to be touched by. She was always expectant, yearning to be seized by grace or aching for religious experience. It sometimes annoyed her how he could just calmly sit whether divine absorption came or not. He just liked the emptiness and the faint sizzle of candles burning out. He relished the smell of incense and old wood. The creak the pew made when he sat down was a cadenza to him.

An old library would have served him just as well. Just squirreling in a cozy desk among the leather-bound tomes of great thoughts and passions mingling with the musky smell of old paper and crypt-like quietude moved him. He stayed there about an hour deliberately not thinking.

And then, things started to pop in his head. He got up, walked out of the church, and headed down toward the Battery. When he got there, he pushed a comma of hair back that brushed his brow from a snippy wind gust and sat on a bench overlooking New York Bay.

The converging waters with their crisscross currents from the Hudson and the East River Tidal Strait worked on him. The churning eddies and small disappearing whirlpools seemed to settle his jumbled brain and invigorate a mind-nurturing thought. He knew that Wall Street was like no other business on Earth. It was the last of the Wild West shows. It was a place where an idea, no matter how crazy it was, could be put into action to see if it worked. It was a place where a phrase like "And they said it couldn't be done" could be spit in the face of conventional thinkers and skeptics. It was a place where a follow-up like "It was just good, solid thinking" could be bopped on the heads of the doubters. It was a place where the personal pronoun "schmuck!" could be barked at the spineless wonders who played the fence and wouldn't take a stand on anything.

He smiled and jotted down some notes on a pad he kept in the inner pocket of his suit. Rereading it, he knew, without question, that it was a good idea. It was simple, straightforward, and workable.

It was a square peg in a round hole, which, in his mind, made a tight fit.

He got up from the park bench, took a deep breath of fresh air, and walked back to the office at a fast pace.

Dee rushed past Pete who questioned, "Where the hell were you? Getting a cleansing at one of them Chambers Street scratch houses?"

Dee didn't respond and slammed the conference room door closed. He started to write his proposal and called Ginnie Mae in Washington to get detailed turnaround times for certificate transfers.

He finished a little after lunch and typed up the proposal himself when one of the ladies in the typing pool took her break. Satisfied, Dee called Pete in.

It was a one-page proposal with an example document attached. Pete read it and placed it on the table. He looked sternly at Dee. "You've got to be shitting me."

"No, I'm not," Dee answered. He had a fully confident demeanor.

"Are you in your right mind? You want to give this to Zollie Kiss?"

"Yes," Dee said, and before Pete uttered another word, continued, "Just call Jerry Parcher."

Pete frowned. "You show this to legal?"

"You kidding? They'll only succeed in fucking it up. Call Jerry."

Pete picked up the phone and called the head cashier. Pete gave Jerry the proposal when he came into the room. "This is what Dee wants to present to Zollie Kiss regarding the Ginnie Maes I spoke to you about before."

Jerry read it over. He looked up at Dee and then looked at Pete. "This is dangerous."

Dee was unmoved by the comment. "Jerry. It'll work."

"I don't doubt that. But pulling it off..." He blew out, by product of a huge sigh. "That'll be the trick."

"I don't like it," Pete said.

Jerry spoke directly to Dee. "You know what you're dealing with here? With Zollie Kiss."

"Yes. I heard he's a nutjob. And when he goes apeshit in his office, his staff calls it the 'Ma's dead' routine." One of the salesmen labeled it based on James Cagney's crack-up performance in the prison mess hall scene in the film *White Heat*. "I just hope he doesn't belt me."

"No," Pete said. "No fisticuffs for Zollie. He's a chickenshit. Though, when his shirt buttons fly off, they can come at you like Screaming Mimis."

"Then I'm okay with it," Dee said. "Should I do it alone? I think I can handle it."

"I'll be there with you," Pete said. Pete then looked at Jerry. "Is it okay with you, the proposal? And you want to participate?"

"Proposal's fine. I'll pass on the audience with Zollie. When he goes ballistic, I feel like smacking him in the head. He's like a goddamned spoiled brat in a temper tantrum."

"I," Dee said, "called Washington and got all the data on transfer timing. If a certificate is presented before noon, it takes twenty-four hours; after noon, forty-eight."

"Good," Jerry said. "Good work. Thanks for the info. That'll help."

"What do you want to do now, Dee?" Pete asked. "You've got plenty of time."

"I want to stay here and look everything over. I want to prepare myself."

"Okay," Pete said. "I'll pick you up ten to three."

Jerry Parcher extended his hand to Dee. "Best of luck, son," he said and left.

Dee drafted some notes for himself to defend his position. Peppered with action words, he wrote pithy approaches to obvious objections. He wanted his retorts to flow naturally with weight and a little touch of the gutter.

Wall Street always had a penchant for the outrageous. It was a surefire way of getting noticed aside from good work habits, which everyone had. Being classified a person with "balls" went a very long way.

Pete picked him up at the precise time. Dee had already used the bathroom and had washed up. He felt calm and well prepared.

Zollie Kiss shook Dee's hand as both he and Pete walked into the office. Zollie's hand was warm and firm, as was Dee's. Zollie closed the door and graciously said, "Sit, please," as his entire bank service department surreptitiously eyed the office seen from their desks, their phones held to their ears with no one at the other end, awaiting the curtain to rise.

"Well," Zollie said in a rather parliamentary tone as Pete and Dee sat on his office couch. He directed his attention to Dee. "I hear you're the new boy wonder."

Dee immediately stood up. "You heard wrong."

Zollie was taken aback by the remark, yet he felt that it wasn't a snap nor was there any disrespect in the color of Dee's voice. Dee omitted the courtesy of the title "mister." In fact, he did not give address to Zollie at all. "I'm just a guy trying to get something done right for this firm."

Zollie felt a little winged. *This kid is brash, but not yet obnoxious*, he thought. This was not the way he wanted to conduct this meeting. "As I understand it," Zollie said, "you're trying to get something right for me."

"You are a partner in this firm. Therefore, you are the firm. That is one and the same as I see it. I want to do right for all parties concerned."

Zollie sat in his chair and took out a cigarette from the gold box on his desk. He then motioned if Dee wanted one. "English Ovals, top-notch Turkish tobacco."

"No thanks. Not my cup of tea."

Zollie smiled, lighting up. "Well," he began, blowing out his first puff.

Dee interrupted. "I would like to get to the business at hand."

Zollie side-glanced at Pete with a cringe of annoyance. Zollie always liked to pontificate a little before a meeting. Pete signaled Zollie, putting up his index finger in a "just wait" sign.

"In that case, young man," Zollie said in a booming voice, "fill the room with your intelligence." He flicked an ash into his ashtray.

Dee, handing the proposal and document to Zollie, said, "Here. This will speak for itself."

Feeling a bit unhinged by Dee's precocity, Zollie ripped the papers out of Dee's fingers angrily giving him a paper cut. Zollie saw the red slice on the finger and ignored it deliberately for the moment. Dee sucked on the cut, his eyes narrowing at Zollie. Before Zollie looked at the proposal, he gave Dee a scowl and, glancing at the paper, muttered, "Sorry 'bout that," offhandedly.

Dee retorted, "No sweat," and sat down.

It didn't take Zollie but a minute to read through the proposal. Scarlet erupted up his neck in contrast to the pure white starched collar he had. He glared at Pete. "You read this?" Pete just nodded his head in the affirmative. "Is this a joke?" He crushed his almost full cigarette into the ashtray jostling out some of the accumulated ashes. "My calendar doesn't say April Fool's Day!" He then stood up and screamed, "This is bullshit! If I call my clients with this proposal, I'll be laughed out of the business! And I'll be goddamned if I have to have my wife become a bag lady because I lost my job and reputation on the Street promoting the shit you're handing me!" He threw the papers at Dee, his eyes popping like that of a stomped-on toad.

Dee picked up the papers and handed them back to Zollie, saying, "Maybe you should read it again. You might have missed something."

Zollie swung his hand and knocked the papers out of Dee's hand. Zollie screamed, seething, "You want my clients, my top clients, to pay a million bucks for a piece of eight-by-eleven typewriting paper with scribble on it! These are not mom-and-pop savings and loans from Bubbleshits, Wyoming! These are top-grade New York Savings Banks!"

"Mr. Kiss," Dee finally said formally, "let me reiterate just in case you misread my proposal." Dee's tone was controlled and louder than the intimate setting needed. "We will," Dee said staring at Zollie, "be delivering a due bill versus payment in lieu of the actual certificate which, at the same time, will be in the process of being registered in your client's name per their instructions. That is our legal obligation. All specifics of the trade will be on the due bill. And when the transfer is completed, we will deliver the registered certificate in return for our due bill." Dee paused. "Most importantly, if our purchase fails on being delivered in, we will still be paid up front on our sell. This gives us free money either to invest or simply fund the business until such time as the original buy comes in to us for payment. That's a plus and a half for the firm. "It's simple, straightforward, and it will work." He ended with a clipped "Goddamnit!" for emphasis.

Zollie was incensed with Dee's insolence. His eyes burned and he rasped, "You know, I don't like your proposal! And I don't like your face!"

Dee stepped right up to Zollie's desk, put his hands on the edges, leaned forward, and said, "Really? Well, I like my proposal! And I'm not breaking into much of a sweat over that kisser of yours either!" He then turned and sat next to Pete fidgeting in his seat.

Zollie shouted and growled and tore at his tie. He was beginning to unravel. He started to pull at his shirt, oblivious to those around him, as if a man trying to escape confinement. He ripped his shirt pocket and then clenched his collar with both hands, fumbling at opening the top button. His frustration agitated, he ripped at the top button until it flew off and then proceeded to tear his shirt right down the middle, the buttons flying helter-skelter and bouncing on his carpet.

Finally ripping his shirt entirely off his back, he angrily threw it on the floor and stepped on it as if on a bunch of scurrying cockroaches. "Goddamn son of a bitch bastard!" he yelled at no one in particular. "Fuck me!" was his final expulsion.

Dee and Pete watched Zollie's conniption. Dee was fascinated by the antics but remained quiet, assuming a mildly bored expression. Pete had seen Zollie's hysteria many times before and scratched his teeth with his tongue as if he had a bad taste in his mouth.

Bare-chested, Zollie then sat down for a few moments, his tomato-red face draining back to natural color. He got up and went to his closet to don another razor-sharp pressed shirt. Aware of his surroundings, he said, "Excuse me, gentlemen," put his shirt and tie on, combed his hair, observing himself in the closet mirror, and, once fully satisfied, turned to them, letting off a sigh as if nothing had happened.

"Again," he said in a very controlled voice, "my accounts will not pay a million dollars for a piece of typewriting paper with gibberish—pardon—the details of the trade typed on it. Bear in mind, typewriting paper is not a fungible security."

"Sir," Dee said, "there will be no fails on the delivery—that's very important to them, and you made that very clear to Pete. There will be no settlement date changes to upset the money consideration. It will be as clean as mother's milk, and I guarantee it. And that's a word we don't readily use on the Street. It will work!"

Zollie said, "I understand. But a piece of paper is not a security. That's the part that's laughable. They will think I lost my mind. They will not buy it. Period. Simple as that. End of story."

Dee knew that that was his exit line. The meeting was over, but he stood his ground. He was going to push the idea one more time even though he felt he was on a flying trapeze between high tension wires. His insides were jumbling like dice in a tumbler.

"Mr. Kiss," he said softly, "if I may…"

Zollie acquiesced in a gentlemanly manner, "Certainly."

"I am told," Dee said, pacing a bit as if in thought, "that as a salesman, you are the best of the best. Top Dog. Some even say you are even better than the best of the best."

"People," Zollie cut in, "are sometimes prone to exaggeration." He lit up a fresh cigarette and leaned back in his chair, his face showing signs of interest.

"I have heard it mentioned," Dee continued, "that your sales pitch is so good that you can sell me the underwear I am currently wearing, nicotine stains and all"—Zollie smiled at the amusing phrase—"and have me walking away not only grateful but snickering that I somehow got the better part of the deal."

Zollie smiled and then glanced quickly at Pete. He pursed his lips and put his cigarette down, saying, "But…"

And Dee jumped right in. "Correct you are, sir. *But* is the operative word. But as you say, Mr. Kiss, but… But if you can't sell this idea, if you can't convince your clients that this is in everyone's best interest, if you can't open their eyes to the sheer…elegance of this proposition, then"—Dee paused with a disappointed bearing on his face—"then perhaps you're not the salesman you're cracked up to be."

Dee then pivoted and sat next to Pete looking enquiringly at Zoltan Kiss, senior partner, Sales, Bank Service department.

Zollie Kiss stared at Dee for a brief moment. There was no malice in his eyes. He then looked up as if in deep thought as if he had memorized something that he was having difficulty remembering. He removed a sliver of tobacco from his tongue, rolled it in his fingers, and placed it in his ashtray. He then began to drum his manicured finger nails on his desk lightly. The right corner of his mouth sidled up ever so slightly after about a minute. Then looking straight at Dee and Pete, he said, "Let me get back to you."

Pete and Dee walked out of Zollie's office after thanking him for his time.

"Pete," Dee said, "I have to go to the john. I have to see if I have nicotine stains in my shorts."

Pete laughed. "Me too."

When they entered the bathroom, Pete checked the stalls and saw that no one was there. "Gotta hand it to you. I think you pulled it off. I think you sold him."

"You think? But, Pete, he's the salesman."

"Dee. Every salesman can be sold," Pete said, patting Dee's shoulder. "Even the best of them. Especially the best of them."

15
CHAPTER

Bea Sharpe waited for Dee at the entrance to 40 Wall Street. She was collecting on a swimming bet she had with him, which she had won hands down.

She wore a green floral-print silk cotton dress that fit her like two coats of paint. It was of midknee length with an unpretentious slit up one side and a modest neckline showing just enough skin to hook a man's eye to ogle for more. Her hair had been done up in a quick fix since she was running horribly late—parted at the left, her waves secured by a petal bobby pin.

He saw her facing the street as he came out the revolving door. "Bea," he called.

Turning, she smiled and said, "Hiya, baby."

He stopped dead in his tracks. He had always known her to be attractive, and when he got to really know her, he upgraded her to gorgeous status. But for a reason he couldn't understand, there was a newness about her now. She exuded beauty. She was absolutely striking. It wasn't the dress or the hair or the way she outlined her lips. It was something he could not place. It was something ethereal, sublime, classic. She was simply a delight to behold. She radiated with a strange body glow.

"What's the matter?" she asked, walking toward him with her sexy, dancer's cadence.

He was so perplexed that he, at first, didn't answer her.

She kissed him lightly.

"I don't know. You're absolutely stunning."

She laughed then purred in her best Mae West, "Betcha tell 'at ta all the goils, Big Boy."

He gripped her shoulders. "You are exquisite. I don't know what you did." She saw awe in his eyes. "But…wow."

"My goodness. You're making my day. I must tell you that I was running so late I just slapped on a face, and my hair? It was a quick and dirty, a one-two-three. Remember?"

Her right eyebrow cocked up.

He covered one eye. "I sorely do. Come…come on," he said excitedly. "Come, I want you to meet the guys." He took her hand and pulled her into the building.

Dee introduced Bea to the security guard who gave her a visitor's pass and then went with Dee through the cage, passing colleagues and clerks doing their jobs. Most smiled as they passed, but all—young, old, and even the jellyfish who never looked up during their day of toil for fear of reprimand—almost broke their necks examining, with relish, Bea as she walked past them, hypnotized by the syncopated gelatin that made up her rear end.

The staff, since they had a great respect for Dee, was considerate and kept their catcalls silent.

Approaching Pete and Stan, both men stood up and cordially greeted Bea. They were gentlemen of the first order.

"I'm very happy to meet you. Dee speaks highly about both of you gentlemen," Bea said.

"He's tops in our book," Stan said.

"He brings a lot to the table," Pete added. "And more importantly, a hell of a nice person."

Bea smiled, proud of Dee.

"I hear you're going to Delmonico's. May I suggest the Veal Oscar. It's a platter conjured up by Oscar Wilde. Nice thin veal cutlet pan fried in sautéed mushroom and onions, topped with asparagus and lump crab meat. Wonderful dish. Tasty and different."

Surprised, Bea said, "That sounds delicious. I'm not a meat eater. Certainly not red meat. But veal is a white meat and I'm game if you are, Dee." She looked at him for approval. "I'm enthused. Thank you for your suggestion, Mr. McKelvey."

Stan chimed in, "I hear you really clobbered him in that swimming match."

"I ran out of steam," Dee said.

"Dee," Pete said, "a fiddler crab should never race a dolphin. No contest."

They all laughed. And when they then said their goodbyes, Pete said, "Ms. Sharpe?"

Bea gazed at him expectantly. "Please call me Bea."

"Bea," he said. "I have to say something. Please don't take it wrong."

"I won't."

"I just have to say that if you look this good green"—she looked down at her dress—"I shudder to think what you look like when you're ripe."

Both Stan and Dee stood back.

Bea, astonished at the remark, smiled broadly and said, "Why, Mr. McKelvey, you are quite the flirt." She went over and placed her hand on his. "You have infinitely better lines than Dee Felico. Forget collecting on my bet with Dee. Maybe I should be going to Delmonico's with you."

Pete actually blushed and cracked a silly smile. Stan had never seen this happen in all the years he worked with him. And then they all laughed. Bea then went over and kissed Pete on the cheek. He was visibly embarrassed but held his ground well.

"Thank you so much for that wonderful compliment. You are a sweetie pie."

As Dee and Bea left and got into the elevator, Dee said, "I never saw that part of Pete. I wonder what got into him."

Bea elbowed him. "He never saw me before. Can't help it if I appeal to older men? Best you take a few lessons from him. If it wasn't for me getting the drop on you, young man, I'd probably be eating a Greek salad in some Queens diner instead of gracing"—she then copped a British accent—"Delmonico's."

"I'll check out his tutoring fees." They locked arms and crossed Wall Street. "By the way, how am I going into the final?"

"A solid C-plus. However, I'm always open for extra credit if you wish to stay after hours." Her smile was delicious.

He laughed and led her down William Street.

The meal was well beyond their expectations.

Not only was the food superb—"Now I know what angels eat," was Bea's quip—but the service, the attentiveness to detail, the regal atmosphere, and the comforting ambiance left them feeling that their blood was truly "blue" and their very presence, a delight for the staff to cater to as if they were Social Register regulars.

Very little was said during the meal. The conversation became nonverbal. A gratifying sound here and there would sneak out on a satisfying savor or eyes might upcast in almost reverential appreciation with a particular swallow.

Finishing, she sighed, "I'm so content. I feel like a princess." She was so overwhelmed that a tear dribbled out of her right eye, and before she could wipe it away, Dee reached over and dried it with a clean napkin. She whispered, "You love me so." She looked at him momentarily. There was so much she wanted to tell him…and so much she couldn't.

He waited for her to speak, but she didn't.

"Is everything okay?"

She shook her head and answered, "I have to powder my nose."

"Sure," he said, standing up as she sought the ladies' room.

Upon her return, she held down his shoulder indicating that his gentlemanly etiquette was not needed and said, "I had to put on a new face. This territory demands it."

"You're as delectable as the meal."

She just smiled at his compliment, but her mind was somewhere else.

Her tone became flat. "I must talk to you. Seriously."

He looked at her unsettled, his lips pulling tight. "All right. What is it?"

"I called your mother."

Dee became pensive. "My mother? She never mentioned anything."

Bea said, "And did you think she would?"

Dee could not answer. "I thought…"

"I called her about the forgiveness retreat."

"I thought you went to that."

"I did," she said. "There is a second one. I invited her. She was cordial. She let me down softly. Issues with the house and all… However, she did thank me. I did think that was nice. And…she said…perhaps another time. And that was all."

"Bea. You have to understand."

"Dee. I do. You don't have to apologize for her. I've forgiven her. I've forgiven her. Truly and sincerely. For the past, now, and for what will come."

"The house thing," Dee said, "is so true. Between you, work, and the house, I'm being stretched to the point that I'm beginning to look like a Chinaman in a fun house mirror. It's so hard to keep things up."

"Dee, I know. And I understand. But I want to tell you about something that happened to me on the retreat. And if it happened to me, I was thinking it might happen to your mother. Dee. I was thinking of her. Her best interests."

The coffee came and broke the intensity momentarily. Dee took a sip and said, "What happened?"

She hunkered down trying to recall all the details. "First of all, the lectures were wonderful. And we were given break time to write our thoughts down or just meditate. I, of course, went into the chapel to pray. And for the life of me, I couldn't. I tried…and nothing, like I had a think block. I couldn't even remember the Lord's Prayer. I never had that before. I had so many distracting thoughts—you, your mother, my parents, all the books I'll never find the time to read, all the places I'll never see. I became so troubled that I left and walked around a little until I came to a little courtyard. It was empty. It had a little stone bench and a fountain in the middle. There were some birds in a tree. I sat there, alone, totally empty. Lost. I was so distraught I started to cry. And when I stopped, I just looked at things with, I guess, with an unseeing eye. My mind seemed dead. And after a while… I don't know if this happens to you, but when I take the train into the city, I always like to look out the first car window at the New York skyline if I can. And depending on the weather, it's usually kind of flat and two-dimensional, but still a beautiful sight. But, some days, through that grimy front car window, when it's clear, the skyline becomes crystal, sharp and vibrant, almost alive with a certain three-dimensional clarity that seems…more, that beams out the spectacular, the majestic."

"I know that," Dee said. "I know what you mean."

"Well, in that courtyard, suddenly everything became crystal. My perception became acute, augmented. The water splashing into the fountain had music in it, the birds flying about looked like they were in some kind of airborne ballet. I actually saw their every feather in flight as well as when they were perched. And I felt outside of myself, there but not there, the oddest sensation I ever had, strange yet natural. I was warm with delight and happiness. The small trees around me seemed like my friends, and I saw every leaf, even the veins in the leaves." She shook her head, her eyes wide open, enthralled. "I was in a complete joy, and all I wanted to do was share it—with a friend who loved me, someone sympathetic, someone deep within my heart—but I couldn't, because I then realized that I was sharing it with someone already, someone so much greater than me, someone who loved me and understood me and was already deep within my heart. It was sort of like a white light. I was aware of it but couldn't see it. And it was very much alive." She looked at Dee with trancelike eyes and continued, "A living light that only I saw…and didn't see." She looked at him questioningly, with a little tilt to her head. "Can you understand this?"

Dee reached out and touched her hand, and she then looked at him as if she just woke up.

"Then it was gone. The skyline became two-dimensional again, Dee. I have never been so happy in my life. The incredible bliss I felt… I can't even say it with words."

"This sounds to me like you tripped out on acid," Dee said.

She smiled. "But it wasn't that. In a very real way something… something wonderful happened to me. It could have been minutes, or even seconds. I actually lost all time. And I want so much to feel that again."

"I think," Dee said, "you had a religious experience. Something like the mystics get or those Buddhist monks that sit half naked in the snow."

"God, can you imagine? Me? The closest I came to that, and it was a long way from it, is after we…after we…"

Dee put his top teeth over his bottom lips and sounded, "Fffffff…"

Her eyes narrowed and she put her finger to his lips. "You know I dislike bad language."

He stopped what he was doing.

She thought for a moment and said, "After we conjugate."

Dee almost sprang out of his seat. "Conjugate?" his eyebrows uplifting.

She peered at him like a schoolmarm, her face serious and emphatic. "Yes. Conjugate."

"Bea," he said. "We are not verbs, nor are we paramecium. Conjugate?"

"Be that as it may," she went on, dismissing his remarks, "the peace, the joy, the words are the same, but the feelings… Dee. In the courtyard it was…pure."

A hurt expression masked Dee's face. "And with us it's tainted?"

She saw the slight and reached for his hand. "Not tainted. Just different. We're human. We're almost perfect, almost."

"Just to let you know, it's perfect for me."

"Dee," her voice just above a whisper. "My parents are away this weekend. Can you stay with me? The whole weekend?" Her eyes lustered. "And strive on the 'almost' to lead me to the perfect you feel?"

His heart pounded like a bass drum. "If I could I would. But I can't."

"I know. I know." She cast her eyes down. "I booked the second retreat this weekend. Am I hurting you by saying that?"

"No. It's something you need. Something you're working out. I understand." He wanted to ask what she would have done had he said "yes" to her offer, but he chose not to add to her burden. Her heart, he felt, was very restless.

"Let me get the tab," he said, changing the topic. "Pete gave me a voucher for car service home. It should be in the front in a few minutes."

"Oh my goodness," she exclaimed. "Just call me Cinderella."

As the car took them over the Brooklyn Bridge and Dee admired the beauty of the city through the car window, Bea asked, "I have a favor to ask. I'm trying to teach the kids at the Dance Center the difference between waltz tempo and foxtrot tempo. Can you put together two songs: one in three-quarter time and the other in four-four time and then throw the songs into the opposite time signature?"

"Sure," Dee said still looking out the window, "provided the melodies accommodate to the time changes." He then turned to look at her. "I wouldn't want any of the songs to sound awkward. Any particular ones you have in mind?"

"Yes," she said, "'I'll See You in My Dreams' for the four-quarter time, and 'I'll Be with You in Apple Blossom Time' for the waltz."

"I know them," his eyes shining in thought. He quickly took his little pad out, scratched out five lines on a blank page as his staff, and plugged in some notes.

"Dee," she said, putting her hand on his pad, "not now."

"Just let me finish this. It's just a thought. If I don't jot it down, I forget. It's a musical reminder."

She leaned over and kissed him. "You're something else."

The car arrived at the apartment house, and Dee let her step out toward the building as he told the driver to park and wait a bit.

Together in the vestibule, Bea said, "Everything was magical. The meal was scrumptious. I loved it." She took the keys from her purse to open the main door. She kissed him gently on the cheek and stroked his face.

"Am I invited up?"

"I think not," she replied. "I have to prepare myself for the retreat."

"If that's what you think's best," he said. He looked dejected.

She saw the pall on his face and said, "What's the matter?"

"You don't know." His tone was so flat that it could have been taken as a statement or a question.

Crinkling a slight squint, she shook her head, unsure of what he was getting at.

It gushed out of him. "How do you think I feel? How am I supposed to contend with competing with God, for Christ's sake?" He threw down his fist, his thumb sticking out. "First, He's omniscient!" His second fingered popped up. "Second, He's omnipresent!" His third finger joined the other two digits. "Third, He's omnipotent!" He took a deep breath through his nose. "He's got a lot more in his bag of tricks than I do. And His pay grade is a hell of a lot higher than mine!"

She started to laugh a deep hearty belly laugh. "Oh, Dee. My sweet Dee." She expulsed between breaths, put her arms around him, and kissed him on the lips, continuing her laugh almost in his mouth. When she momentarily checked herself, she said, "You certainly got Him beat on kissing."

He smiled and returned her kiss, holding her face.

Finally calming down, her eyes shone as sultry as a cat's. "Dee Felico. You are a persistent and persuasive one." She then held both his hands. "I love you so much."

"And I, you," he said.

"'And I, you?'" She then repeated the phrase, enunciating each word, "'And I, you?' Where'd you get that line from? Some bad play?" She laughed again. "Nobody talks like that!" She continued to laugh quite heartily finding it hard to contain herself.

She unlocked the front door. "Come," she said still laughing, "Let's go upstairs"—a shocked expression crossed his face—"and strive for perfection, you naughty boy."

Once entering the elevator, she turned to him, squeezing his hand, her smile wide and her eyes actually tearing in glee. "You have another one-up on God."

"I do?"

"You know, you really, really make me laugh," she said as the elevator door opened into the apartment.

16
CHAPTER

Talk of the meeting between Zollie Kiss and Dee Felico spread quicker than the 1918 influenza pandemic.

By the time Pete and Dee arrived back at their desks, Stan had just hung up with Zollie Kiss. "What the hell's going on? Had so many goddamn calls for you the inside of my head feels like an echo chamber. Zollie Kiss just called. A bunch of trading desks called and Vance Barlow too. On his own no less. Twice. Next time you stir up shit, get a secretary. I got fuckin' deadlines to make!" Stan went back to his job.

Pete immediately called Vance Barlow on his private line. "I need to see you now," Vance said, bypassing his normal phone etiquette.

"Be there in a flash," Pete said and hurried toward the elevators.

"What happened?" Vance asked as Pete walked in the office.

"The kid did a job on Zollie."

A surprised look overcame Vance's face. He stood up and quietly waited as if for a jury's verdict. "And?"

"He kicked Zollie in the balls and basically told him to stand up straight. I am goddamn proud of that boy. It was like watching a triple play win on the last inning of a World Series." Pete was actually bouncing on the balls of his feet.

"Mr. Barlow," Vance's secretary broke in. "Zollie Kiss on the phone."

Vance picked up. "Zollie. Hold onto your herman. I'll be with you in a few." He then hung up.

Vance then sat next to Pete on the couch. "Pete. Tell it to me slow. I have a feeling I'm going to really enjoy this." And with that, Pete related in detail the entire episode.

"I think I'd like to put him on the Ginnie Mae desk; it'll get his feet wet on the trading end, and if he ever wants to jump into sales, he'll have a complete picture under his belt. He has the ops down flat already. What do you think, Pete?"

"I concur. It fits the ticket. Just let me have him till the end of the week. And let me give him the good news," Pete said.

"Fine. I'll call Brian Devlin and tell him Dee will report to him on Monday. Brian's a task master."

Pete cut in, "No more so than me."

"Pete," Vance said, "you're in your own category. Plus you're a ball buster."

Pete shook Vance's hand. "Done."

"Pete," Vance asked, "I think this calls for a lunch. What do you say?"

Pete jumped up. "You nuts? I'm down a man! And you want to dawdle on a picnic? What's the matter with you? Seriously!" He started to twitch. "I gotta go." He left shaking his head in disbelief.

Vance laughed loudly.

Pete touched Dee's shoulder lightly and startled him since he was working intently on a rather sizable bond interest claim. "What? What's up, Pete."

"Come," Pete said, walking toward the conference room.

Dee followed Pete, and as he entered, Pete, closing the door, said, "You caused quite a stir with a lot of top dogs." He smiled. "They agreed to use your proposal. Zollie even bounced it off legal just to play it safe. They know how he is, and they tiptoed around it but ultimately agreed that if the clients want to shell out big bucks for a piece of paper, then who the hell were they to say they couldn't? We're legally bound to the trade any way you look at it." Pete then lit up a cigarette. "Also, Vance wants you on the Ginnie Mae desk Brian Devlin started up. You start Monday."

Dee was stunned. "But, Pete..."

"That's all. Just don't fuck up. That'll reflect on me."

"Pete. I didn't ask—"

"It's done. You did an outstanding job on this and it's being recognized."

"Did you…?"

"You did everything on your own. All's I did was walk you into Zollie's office."

Dee was beside himself. "I don't know what to say…"

"'s'nothin' to say. Get your ass back to your desk. You got work to do. And…take the Ace Coupon Chimp plate off my desk. You put it on yours. Always'll let people know where you came from."

"Pete," Dee said, "I can't take that. Old Man Barlow gave that to—"

"A million years ago. And you're not taking it. I'm giving it to you as a kind a decoration. It ain't up to the Good Conduct Medal…" He thought a bit. "Something on par with a campaign ribbon—without any battle stars. I got it. An 'I Was There' medal."

They looked at each other for a long time. Nothing was said, but plenty was understood. "Now, get the hell out of here before my nose turns red!"

Dee got up, paused over Pete quietly sitting and taking a drag on his Chesterfield, touched his shoulder, and left the room. Pete did not look up. After Dee closed the door, he sniffed heavily twice, blew his nose like a bugle call, muttering, "Goddamn air-conditioning," picked up the phone, and called Vance Barlow.

17
CHAPTER

Dee was very pleased with the time-signature changes on the songs Bea had given him in the car. It was done in a rush after he had gotten home from their tryst. He smoothed out the piece the following morning making it printer-ready for the musical director to read and not guess at his scrawl. He embellished it with some Gershwin harmonies to give it a jazzy tang. The songs were simple melodies, and he thought Bea would like the spice-up. He gave it to her after they attended early morning Mass that Sunday.

"So soon?" she said. "I didn't need them till—"

"It gushed out of me."

She inwardly smiled. "Did I have something to do with your inspiration?" she purred.

"What do you mean?" he said thoughtlessly and then closed his eyes realizing his error. He flubbed out, "I... I only had one fast cup of coffee this morning."

"I think you're chock full of nuts already." She let go of his hand.

"Come to the house. I'll play it for you." He hoped she would consent since he had some tar work to do on the roof as well as hang a new fixture in a tenant's apartment. He knew that after he played her the rendition she would leave since his mother was home doing a barrel of laundry, and to have them together too long could create a Russian roulette situation he was not willing to risk. Their association was still at arm's distance.

"No. We'll go to the diner. You need your second cup to wake up. I hope you paid attention at Mass."

He knew she wasn't kidding. Recently, she ruffled easily and became unusually sensitive when he made a remark off the cuff that didn't sit well with her. This was something new. Yet even though it was happening more often than not, he did not think it was necessary to address. He merely chalked it up to stress.

She was loaded down with course work. And with the pressure of putting together syncopated dance steps for little kids in a production number to satisfy their tuition-paying parents, he felt that anyone's nerves would start to fray under those circumstances. It was a simple case of fatigue and overwork, and a snappy response seemed quite the norm. So he let the matter go.

He just hoped, walking with her, she wasn't going to quiz him on the homily or scripture readings. He never knew where her head would be after Mass. He had daydreamed through the entire service and went through the ritual motions like an old horse on a milk route with the driver fast asleep.

At the diner, Dee chugged down a coffee which he made extra light to cool it and asked for another before the waitress took their order.

"That's your heroin," she said.

"I do need the hit in the morning, but after that I'm okay. You know that."

They remained quiet for a while until their order came as Bea sipped water and he nursed his coffee.

"Dee, I've been having some problems sleeping."

"You're overworked."

She slammed back, "I am not!"

He looked at her with concern. "You have a big load on your shoulders. Maybe you're trying to accomplish too much in too tiny a time frame."

"And," she said loudly, "you're saying I'm not up to it!"

"No. Take it easy." He then rearranged his thoughts. "You can do it all. You just need some rest time. A power nap. Some daydreaming." He smiled to himself. "A cosmic caesura."

She took note and interest in what he said. "Mmmm. Yes. Cosmic caesura." She liked the phrase. "My...heavenly rest."

"Yes. That'll give you the recharge."

She mulled it over for a moment and then confessed, "But I have horrible dreams. Weird. Sometimes violent ones. Dreams filled with...dread and...desperation."

"Maybe you're reading too much Kierkegaard."

Her eyes became steel points. "I'm steeped in all the philosophers!"

"Bea," he implored, "I'm not judging. I'm only responding, trying to help. I know you're big on prayer. Have you done it? I think you're going through some kind of crisis...maybe a spiritual crisis? I worry for you."

"Yes. I do!" she sighed in exasperation. "On my knees! In front of my 'garbage-picked grotto,' as you call it! And to no avail! I'm all knots inside!" Her face was etched with defeat.

"Can you pinpoint what it is that ails you?"

"No. I can't."

"Do I," he said, reaching out his hand, "calm you in any way?"

Her face softened. She held back tears and clasped his hand. "You do." And then she turned her head in questioning thought. "By and large, but not all the time...not all the time that I need." She swallowed hard. "And I'm not needy, mind you!" Her eyes cleared and she let go of his hand.

"Maybe you're being prepared for something. Ever think of that?"

It was something she had never thought of. She seemed to contemplate the thought, shaking her head ever so slightly, whispering to herself. The waitress brought their order.

He patted her hand. "Eat up. Slowly. Savor each piece. You don't want it to get cold."

Following his instruction, she picked up her fork and knife and cut up her vegetable omelet.

Halfway through the meal, she looked up at him and said, "You're the one that's blessed. Not me. I envy you. And I hate myself for being envious. But I can't help it."

"How'm I blessed?" he said, his mouth full of home fries.

"That 'infernal machine,' as your mother puts it, playing that same record over and over a million times. Ad nauseam."

"That," he said, swallowing, "is my caesura. I think it's the repetition, sort of puts you in a different state. It's something akin to the rosary, the Jesus Prayer, that Indian 'om' sound, a whirling dervish. It's different for different people. And it varies by degree on where you are in your mind. It's certainly not the threshold in the garden you experienced. For me, the music brings me to a high plateau. At best, it calms me on a cloud. Not a mini salvation. Far from that. It doesn't reach that mark. But it comforts me." He took a sip of coffee. "What you had was much, much more. Way and above anything I ever encountered." He looked straight at her. "So who's blessed?" He then shrugged his shoulders.

"I'm looking for answers, Dee. And I'm not getting any." She wiped her nose with her napkin. "I need some."

"Maybe," he said, sucking his tongue against his teeth to clear a morsel of bread, "the silence is the answer. Ever consider that? You've read the mystics. It's not unusual, you know."

She put her knife and fork down and gazed out the window for a long time. He saw she was deeply troubled. He remained quiet.

Suddenly she turned to him and asked, "What would you say if I got a tattoo?"

"What!" he said, totally bewildered.

She took his reaction unkindly. "Yes. Tattoo." Her sarcasm unleashed due to his affronting tone. "I will wait until it sinks in." She had a steely look about her. "What would you say?"

He didn't know if this was a tease or a test. To figure out what prompted this, he thought, would be trying to figure out the proof for Fermat's last theorem. And even if he did figure it out, he was dead certain he would probably be wrong.

"I'd say," he said, taking a deep breath because he knew he was on his way under, "that you're either joining the Navy or the Ringling Brothers Barnum and Bailey Circus."

Her eyes turned to fire and her mouth opened. "It's just like you to say something crass like that!" Her words shot out like dumdum bullets.

"If you knew that, why did you ask?"

"I just thought, and pardon me for saying so, Mr. Felico, that you might have expanded your progressive thought process."

Her indignant manner bothered him. "Bea, you know what I like and don't like. This is not our first encounter."

"And you don't even ask what type of tattoo and where?"

She was starting a row. He had no idea why. He felt he was just being the whipping boy for her internal exasperation. She had more twists and turns in her than a tangled fishing net. "Okay. What and where?"

"On my ankles. Treble clef on the right and bass clef on the left."

"And a melody in your heart?" he spouted out.

She smiled tentatively. "As a matter of fact, yes."

"Body art does nothing for me."

She shook her head. "Not even one ounce of serendipity! How can you live with yourself?" she said with harsh disappointment. "And the art is for me! Not you!"

"I haven't gotten any notions to commit suicide recently. So. So far, so good."

"Well! For that matter, I am going to do what I want to do! Anyway! So don't tell me!"

"I'm not telling you. You're telling me."

She steamed out with, "I'm sick of this. I've had it with you and your merry-go-round talk." She abruptly got up. "I'm leaving!"

"Wait, Bea. Let me pay the bill…"

"I'm going now! And just to let you know, there's something wrong with you!" It was not a statement; it was a declaration, a fixed label.

She started to leave and he grabbed her arm. Pulling it away, she said, "Let go!"

"Here," he said, handing her the music he had written for her, "you forgot this." She hesitated momentarily then snatched it from his hand. He remained in his seat as she left.

From the window of the diner, he saw her run down the stairs, briefly looked at him, and mouthed "thank you" as she flicked up the envelope holding the music. Then she turned and hurried toward the el. She never saw his acknowledging nod.

The waitress came over, noticing not everything was eaten on Bea's plate. "Problem with the food?"

"No," he said. "It was fine." He pulled out his wallet. "There's just something wrong with me." He then paid the check and went home.

18
CHAPTER

When he met her at St. John's Chapel, he became visibly shaken.

She had lost weight and her hair was cropped shorter than ever before. By his estimation, she looked ten years past her best moment.

They hadn't seen each other in well over two months; their schedules hardly ever overlapping. And when on a fluke their timetables aligned, a last-minute derailment usually occurred. He missed the dance recital due to work and was briefly told by Bea that everything went over famously including his renditions of the songs, which hit the local paper and were footnoted as "fresh face lifts on two old standards." When Dee heard this, his response was that the writer probably had a tin ear.

She smiled genuinely from the heart when she saw him, but it came with some effort as if interrupted from something important. She said, "Hiya, baby."

He kissed her on the cheek. "Are you okay?" He wanted to hug her but felt a little ill at ease to do so in church.

She stroked his face. She looked drawn, tuckered out as if after an illness. "I'm fine, baby. Just inundated. Had to quit the Dance Center after the recital. Senior seminars, retreats, my thesis—I'm all over the place. I'm lucky I'm breathing."

He missed her so much—the feel of her against him, the safeness he had with her touch, and those long rambling conversations, crackling with wit and deep insight that really went nowhere but gave him such a feeling of refreshment and joy that to end it seemed almost sinful. He also missed just looking at her and wondering how such a beautiful thing blessed his life.

"I tried to get you on your birthday. Your phone rang, then I tried again and it was busy. I even tried to come to the house. I rang the bell. There was no answer."

"I know," she said. "I took the phone off the hook. I didn't answer the door."

He was incredulous. "Bea? Why would you do that? It was me. You knew it was me.

"I needed," she said, "my solitude. I was fasting and meditating."

Confounded, he tried terribly to understand but couldn't, even though his heart of hearts accepted her behavior out of love. He muttered, "I understand." He was hurt. No apology came. It was not that she didn't want to or couldn't. There was simply no reason to do so. What she did, what she was involved with, mattered more—more than him. That confused him.

A pang hit his stomach. He remained quiet about the issue.

He sat next to her and she took his hand in hers. "I'm okay, Dee. There are just some things I have to do, have to find out."

He noticed that on her left hand, on the ring finger, there was a blue tattoo of a cross. "You did get a tattoo," he said.

Delightedly, she said, "Yes. And by the way, look." She showed him her ankles. There was a blue cross on each ankle. His puzzled face led her to say, "I've always had a softness in my heart for the two thieves." She smiled.

"Well," he said, really not knowing what to say, "it's certainly a lot different than what you actually intended. Did it hurt much?"

"It pinched." She put her hand to his cheek again. "Are you cross with me?"

He laughed. "Are we playing on words?"

"Yes." She chuckled to herself. "I didn't realize I said that. I suppose so."

He didn't know if it was a good place and time to do it. He figured that he had nothing to lose. It might even brighten his spirits. He reached into his pocket. "I have a birthday gift for you."

A surprised look came across her face. "You know I'm not into material gifts." She looked at him sternly. "Dee? Dee, you know…"

"I wanted to. It's as simple as that."

"I can't," she whispered, spying the small ring box.

What she did not see immediately was a swatch of birthday wrapping paper and a small plastic scotch tape dispenser that he took out of his other pocket.

He handed her everything, saying, "I don't wrap."

She burst out laughing, looking at him. "You're something else." She laughed louder than one should in church, but it really didn't matter since no one else was there.

She opened the ring box and gasped. "Dee. It's beautiful." It was a scorpion ring with an amethyst stinger. She put it on the finger with the tattoo. It fit perfectly. She was speechless for several moments.

"Scorpio," Dee said, "the scorpion. It is the lady."

She touched his hand. "Yes, yes. It fits so well. In every instance. It is me." She then inspected, studied, and admired it, stretching her hand out at arm's length, wiggling her fingers. "It is me." She then queried, "How...?"

He jumped in. "You sometimes wear that large paper clip on your finger as a ring. When you were washing up a while back, I sized it on my finger and used it as a guide." He smiled. "The caper worked. Do you really like it?"

She continued to stare at the ring.

Peering up at him, she said, "I love it. But, Dee, I can't accept this. It's so expensive."

"Take it and keep it. I wanted to do this for a long time. And... I'm glad I did."

She put her hands on his face and looked deeply at him. "What am I going to do with you, Dee Felico?" She then kissed him very chastely on the lips aware that the Lord of hosts was watching, or so she thought.

"You can take me home with you."

"I could. In fact, my parents are away in San Francisco, another mission, something having to do with the Indian occupation of Alcatraz. If it isn't a demonstration, it's some kind of relief effort. That's them. And the better part of me wants to desperately, but I won't. I need this time. I need this time. I need alone-time."

He felt a little dashed by the comment.

"I've missed you terribly. This would be a perfect opportunity to catch up."

"I really need the quiet time."

"I'll be quiet," Dee said.

"Dee," she said, putting her finger on his nose. "Stop."

"Did I do something wrong? Because, if I did…"

"For heaven's sake. No. You did nothing wrong. It's me. I'm involved, and I really…"—she gasped somewhat in annoyance—"don't press me. I can't talk about it," she said.

He tried to hold her arms, his thinking completely rattled. "Bea? Is there someone else?"

"No."

"Tell me the truth. Is it somebody else?"

"No," she said, touching his hand. He then held her tightly as she whispered in an indistinguishable sighing breath, her lips kissing his hair, "It's another." He only heard her sigh.

He tried to kiss her, and she gently pushed against his chest with her fingers even though she saw the pain in his eyes. "This," she said, her eyes downcast, "is neither the time nor the place." She paused. "I know you will understand this: think of me as Mariah. They call the wind Mariah. I'm a wayward wind, a restless wind."

He cringed. "My god, has it come to this? Swapping lyrics as explanations, or excuses?" He shook his head. "Should I now say 'the song has ended but the melody lingers on'? This is worse than exchanging footnotes from 'The Wasteland.'" A sour look etched his face.

"I'm not trying to be funny, Dee. And don't mock me."

"That's not the intent. I'm just frustrated. This is so beyond my comprehension." He sloughed it off, saying, "Whatever," in a disappointed tone.

Peripherally, she saw him coming and got excited. "My confessor is coming. He's my grade advisor and my mentor as well, and he's also my friend. He's a Jesuit and brilliant. I want you to meet him. That's why I asked you to meet me here. He's wonderful. I'm in awe with his intensity."

She got up and waved to him as he came in the chapel door. He acknowledged her with a slow wink of the eye. He did not genuflect or make the sign of the cross. He just nodded briefly at the altar as if passing a student in the hall.

He was tall, regal in bearing, and walked with a strange gait, a sort of glide or slithering to mask a gross limp caused by a childhood ailment or a war wound. He had on traditional black priest's garb that looked more custom-made than off the rack. His black eyebrows were long and comb-able, arching like a falcon's wings in flight, and his mustache traveled, sleek and waxed into end tips pointed upward over full pouting lips. His beard came to a severe point. But it was his eyes that intrigued Dee most. They were amber in color with orange specks, and there was something about them that Dee suspected was unbecoming his vocation. His hair was jet black and combed back severely with a patent leather sheen to it. Had a caricaturist done the priest's portrait, it would have taken on the facial characteristics of a timber wolf.

"Democedes Felico," the priest said in a heavily accented voice, perfectly pronouncing his name with the proper inflection. "Much have I heard of you." He extended his hand.

The hand seemed withered and small, and the grip weak and somewhat slimy like that of an octopus tentacle. His fingernails were manicured and had a clear polish on them.

"Favorable commentary, I trust," Dee said.

The priest laughed showing rather jagged, yellow unkept teeth, peering down at Bea yet addressing Dee, "Yes, yes. Very positive. Very." He spoke slowly, methodically, awkwardly manipulating his mouth and tongue to pronounce the words so foreign to him. Watching him speak was as unsettling as a fiddle player viewing a left-handed violinist performing. It went against the grain like the whine of a dentist's drill.

"Dee," Bea said, "this is Father Valentin Negrescu."

"Little friend here—yours—is my finest student. A crown jewel. A rare gift," he said.

Dee suddenly clasped Bea's hand, which unsettled her. "Yes, Father. I agree. She is a rare gift."

"And...you are a Vall Streeter, hmmm, I hear."

"Yes," Dee said. "I work on Wall Street. And I'm finishing up school too like Bea."

He mumbled, seemingly translating the Romanian of what he wanted to say into English before he spoke. "A manipulative business." He articulated *business* into three syllables. "This... Vall Street."

It was hard for Dee to understand whether an affront was being made or just a badly fractured translation from Romanian. "Yes. As are many enterprises," Dee said.

"True," the priest said, rolling the R and extending the sound of the word as if in song.

"If one would consider, Father," Dee forwarded, "the church as a business, it too might fall under the same category."

Bea squeezed his hand irritated by the comment.

The priest laughed loudly, an odd staccato sputtering, and cocked his head. "Vell...interesting observation. Ve," he postured, "however, hmmm...gain from...the saving of...souls."

"By manipulation?" Dee queried.

Bea stuck her thumbnail into Dee's hand in anger while maintaining a normal facial expression.

The priest continued to laugh. He then addressed Bea. "Your friend... I like, Beatrice. Very clever. You should...hmmm...audit my class." He then looked at Dee. "Your courage...is vitality—no, no...hmmm...is refreshing. Effervescent. Now." His voice became pedagogical in tone. "Ve but correct, Democedes Felico, and instruct the uninformed, the souls ve save." His smile looked like a snarl. "Your means to ending is for, how you say? Remunerative splendor, profit? Yes. Profit. Ours"—he widened his arms in the gesture of proclamation—"is for greater glory of God." He raised his voice then snickered into a laugh as his ending point.

"I see," Dee said. Bea took her hand from his.

Suddenly agitation crossed his face. "Ach!" He patted his vest frantically until he found his pocket watch and opened it. "I must...rush...please," he said, slightly bowing to them. "My forgiveness to you. A colloquium I must attend. I am joyous to meet you, Democedes Felico. Perhaps with more time, more conversation. Yes?"

"I look forward to it," Dee said

The priest placed his hands on their heads. "A small blessing for you both, if I may." He whispered his prayer in Romanian. Upon completion of his blessing, he cupped Bea's face in his hands and gave her a slobbering kiss on the brow and on both cheeks European style with such audible smacks it sounded like someone sucking marrow out of a bone. He then, with his thumbs, wiped the moisture from his lips on the three areas he kissed. He gazed at her momentarily then turned to Dee and said, "A ravishing creature, so comely a sylph."

Dee thought the comment and the sign of affection inappropriate, whether it was his custom or not, and the priest saw the heat in Dee's eyes.

"I have," the priest said, "come late to this language of yours. A testing...it is...to me, much like the Trinity. Fantastically difficult. Pardon, hmmm...your English to me does not come...easily as with other things. Alas, hmmm...they remain products of yes...original sin. Please to forgive." His parting smile was ugly.

Dee nodded in acknowledgment but sensed sincerity held no weight in his words. He shook Dee's hand. "A pleasure."

Dee said, "Thank you, Father. Best of luck."

When the priest floated away, Bea was livid. "You are incorrigible!"

"What!" Dee exclaimed.

"How embarrassing! You should be ashamed of yourself talking to him that way!"

"Embarrassing? How?"

"Picking at him like that, antagonizing him...about the church! Manipulating minds! How could you!"

"He's a Jesuit!" Dee said strongly. "They live on challenge! What's the big deal?"

"The big deal?" she rasped, keeping her voice down aware that she was in church. "What now will he think of me?"

"What? Because you're with the likes of someone like me? Get off it!"

"Get off it?"

"It should have no bearing. He should, if he's worth his weight as a true Jesuit, accept you for who you are. Totally. Regardless of your…proclivities! Me, being the proclivity in question! There should be no guilt by association!"

She shook her head. "I just don't sometimes understand you! That's so mean-spirited!"

Dee abruptly said, "Mean-spirited! What don't you understand? Bea, I didn't like the way he leered at you. I didn't like him kissing you like that, like he was the Marquis de Sade! I didn't like him referring to you as a ravishing creature—creature, mind you I…and a comely sylph! I didn't like that! In fact. If you asked me, looks like he studied dramatics under Bela Lugosi for Christ's sake! He even looks like Dracula! I'm sorry! I don't like him, genius or no genius!"

She flicked her finger on his mouth. "You're in church! Watch your mouth!"

"And just to remind you," Dee continued, "he's a Jesuit. An ordinary man! Not a secular saint! Not a deity! A Jesuit! One of the pope's men! And those fuckin' guys are apt to do anything for the greater glory of God! They stretch the rules like saltwater taffy." He took a breath. "I wouldn't be surprised if he broke every goddamned vow!"

Bea slapped his face.

Shocked, fury initially raging in him, he glared at her and seethed, "If you ever hit me again, I'll brain you like baby seal on the open ice!"

She pulled back, startled. He had never spoken to her in that manner before.

He then turned and slowly walked toward the chapel door, a desolate emptiness ravaging him. He felt something hit his ear. When he looked down, he saw the ring on the carpeted floor. He picked it up not looking back and rolled it mindlessly in his fingers and then placed it on the arm of the last pew and walked out.

He sighed heavily when he got outside, the world before him just flatness and drab color. Moving toward the curb, he suddenly started to cry bitterly.

She saw him crying through the tinted glass windows of the chapel and realized what she had done. Instantly she ran out to him, picking up the ring before she shot through the door.

She touched him and he pulled away as if brushed by the thorns of a rose bush. "I'm wrong. I'm wrong. I'm so sorry. I'm such a miserable bitch. You were looking out for me. You were trying to protect me. I tried to control myself... I can't..." She couldn't speak and started to cry also.

He walked away from her and sat on a concrete step overlooking the track field. She followed him. "Just leave me the fuck alone," he said.

She sat near him but not next to him. They remained there a long time. She put her face in her hands and cried. "It's me. I'm the poison."

He said nothing and continued to stare at the field, the buildings across the way, and the gray sky.

"I've tried so hard...so hard..." She was in total resignation. "It's a plague in me. It's in my blood. I'm diseased. Nothing quells it. There are no remedies. All the calm, the quiet, the meditations, the retreats...the prayers—useless." She cried in anguish. "Fucking useless!" She slammed her fist on her knee.

He turned to look at her. He had never heard her use harsh profanity before.

"I'm cursed. I'll never be able to complete myself as I want to. I'll never be able to salvage my soul and no one else will either." Their eyes saw nothing but each other's. "Maybe my mother made the mistake. Maybe the blame's on her all along. Maybe the pinprick would have been the more humane thing to do." Her bottom lip quivered. "Oblivion would have been paradise compared to this." She then put her face in her hands.

He still loved her, poison and all. They sat in silence for a long time before he remarked softly, "If that were done...look, look what I would have missed." He extended his hand to her.

She touched it from afar, the pain so much within her. "How I'm loved," she sighed, tears dripping down her cheeks, not talking to him but to herself, the words projecting outward toward the vista before her, the world around her and all that it meant, and that safe harbor she desperately yearned to be invited into one day.

"I'm lost. So lost," she said. "Don't you ever feel lost?"

"No," he said.

"Is there a trick?"

"A trick?" Dee paused. "I don't think so. Maybe the trick's not minding what comes next. You see, you can't get lost if you don't care where you are. You're trying too hard to find it. I don't look for it. It finds me."

She heard and absorbed his words but didn't understand it.

"Bea. You're dog-earing your own page. You're not letting the story complete itself. You're trying to do it yourself, force the story and it loses its flow, and that puts you in the bind."

She put her brow on her knees.

He went to her. "Come. Let me take you home."

He helped her up and they left the campus.

Little was said on the commute home. Upon arriving at the apartment, she said, "I'm so tired. I have to lie down."

"Mind company?"

"Dee. I'm really not in the mood."

"Me neither. I'm emotionally spent."

Weakly smiling, she held his hand. "Okay. Come."

They faced each other on the bed. She fought for slumber, but her mind was a tornado.

"I'm sorry about the priest thing. I was upset with his manner, and knowing what he knows about me and you…through your confession, that is. That bothered me."

"All," she said, her eyes closed, her voice just above a whisper, "he's privy to is our surface stuff. And nothing else."

"I don't follow."

"I have other confessors, visiting priests, one-shot deals. I choose who I confess what to." She looked at him, her eyes wide open.

"So…" Dee began connecting the lines.

"He knows nothing of our…underground doings."

He kissed her on the cheek. "I was upset. I was scared. I'm sorry. But I do feel better now." He then hugged her, feeling the bones in her back. "Please don't lose any more weight. I feel your bones. Don't get brittle on me. I'm afraid for you."

She was amused by what he said. "I'm just cleansing myself, ridding myself of all artificial things. It's high time. I want everything in me to be totally natural. I'll never be pure again, but I'd like to get as close to that as I can. I want to be burden-free. I have so much to do, and I need to be in tip-top condition—in mind, body, and spirit. And I'm blotting out any and all…distractions."

He touched her. "I think I understand."

"I think you do," she said, gently removing his hand from her thigh.

"Bea. I missed you so much."

"I've missed you too. I dream of you."

"Do you, really?"

"Yes. And they are very sweet dreams."

"And the bad dreams are gone?"

"They come and go. But there are less of them than before."

"I love you, Bea. I want to spend the rest of my life with you. I want to take care of you."

She covered his mouth with her palm. "I know. But this is not the time. I have to do what I have to do. Please. Please let me do it. You're making it very hard for me."

His mouth suddenly became dry. "Am I losing you?" He said it even though he feared the words. It was the hardest thing he ever asked her.

She did not speak immediately. "I don't think you'll ever lose me." She combed her fingers through his hair. "I'm going during Christmas break and also during intersession to San Francisco to check up on my parents. It'd be good to see them again. I do have to keep tabs on them. Sometimes they get a little rambunctious with their civil disobedience. They are old radicals. I wouldn't want to see them get thrown in the hoosegow."

He laughed. "In this day and age, it's usually the other way around. Keeping the kids out of the clink, not the parents."

She looked deeply into his eyes and lightly stroked his hair and, in a wispy, half-sung, half-spoken voice, began, "'I'll see you in my dreams. Hold you in my dreams…'"—her eyes, serene, soft—"'Someone took me out of your arms. Still, I feel the thrill of your charms.'" Her breath was warm, hinting of lilac. "'Lips that once were mine. Tender eyes that shine'"—her finger trailing down from his hair to his mouth—"'They will light…my way tonight,'" then sighing, whispered, "'I'll see you…in…my dreams.'" She then kissed him very tenderly.

He had all to hold back tears. "I don't think," he chokingly said, "I've ever felt so happy in my life."

"I hope I was in key," she said, touching her nose to his. "You and that perfect pitch of yours."

"You were. I heard with my heart."

They embraced and held each other for a long time.

The moment could have been holy had he been in prayer, but he wasn't. It just happened. His reedy baritone lifted out, "'I'll be with you in apple blossom time. I'll be with you…to change your name to mine. Someday in May, I'll come and say… Happy the bride that the sun shines on today'"—his eyes spilling into hers—"'What a wonderful wedding there will be'"—fingering her dimple—"'What a wonderful day for you and me'"—touching her, kissing lips—"'Church bells with chime. You'"—tapping her nose—"'will be mine'"—then slowly, majestically, with schmaltzy emotion, she harmonized with him the final lyric—"'In apple blossom time.'"

Ending, they looked at each other in silence and then suddenly erupted in unison into hysterical laughter. They had to quickly sit up in bed to catch their breaths.

After a time, their laughing jag subsided only to be retriggered by a coaxing, casual knowing look. By the time they regained their composure, their sides were like battered bulkheads.

Dee sputtered, barely getting out the words, "We sounded like the ghosts of Jeannette Mac Donald and Nelson Eddy—on a bender."

"Dee," Bea gasped, "I don't remember the last time I laughed so hard. I hope I don't have to go into traction." Happily exhausted, she continued, "I really needed that," and looking at him, ended with, "We both did."

He got off the bed. "It was a good one. But I best be going now. I have a shitload of stuff to do. You don't have a monopoly on that."

"Can I get you anything? Something to eat? Drink?"

"No. I'm good. When will I see you? When you're back from your visit?"

"I'm going into self-imposed exile on this last academic leg. So, so many things to do and square away." She licked her lips. "I'll call you."

His face became drawn.

"I really mean it. I'll call you."

She got up off the bed, held his hand, and walked him into the living room where the elevator was.

"Send me a postcard. From San Fran. And don't forget to say hello to your parents for me. And…if you need any help…"

She squeezed his hand. "I know. I'll send you a postcard. And I'll give them your regards."

He held her face in his hands as the elevator doors opened when she pushed the button. His eyes were sad. "I love you, baby."

Her eyes flashed. "You never called me 'baby' before."

"I hope you don't sue me for plagiarism."

She giggled. "You are a funny one." Her hands went to his face and pulled him down and kissed him soulfully.

He then went into the elevator holding her hand to the very end. She said, "Bye, baby."

He watched her and sidestepped with the moving elevator door to look at her until the very last second before it closed. His heart had lost its Shangri-la.

He never saw her again.

19
CHAPTER

Violet Wagner was a Broadway gypsy, a few bad hands past forty, three husbands down, living on upper Madison Avenue with a mother still saving for the next Depression. She shilled Park Avenue real estate part time while moonlighting in a nudie musical off off-Broadway.

While entertaining a group of redneck Muni brokers from Memphis, she caught the eye of Zollie Kiss. He immediately saw her assets as a beautiful business lure and, after the show, went backstage with business card in hand and offered her a job on the spot as coordinator and receptionist for the executive dining room.

On a lark, she went down to his office the next morning and found to her shock that the job was legit and the eye-popping salary that was assigned to it forever eliminated the words *struggle* and *poverty row* from her vocabulary. When she told her mother, the old lady opened up a bottle of elderberry wine and threw away all her bank deposit slips.

She snapped up the job like a frog bagging a dragonfly, quit the real estate game, but stipulated to Zollie that it was imperative to continue with her nightly theater gig since she had a "run-of-the-play" contract. Zollie ironed out that compliance issue without a hitch and took full credit for his new "discovery." He also bought a group of seats in the small, intimate theater on the corporate account assuring continued attendance by his out-of-town players whose future business would not only offset Violet Wagner's salary and bonus but add a nice piece of change to the bottom lines of Barlow Brothers, the theater, and the actors and actresses on the stage. In his mind, Zollie Kiss dubbed himself an entrepreneurial patron of the arts.

She became acquainted with Dee Felico when he moved up to the Ginnie Mae desk. She found him to be a charming young man and was a little dashed when she found out his age. His mustache belied his years. She was attracted to him but just satisfied herself with a little good-natured flirting here and there. He played along very nicely. She found him to be a good sport and knew he didn't consider her a broken-down broad.

Being a new security, the Ginnie Mae desk was run by younger men a bit more refined than the rowdy cowboys that manned the other trading desks. All of the members of the Ginnie Mae desk were very kind and gracious to Violet save Howie Bernstein, who was a discarded relic from government bond trading. Howie was a slime-ball who never made it above sewer level. He was a crackerjack on pricing an issue, but aside from that, he was living proof of what bad taste really was. One of the oldest traders on the desk, he wore suits that looked like he slept in them and had a greasy bald head flanked by steel wooly gray hair that, after the hair spray wore off, flared out like Larry Fine's of the Three Stooges.

Violet was serving the desk a new brand of coffee she got samples of from a coffee taster she had become acquainted with at 99 Wall Street. Howie was scrutinizing *Hustler Magazine*'s centerfold as she placed the cup of coffee next to him.

Peering up at her, he said, "Something, huh? What do you think?"

Violet merely said, "Looks familiar."

He wiggled his eyebrows. "Nice."

"Is that necessary for you to look at now?"

"Yes. Getting ready for lunch. My kind of menu," he said flatly. She turned to the desk partner. "Brian. Can't you fire this bozo?"

Brian Devlin said, "He's the bane of my existence. I must have done something terribly wrong before I was born to get this albatross. And the answer is no. I didn't hire him. He was here long before me. He came with the cornerstone of the building. I wish I could put him in a time capsule for some future civilization to figure out."

She laughed and then served Dee his coffee.

"Thank you, Vi," he said.

"Give it a taste."

Dee sipped it and smacked his lips. "Wow. Is this delicious." Turning and looking up at her, he said, "Where'd you find this guy?"

"Stage door Johnnie. Just came to see me after the show to say how much he enjoyed it."

Dee squinted a little. "Was that his entrance line to delve into other things?"

"No, dearie. He's an out and out Renaissance man. He brought his boyfriend next time he came. He was testing out the play. Didn't want it to be overly risqué for his candy stick. I must say his partner was gorgeous."

Dee chuckled, taking another swig of coffee. "I understand. The perfect escort."

"Yes. We then got to talking—theater talk amongst other things—and then he said he was a coffee taster, not your run-of-the-mill job, and he showed me his operation, just down the block from us, 99 Wall, and he suggested giving me some samples of coffee to get a public response. So you guys are the guinea pigs. Very interesting setup, it is. He has a big metal circular trough. It's a slurping and spitting and note jotting business. His taste buds must be extremely acute. What a strange occupation. My mother even likes him, and that's saying a lot. Must be the free java." She giggled then paused. "Zollie booked a slew of seats at every performance till the cows come home. I've never seen you there."

"I have a lot I'm doing." He was being polite.

"Dee. It's a show. It's not raunchy. I'm in character. And it's funny. I won't be embarrassed if you see me."

"But I might, Vi," he said. Even with his dark complexion, she saw a rushing blush on his neck.

"Oh," she sighed, totally touched. "You are such a sweet one." She gently placed her hand on his shoulder and continued to serve the coffee to the other traders.

His phone rang. "Ginnie Maes, Dee Felico."

"Dee. It's me, baby."

He jumped up, the desk staff and Violet noticing his abrupt move.

"Where are you? I haven't heard from you in months. I was sick with worry!"

"I'm so thrilled. I think…no, I know I found it. I had to tell you before I go."

"Go!" Dee was shouting. "What do you mean go?"

"It happened so fast. The decision's made, Dee. I love you so much, but I'm so happy it's happened."

He was frantic. "Where are you? Where are you!"

"Wait. I need more coins for the phone."

He was almost screaming. "Where are you!" He heard the operator cut in to request more change.

"The airport. My plane leaves in a jiff. I gotta go. I love you, my baby. I'll see you in my dreams, and I'll be with you in apple blossom time."

"Bea! Bea! Where are you going?"

"I gotta go. The plane is leaving."

"I never got your card!"

"Oh, Lord. I forgot. Bye, baby… I'll see you in my dreams, and I'll be with you in apple blossom time."

The phone then went dead. "Bea! Bea!" he screamed, tears coming out of his eyes. He slammed the phone down so hard he broke the receiver. He collapsed, his face in his hands, moaning and grunting in sudden anguish.

Violet put her arms around him, sitting next to him as the other traders came to help. Howie Bernstein just said, "Somebody musta fuckin' died."

Violet rubbed his back as the others stood around him. The commotion jarred the other desks to peer over speculating whether the outburst was caused by breaking a trade or the result of bad drugs. "Come, honey. Let's go to some place quiet." Both Violet and Brian brought him to the executive dining room. Violet sat next to him on a couch while Brian, squatting in front of him, put his hands on Dee's knees and softly said, "What happened, Dee? What happened?"

"My girl...," he choked out. "My girl is...gone... I don't know... I don't understand."

Brian looked up at Violet who nodded that she would take care of him. Brian said, "Vi. If you need me..."

Their eyes showed concern. Brian got up placing his hand on Dee's head. "You stay with Vi. We have everything under control. You just take it easy, my friend. If you need to hit the road, no sweat. We have everything covered. Take whatever time you need."

It was quite some time before he sat up and stopped crying. Violet held his hands. They were ice cold. "Tell me, honey. Tell me all about it. Get it out of your system."

Dee looked at Violet's pretty face, her eyes soft with under-standing, and then, somehow feeling the comfort only strangers can give who ultimately only care to help without knowing the details, dropped all his guards and told her the story.

When Pete McKelvey found out, he became livid. "How a pretty thing could do that to my boy I'll never know! They're all cats! Fuckin' cats! Nice to look at, but when you go into their cages, better have a whip, a chair, and a fuckin' gun."

Dee's mother, Margo, at least showed some sympathy for her boy. "She was a very pretty girl, but she was troubled. I felt that from the start. I hope she finds what she's looking for. In fact, I'm going to light a candle for her." Dee's numb mind knew it was about as kind a gesture that his mother could make about "that" Bea. He just won-dered if the votive candle-lighting was for a prayerful intercession for Bea, or a thank-you to God Almighty for her not being in his life any longer.

20
CHAPTER

Vietnam was a bivouac inside Jimi Hendrix's orgiastic guitar-screaming feedback, discord and static. And once smashed and burned, it was loud. Even the quiet was loud. Loud enough to sustain a C-sharp in one's ears during anesthetized sleep, if one can call that sleep "sleep" and not that palatable exhaustion that hangs on you like tattered clothes on a forgotten clothesline.

If one saw it as a movie, it was Oz jujitsued, the wizard and the Emerald City smoky visions culled from the Montagnards' legendary grass, and the "We're off to see" skip, a constant call to the nowhere that didn't want you, the nowhere that shooed you away with hordes of poisonous insects whose names were calibers and stingers lethal.

It was a violent cartoon; an indoor/outdoor musical, sloshed in harsh Van Gogh colors, conducted by a spastic corpse. And if you were a salaried extra playing soldier, you moved at the puppeteer's whim with everything depending on the tautness of the strings provided the strings had not been worn off by exposure. But, either way, you were basically on your own. Your training, your guns, and your rabbit's foot showed you, most times, to follow what you thought was the yellow brick road.

Vietnam produced two things amid the blur and nightmare: the one and only letter Dee ever received from Pete McKelvey and a four-part blues Dee wrote as a memory lament for Bea.

The letter, handwritten on Barlow Brothers stationary, informed Dee that Stanley Conn had dropped dead at his desk of a stroke. "Stan went in midsentence," Pete wrote. "I don't think he knew what hit him. He was dead before his head hit the desk. He was asking about you—hoped you was okay. I'm going to miss that bastard. It'd be just like him to pull a stunt like that on me. Best treasury interest clerk on the Street. Sorry to be the town crier on this with you. But you had to know, and it was my place to do it. Keep your head down. And make sure you come back with both cheeks on your ass. Pete."

It saddened Dee to think of Stan gone. He complimented Pete, was a tad softer, and liked him very much. He had taken his advice regarding the .45. He packed two of them, one issued and the other pinched from ordnance, when he went out on patrol. And now with Stan dead, the second .45 became Dee's mojo, a gat loaded with Stan's spirit, chambered with silver bullets.

The blues he wrote in snippets on a little memo pad he kept in his helmet. He did it between patrols and the sleep that never seemed to come.

It was forged by an adrenaline that never cooked on simmer. It was angry and bold, a string quartet with lightning cadenzas sometimes perching on sustained blues notes that ended in scratches that only string players could make pressing a bit harder on the bow.

It captured canary trills for the caged bird he thought he was and donkey brays on the jackass he knew he was. He was the blues, its harmonies countering between dissonance and plushness. He was the blues in the jungle, stalking on leopard's feet, as out of control as control can be, agitated in a twilight sleep, yet primed to kill as the Cong, and land the fire on the downbeat. It told his story as no one would be able to read. It told his story as no one would be able to hear. If he ever became musically famous, maybe the music critics might piece together the story, but it probably would be wrong and wind up a myth. He wanted it to be self-contained. He wanted it to be his. And if he burned it in his helmet with his lighter, it would always be fresh for a ready performance in his head. That would be his settlement and final statement.

And he did, upon completion, burn each manuscript page nightly in a ritualistic catharsis, the notes on the paper melting into the browning of the paper with the flicker of the flame. Dee manipulated the paper so that it would burn evenly, measure by measure, until the paper carbonized into the black, curling feather ashes that blew into the blackness of the night, his painstaking effort of composition, as it were, cauterized as a medic would do on an open wound into a mock healing; the notes, the lines, the harmonies burning outright, but still smoldering in his brain.

He would never again see the youthful jottings of the music from the eyes of an old man, but he would always remember the piece, the sound, in what pass or paddy a certain phrase came to him, in what village or what ravine or gnarled valley a certain riff entered his ears. And he knew he could produce the piece in its entirety from memory, but now he was returning it to the wind and the spooky mists that fumed up from the valley swallowing the light to the place he didn't belong.

He burned it every night until it was complete, and when it ended, he cried bitterly at his loss and his hope for the end of loss, but he knew within his sinew that it would always be there until he died, and then…who knew? Even though he had a funny feeling he did.

They started the patrol during the violet hour.

Night patrols gave Dee the willies. He had been on many patrols and had been in a few firefights as a support effort for another patrol under ambush, but night patrols brought fear to a higher level.

Spaced apart they moved cautiously with the speed of a caterpillar. They ambled through the virulent jungle. Save for their steps and breathing, the sounds of the jungle augmented as they delved deeper. Droplets hit broad-leafed plants sounding like the reports from a pistol with a silencer, and wayward crickets chirped as loud as police whistles, oblivious to the land's terror, shooting flashes of anxiety into the loins and the jaws of the men.

Only the moon was neutral. It gave spotty illumination through the dense foliage.

Suddenly, as happens every so often, as if some prehistoric wand was waved over the area, all the sounds of the jungle ceased. It reminded Dee of the movie *The Naked Jungle* where army ants suddenly go on an eating rampage in some South American country through the undergrowth and all living things hightail it. The acid reflux in his throat was as hot as napalm, his fear beyond itself.

With the triggered booby trap, the explosion ripped up and the enemy popped out of the ground like the gopher game in an arcade. The soldier ahead of Dee caught the bulk of the shrapnel and banged into him knocking him down. Bowled over, Dee felt the M-16 ripped out of his hands. He heard the clang on his helmet and then a searing pain on the left side of his brow.

He grabbed the .45 from his shoulder holster as a moving body with the rank of fish straddled him. He thrashed at it with the gun hitting straw, flesh, and bone until his muzzle flash exposed a bobble head face exploding. He then, rolling up to a kneeling position, fired succinctly at the flash reports from the jungle. He pulled out his other .45 and shot at the flashes, lining them up as targets, guns in both hands.

A brief lull allowed Dee to pull the man hit by the booby trap back with one arm, shooting with the other and briefly pausing to reload. He dragged several other wounded to safety while executing accurate and devastating fire. Retrieving his M-16 and suddenly being overcome with an eerie sense of calm, everything lumbering in slow motion, he radioed in support at his first lieutenant's call, using the radioman's dead body as a shield while firing his M-16 in short discriminatory bursts. He couldn't see out of his left eye but paid it no mind since his aiming eye, his right eye, was perfectly on the mark.

Both he and the first lieutenant worked in concert fending off the ambush, corralling the men, and setting up a defense position for the medevac.

When the helicopter arrived, Dee engaged the enemy with suppressive fire, allowing the wounded to be extracted, and routed the enemy out of firing range.

Running back to the helicopter, he jumped up as the copter was lifting into a bunch of friendly arms who hurled him in. He turned and looked out the open bay of the copter as it pulled up and moved out. It was then that he felt a tremendous pain in his head. He vomited as someone took the gun from his hand. He sat rigid as steel in cement. He took one deep breath and fell face forward, breaking his nose, on the steel deck of the aircraft, unconscious.

"Felico. Felico."

He heard his name and he opened his eyes. His hearing was muffled as if his ears were plugged. His vision was slightly out of focus, but he saw his lieutenant. "Hey," he whispered, wincing a smile.

"How you feel?"

"Like someone's working a jackhammer in my head. And my left eye's out of whack."

"Lucky you still had your helmet on. You took a bad bash on the head. That gook's bayonet point put a pleat in your skull. Your left eye will be okay. It just filled up with blood and caked from your head wound."

Dee was in pain but asked, "The guys? Who..."

"Henshaw and Pasterino," the lieutenant said just shaking his head. "Parker, Jack, and Hughie will be on a plane with you going home. The rest? Okay." He sat on the bed near Dee's legs. "Who's Stan?"

Dee didn't understand his question. "Wha...?"

"Who's Stan? You kept thanking him in the copter."

"Guy I worked with. He died. I don't remember talking about him."

"Must have been a hell of a guy."

"One of the best. I guess he's my guardian angel."

"Dee. You did some real good shit out there."

Dee said, "You weren't too shabby yourself."

"Say. I always knew you were a crack shot with a pistol. Where'd you learn that shooting?"

"Coney Island."

The lieutenant reared back. "Get the fuck out of here."

"No shit. My old boss and an FBI pal of his took me many times to a shooting range there. They loved playing around with .45s."

"Well," the lieutenant said, "I just wanted to come by and see you, and tell you that I put you in for the Bronze Star with V devise. The Purple Heart comes with the wound."

"C'mon. I don't deserve that."

"Yes, you do. And in spades." He sighed. "You see, they put me in for the Silver Star." He let that sink in. "Can't take all the credit." He smiled.

Dee laughed in pain. "And I'm one rung lower to balance out the field report and add credence to the action." Dee dwelled on it a second. "I love it. In keeping with Army tradition, right?"

The lieutenant patted Dee's knee. "That's how you play ball." He leaned forward. "Thanks. Be well, buddy. And wherever you're reassigned, please don't shoot up the place. You're a dangerous fuck. Good luck."

"Say," Dee said, reaching out for the lieutenant's arm. "Who busted my nose?"

"The floor of the copter. You wanted to kiss it, but your schnoz got in the way." He got up and said, "See ya before you ship out," as he left.

When he was released from the hospital and sent home, Dee Felico was reclassified and reassigned for the duration of his service to a finance battalion where he utilized his numbers skills to help tighten internal and policy controls.

It was lackluster work, but it allowed him slowly to get back into a climate of some normalcy. The work was predicated on typical Army structure. It was mundane and predictable but a haven to an old combat vet who didn't have to duck every time he heard a loud noise.

*****

"It's the Greeks," Dee said softly, shaking his head. "Such backward thinking." He looked straight at Pete. "And from people who basically created thinking, no less."

"It's not the Greeks. It's just old-fashioned thinking. Scared thinking."

"I mean, how could she think that by keeping it quiet and forgetting about it, it would go away?" He was all cried out. He had cried a barrel of tears. Tears wouldn't even come now if he stabbed himself. "And telling me that it was her allergies acting up. 'Don't let anyone tell you different. It's allergies,' she'd say. Even now, I can't get over it. And from such a smart lady too."

"It was," Pete said, "her way of protecting you. Taking the weight off your shoulders. My mother always said everything was just fine." He snickered. "Everything was in shambles." Pete reached out and patted Dee's hand; it was the best he could do at comforting him.

Dee was in a Job moment. One of many. It would make a second combat tour in Vietnam look like skipping down the street.

"Why didn't you call me?" Pete asked. "I could have helped."

"I don't know. Pete, it had nothing to do with you. I guess I considered it my detail. Didn't want to put anybody out. When I came home, she looked like a waif—death lukewarm. I couldn't swallow. The bout with pneumonia was one thing—that took a toll. But when I took her to the hospital for the X-ray—doctor's orders—I thought I had a war in Southeast Asia. She was like fighting a Giap battalion. Christ! Where she got that energy from with all her yelling, I'll never know. And then the diagnosis: inoperable lung cancer. On the outside they gave her six months. She didn't even make half that. She was already eaten up inside before they had a chance to do anything." He just sat then quietly, looking down.

Pete said nothing. He gave Dee pause. When Dee looked up, exhaustion in his eyes, he said, "And what happened to you? Retired? Didn't think that word was in your vocabulary."

Pete had a sheepish look on his face. "Call it a plea bargain. I was up in the trading room. Needed to ask Brian Devlin something, and this new kid, some shit that came along with the merger, calls me 'Squeeze Balls.' He says, 'Hey, Squeeze Balls, go get me a light coffee.' And I don't know he's talking to me, and he then comes to me and says, 'You hear me, Squeeze Balls?' So I says, 'What's Squeeze Balls?' And get this, he says, 'Squeeze Balls is what I call old fags like you.' He then struts back to his desk and wise-asses with the other guys. So's... I picked up a chair and slammed it on his head. Busted his clavicle and gave him a fuckin' concussion." Pete chuckled a little. "Vance suggested retirement to avoid a lawsuit, and since Stan died, things...you know the things we did, how we got along...well, things just weren't the same. So there you are. Vance has me trying to reconcile the 'Unclaimed Dividend and Interest Account' before we have to cough the funds up to the state. I'm at the Brooklyn Warehouse two, three days a week. He pays me off the cuff. Otherwise, I putter around."

Dee blew on the coffee before sipping it. "What else is going on?"

"Deegan cashed in his chips. Didn't want any part of the merger. Said a lot of the incoming parties were empty suits."

"Well," Dee said, "I'm sure he not only has his first dollar but a lot of the ones in between."

Pete laughed. "What he has stashed would make King Solomon's mines look like a gold crown on a back molar."

Dee smiled at the line. "Who took Deegan's slot?"

"A first class piece of shit by the name of Chuck Mercer. Ex-Green Bay Packer. Linebacker. Looks like a refrigerator with a crew cut. If you kiss his feet, he'll show you his Super Bowl rings. Everyone hates his guts. He pits people against each other. Has sales barking at the trading desks. We never had that before. Also berates managers in front of their staffs. Likes to see people squirm. Brian Devlin calls him the Antichrist. He creates dissension. No give-and-take. No teamwork. He has no business in that role. What a fuckin' kettle of fish."

"Wow," Dee said. "That's saying a lot."

"And that Violet broad...boy. She's still with us. That show finally closed. Rumor has it—now you know I don't sniff out gossip—that Zollie was popping the shit out of her and one of the cleaning ladies caught them."

"But I thought Zollie has the trophy chick. The young wife."

"You gotta understand, Dee, Zollie is hornier than a two-peckered billy goat. Can't help himself. It's in his blood. Like the Kennedys."

"Why's she still there?"

Pete said, "Don't know. Zollie promoted her to be his executive secretary. And get this: Violet and Zollie's wife are chum-chum together. They go to lunch. Like sisters. Very peculiar." Pete momentarily paused in thought, "You think it might be one of them triangulated things...you know?"

"A ménage-a-trois?"

"Yeah. Something on that order."

Dee laughed. "That's one way to keep Zollie on a short leash."

"All and all, firm ain't what it used to be. I miss the old days, and especially the action. Don't miss the bullshit."

Dee paid for the coffee, and they both got up and walked outside. "And thanks, Pete. It didn't go unnoticed."

"What?"

"You didn't light up."

"Oh," Pete said. "I was trying to pay some respect."

"Go ahead. Have a smoke. Clean air will kill a guy like you."

"Not New York air. Breathing that," he said, snorting in a lung full, "is like smoking two packs of filtered cigarettes." Pete lit up a Chesterfield and sucked the smoke deep. "These," Pete said, showing Dee the unfiltered cigarette, "make me think better."

As they walked, Pete queried, "Any word from the girl?"

"No."

Pete shook his head. "Now that's a real kettle of fish." He blew out some smoke. "Out of sight, out of mind."

"Just out of sight, Pete. Just out of sight."

"I hear you. And I feel for you, son. I feel for you."

They walked several blocks not saying a word. Dee felt very comfortable being with Pete.

"Maybe I'll stop over, Pete, and we'll watch a Knicks game together."

Pete almost became joyous. "Any time, Dee. Any time. I'll supply the hooch and the eats. And if it runs too late, you can sack out on the couch. No worries. Any time."

"I'll let you know."

"By the way. What you gonna do with the house?"

"I spoke to Mike at 40 Wall, the old custodian. His brother escaped with the wife from Poland and has been staying with him. He's a building engineer. No papers. I told Mike he can super my house. Free rent. Just mind the other apartments and tend to the

garbage and snow. And if his wife wants to do a vegetable garden...
well, I said, the backyard is hers. He jumped at it. I'll keep the house.
If the neighborhood goes down the drain, I'll sell—it's paid off free
and clear—and if the area prospers, I'll have a gold mine as a nest
egg. Meanwhile, I got me a two-bedroom duplex on Bank Street, just
far enough from the office to take a breath and close enough to hike
to work."

"The Astoria house will be your diamond—twenty minutes
from Bloomingdales. Nice sales pitch when you're trying to rent an
apartment," Pete said.

*****

When Dee returned to work at Barlow Brothers, he was given
a very gracious welcome. He reinstated himself back on the Ginnie
Mae desk and quietly got back into the trading game. His introduc-
tion to Chuck Mercer was not exactly a sterling event. Mercer shook
Dee's hand with an extra tight grip and said, "I heard a lot about you.
I'll give you a little time to get back to speed. But not that much time.
This is not the home of the wayward boys, I want you to know."

"You won't be sorry," Dee said calmly.

"I don't wait for sorrow to hit. I blow it out when I sense it
coming."

"Well, I guess that's the way football players think," Dee said.

The comment did not sit well with Mercer. His mouth turned
down as if he sniffed a bad odor and walked away.

Mercer's handling of the desks was an exercise in pandemonium. He created discord and animosity between all parties leaving
the trading area a generalized free-for-all. Even Zollie Kiss had problems with him. And Zollie Kiss could negotiate a deal with the devil
and not get his fingertips burnt.

"I don't understand him, Dee," Brian Devlin said to Dee.

"Maybe there's nothing to understand. Ultimately, does he
really know what he's doing? When he ran trading at the other firm,
did he really have a claim to fame other than the NFL accounts he
brought over? And as a football player, I find his approach insane,"

Dee said. "If he wants everyone to free-think, think out of the box and not go by a corporate or desk mindset; he should say it straight out and not trip booby traps in the hopes that we get his drift. This may be brilliant to his lackeys, but it's dangerous to me. We had an officer in 'Nam who did things somewhat similar to Mercer."

Brian said, "In war? Really? How'd he fare?"

"He was killed." Dee looked directly at Brian. "Shot in the back five times, I was told, by accident. Friendly fire." Dee took a sip of water. "And Brian, one more thing. I really wish you'd tell him what you think. You're a smart guy. He rides you like a jackass, drags you over the coals, and you don't even own an asbestos suit, and then you come back here with your tail between your legs like a pooch. Shouldn't let him treat you like that."

"Because I got a wife and three kids and a mortgage, and frankly, I'll tell you—he scares me. I don't want to lose my job. He really scares the shit out of me. He's intrinsically evil."

Dee was a bit disheartened by Brian's comment. "I'm in a different category. I may go down and talk to Vance about him."

"Vance hired him, Dee. I wouldn't do that if I were you. It's all about the NFL accounts." Out of the corner of his eye, Brian saw Mercer coming their way. "On the horn, Dee. The fuck's barreling this way."

Dee picked up the phone as he was told and merely dialed the weather bureau.

Dee's reentry back into the trading arena went rather well. He came in early, one of the first in, and went home long after the other traders left. He liked to touch base with the investment bankers and the research guys to glean any new tidbits that might make a trade or a position profitable or just hang around for the company and shoot the shit. He had no commute to speak of, and his personal life was solitary, and he preferred it that way at this point in time.

One early morning Chuck Mercer came by his desk. "Felico."

Dee looked up; Mercer's disposition was like that of a loose bowel movement. "Yes?"

"In my office. Now! Pronto!"

Dee got up and walked into Chuck Mercer's office seeing no apparent reason for the hostility in Mercer's voice.

"You take notes during morning meetings?" Mercer asked.

"If I have to," Dee responded.

"From now on, do it!" Mercer picked up a position report and handed it to Dee. "This yours?"

"Yes, but—"

"No buts! We have hedge accounts for treasury trades."

"I know."

Mercer grabbed the position sheet from Dee's hand and pointed to the treasury position in question tapping the computer paper so hard he almost put his finger through it. "And what the hell is this! A treasury position comingled with your Ginnie Maes!"

"It's not my position. That treasury position is not my trade."

Mercer frowned at him, masking his confusion. "Then what the hell is it doing in your position?" His eyes were fired up.

"Firstly," Dee said in a lecturing tune, "you're looking at last night's position. This morning's doesn't have it in my account. I transferred it out. It's your pal Josh Gray's trade. He put it in my position by mistake. And this was no key punch error. I'll show you his ticket. He just wrote the wrong account number on it. Had he checked his day's work at end of day he would have found it. Obviously he was in too much of a hurry to meet you at Harry's."

"Just watch your mouth, Felico," Mercer snapped.

They looked fixedly at each other for a minute saying nothing.

"Okay?" Dee said as an exit line. "This meeting over or what? I've got stuff to do."

"No. It's not okay. And it's not over till I say so! Now, you listen to me, Felico. I just want you to know that the only reason you're back here, and Barlow gave me full discretion on this, is because you're a crippled vet and Barlow has a warm spot in his heart for guys like you." Mercer then crumbled up the computer run and threw it in the garbage." Now, get back to your desk. You're off the hook."

Dee stood up, looked at him with almost no expression just long enough to tease Mercer to make a comment, but before he did so, he very calmly said, "You'd better have a little sit-down with your buddy boy Gray. I'm paid to make money for this firm, not clean up his shit. And just for the record, I was never on the fucking hook." Dee then turned and strolled out of the office before Mercer had a chance to respond.

*****

No matter if the market zoomed or spiraled down, fun was to be had in every Wall Street trading room. There was always a ripple of laughter which spotted the area. It could be gallows humor as when a preferred stock trader took a position that lost the firm three million dollars in a day and then had delivered to him a Kentucky Derby-size horseshoe wreath full of dead roses by the firm that sold him the stock as confirmation of the trade or a salesman crossing a trade with two phones propped against his ears by his arms as he tried to squirt some mustard on his hot dog and winding up getting a yellow glob on his Sulka tie as well as his eyeglasses. But regardless what was going on the floor, one of the great moments of the day, every day, at Barlow Brothers, was the arrival of Tyrrell Balthesar Johnson, affectionately called T-Bone.

He was a retired postal worker who graced the floor each day hand-delivering the mail singing as his mood struck him everything from *Rock of Ages* with a basso-profundo timbre to the "Crab Man" Street call from *Porgy and Bess*, executing the three-octave yodeling glissando with complete perfection.

He ran the mail room with the firmness and efficiency of a buck sergeant. He was also a preacher man, a self-proclaimed pastor and spiritual advisor to lost ladies, with a little storefront church near the projects in the Crown Heights section of Brooklyn.

He found Jesus at the Apollo Theater after a Lady Day concert when he viewed a film clip of Billie Holiday wailing "God Bless the Child." The song and Billie's sultry voice changed his life. Most of his flock resided in the large project where he had a one-bedroom apartment. He had six children with four different women ranging in ages from six months to thirty years. His primary wife, Earth Mama, he called her, was barren, so he convinced her that since Old

Testament Sarah gave Abraham the blessing "to wife" her handmaid Hagar to bear him a child, that he be giving the same opportunity to be fruitful and multiply with those misdirected sisters of love in his apartment complex who needed his spiritual guidance and willingly assisted him, in his words "of proliferating my progeny."

At 11:00 a.m. sharp, T-Bone would arrive on the floor, usually garbed in a candy-apple red velour suit with white spats, proclaiming, "Neither snow nor rain nor heat nor gloom of night stays this courier from the swift completion of his appointed rounds!" And a moment later greeted the throng, "Bless you, my children, my brothers and sisters." And with a powerful voice would announce, "Mail call…in the house!"

Once the entire floor responded with a resounding "Amen!" he proceeded to hand out the mail.

His smile lit up the entire trading area. He sported two gold-capped front teeth which he kept as a reminder of his past life of iniquity before Jesus freed him from the bonds of debauchery and degradation. He often mentioned that he had had a dream that the gold in his teeth had actually been forged from the very golden calf Moses destroyed as a heathen god upon his return from his encounter with Yahweh on the mount.

Much of the banter with T-Bone by the traders concerned his potential parishioners because traders, by nature, were gossip-mongers. The juicier the dirt, the better to pass on during a trade negotiation.

"So, Bone," one trader asked, "any new acolytes in the wings?"

And when T-Bone spoke, all heard whether they wanted to or not since his voice boomed like a PA system. "Indeed, Brother William," he said to the trader. "Bless that child. Wykeeta, a Nubian, blue-black of skin tone, distinctly of African origin, pure as the untamed nature she sprang from. Epic in proportion, I may add." He closed his eyes and hummed, "Mmmm. Mmmm. Mmmm, mmmm, mmm!" like he was tasting a sweet peach. "Her skin, polished mahogany. I can see her in my mind." He paused, smiled, and said, "She is attending my religious instruction. We are getting to know each other…in the biblical sense." He winked to the trader. "I must confess, she is a bit of an eager beaver. But these things can't be done quickly. These things take time…and practice." He then laughed. "But, mind you, Brother William, a veritable banquet of 'in-no-sance,'" his pronunciation of innocence being his own, "and enthusiasm."

"But, T," another trader chimed in, "When does the course work begin? You're in early and do the late-night drop at the post office."

"Brother Sal. I am a nocturnal guide. God's work must be done delicately in the quiet hours when the moon is bright and the stars twinkle. Praise God! And now, allow me to continue my postal mission, God love you all."

T-Bone moved past Brian dropping his mail in front of him. Brian was on the phone and gave T-Bone the high sign as a thank-you.

Next he stopped by Dee. "Brother Dee. Ask."

Dee followed the litany: "And it shall be given unto you."

"Seek."

"And ye shall find."

"Knock."

"And it shall be opened unto you."

T-Bone smiled, shaking his head with glee. "Truly a learned soul."

"And now for you, Reverend. If sinner's entice thee?" Dee asked.

"Consent," T-Bone bellowed, pausing just long enough for an eyebrow to be raised. "Thou not!"

Both laughed for different reasons.

"Brother Dee. The usual mail, however, you have a post card here. Seems foreign considering the stamp." He handed Dee a post card. It was a twilight picture of the white limestone Bridge of Sighs in Venice, and beneath it was a gondola with a man and woman embracing.

When Dee turned the card over, he gasped as if hit with an electric shock. It was Bea's handwriting. It read: "Hiya, Baby: Found streets filled with water. Please advise. I didn't forget this time. Love, until you hear different. Bea." He was totally frozen. He heard nothing. He saw nothing. He was stunned. He never heard Mercer bark, "Get on the phone, Felico!"

Dee was totally in a state of numbness until the card was snatched from his hand by Mercer. "Get on the fuckin' phone!"

Dee turned around and said, "Give me back my card."

"On the phone!" Mercer yelled, walking away with the card.

"Give me back my card." Dee was returning to reality.

"Later!" Mercer said, continuing to walk away.

Dee stood up. "Give me back my card, you lousy son of a bitch!" Everyone on the desk became silent.

Mercer turned, shocked, and said, "What did you say?"

"I know one thing. You're not deaf. Now give me back my card!"

T-Bone jumped it. "Give him back the card, Brother Chuck. Confiscation of another's mail is a federal offense. Give Brother Dee back his card."

Mercer leered at T-Bone. "Shut up!"

"Jesus loves you, Brother Chuck. Jesus loves you."

"If you don't shut the fuck up, you're gonna see Jesus!"

Several traders joined in by saying, "Give him back his card."

Mercer ignored them. "Felico! In my office now! I gotta take a piss! And then I'll deal with you!"

Dee turned and walked toward Mercer's office. Some traders went to Dee, but he brushed them off. He went into Mercer's office awaiting him.

Mercer stormed into his office after his visit to the men's room. Before Mercer could say anything, Dee said, "Give me back my card!"

Mercer said with a smug expression, "You want it? Come get it. But be advised. I used to make my living knocking people down. I got two Super Bowl rings to prove it." He was posturing at his best to intimidate Dee.

Dee suddenly relaxed. The same feeling hit his system in war. He fell into a calmness of mind and body. He said very slowly and tersely, "I was awarded a Combat Infantryman's Badge and a Bronze Star with a V-devise, which is for valor, just in case you're unaware of military decorations. I got paid to kill the enemy." He looked squarely at Mercer. "And I got pretty good at it." He stepped closer to Mercer and stood his ground, his hand held out awaiting the card. "Give me the card."

Mercer, to rattle Dee, picked up a square glass ashtray and held it at Dee's face to scare him. "You want to see what I could do to you?" Dee did not flinch and looked at Mercer with an almost invitational gaze, a slight smile on his face as if welcoming him into a safe harbor. Mercer swung with all his might, the ashtray in his hand, and aimed to stop short of hitting Dee with it to see him duck or cower. Dee did not move. Mercer miscalculated his thrust and stopping power. The pointed edge hit Dee slightly above the cheekbone as five traders rushed into the office and took the ashtray away from Mercer screaming at him. It didn't do much physical damage and barely jolted Dee, but it did create a gash.

The cut on Dee's face dribbled blood down his cheek onto his shirt collar.

"When you go home and say your prayers tonight, I want you to thank God that you didn't hit me with full force. Today you are a very lucky man." Dee stuck out his hand again. "Now, give me back my card. I am going home."

Mercer gave the card back to Dee. There was a slight tremor in his hand, and his wide-open eyes had a flintiness of apprehension in them.

Dee walked out as Vance Barlow, Zollie Kiss, and Violet Wagner rushed in. "Violet. Take him to Beekman Hospital. He needs a stitch," Zollie ordered.

"Zollie. I'm okay. I want to go myself. No damage to speak of. Just a little cut." Violet ran to get a small first aid kit.

T-Bone interjected, "I'll take him, Brother Zollie. He will be in my care."

Both Zollie and Vance acquiesced and then scurried into Mercer's office.

Violet came back and tended to his wound, then T-Bone and Violet walked him to the hospital which was only a few blocks away. When they left, the floor was in a total uproar.

A butterfly stitch was all that was needed and an ice pack. He was going to have a shiner one way or another.

He stayed home two days and was only interrupted once by the police knocking on his door at two o'clock in the morning. He was playing the phonograph too loudly and the neighbors complained. The police did not smell any liquor or pot and saw that he was talking very lucidly. His eyes were red because he was crying. One cop did ask what the problem was, and Dee responded that he had lost someone that was very dear to him. He complied with the officer's request, apologized, and played the record at a lower volume again and again until one of the tubes burned out. It was only at that point that he finally went to sleep, the card tucked under his pillow.

When Dee Felico returned to the office, Mercer's office was occupied by Vance Barlow and Zollie Kiss. They both looked ten years younger than their years. There was enthusiasm, vigor, and vibrancy in their dispositions like a finger snapping to a real great jazz bridge.

"Dee," Brian said. "You have some shiner, that ain't no mouse, and I'd regard it as a badge of honor."

"Well," Dee said, "at least that's over with."

"You call Pete?"

"No. Why?"

"Somehow or other he got wind of the whole incident and barged into the office dressed to the nines; went into the room with Vance, Zollie, and Mercer; and backhanded Mercer right in the snoot. I think he busted it. There was a lot of blood. He kept saying, 'Don't you ever hit my boy again!' Parker and some of the other security guards took him into the mail room with T-Bone. I think they calmed him down with a couple of Scotches. Parker took him home by car service."

"No kidding." Dee shook his head. "Boy'd I cause a riff."

"It was waiting to happen. Only a question of time." Brian touched Dee's shoulder. "And, ultimately, it was for the good. But more importantly, you okay?"

"Yeah," Dee whispered. "I'm okay."

*****

226

What Violet Wagner couldn't do in twenty years as a Broadway gypsy, Zollie Kiss did for her in two months. He made her a headliner, top billing.

Getting rid of Mercer and some of his crew was not the problem. Maintaining the NFL accounts at Barlow Brothers was the concern. The incident was, in the conversation to the NFL accounts, spelled out accurately and, depending on the portfolio manager, was either in lurid detail or legalistically approached. The NFL parties all loved Mercer—he was one of their own—but they all did agree that he overstepped his bounds and was totally out of line and collectively, after much discussion and cocktail soirees, gave Barlow Brothers, out of courtesy, the opportunity to woo them for better trade execution, research, and intelligent ideas, since as their head portfolio manager said, "Bottom line is...bottom line, and it is absolutely contingent on what her bottom looks like. That's what really matters."

Violet Wagner's name was put up in lights. She became a part of that bottom line. Under Zollie's tutelage, she studied football stats, politics, and spoke authoritatively on black powder firearms, which had the backwoods portfolio traders drooling for a target practice session with her, any time, any place at their expense, preferably au naturel.

She was smart, sassy, as only an actress can be, and sexy without being vulgar. She lost some weight but was still "front an' center," as one manager dubbed her, and at forty-five could rightly still be considered a babe; one comely dame, piping hot.

Zollie's approach to capturing and maintaining the NFL accounts was based on a German strategy straight out of the Battle of North Atlantic in World War Two. He, along with his wife, and Violet would descend upon the conferences and seminars like a wolf pack on a convoy. They would firstly pick out the most vulnerable account and then once captured, proceed to the prime targets, the big honchos.

Violet's passionate approach, based in part on what Zollie thought was the Stanislavski method, sold them like rube's buying the Brooklyn Bridge and then shaking the hayseeds out of their hair not knowing what happened. "It," according to Zollie, "was esthetically delightful to watch and magic when they 'rendered unto Caesar' through Violet's charms, the big bucks. She deserves more Oscar's than Kate Hepburn and Bette Davis combined. I am told, in confidence, by the head portfolio manager that her very voice on the phone has him standing at attention." Zollie was proud of himself, and, of course, Violet too.

Rumors abounded about Zollie, his wife, and Violet. It was said they even went on vacation together and Violet's mother was part of the traveling package also. The rumors were just small talk that seemed to come up between cigarette light-ups. And the small talk remained just that: small talk. No pictures ever cropped up and the speculations were about as sure as a mine that produced licorice. But it did have to be noted that they were a profit desk unto themselves, and a big one to Barlow Brothers, a Nairobi Trio, dressed in monkey suits playing their jazz ensemble stuff piping the right pitch, just the right pitch, to the right ears that brought the money in barrels into the house.

Zollie's wolf pack maneuver worked. Barlow Brothers kept all the NFL accounts.

A few weeks later Zollie stopped by Dee's desk. "Here," he said. Dee looked up. "What's this?"

"Two floor tickets to the Knicks. Take Pete."

"Thanks. He'll be thrilled."

"You know, Dee. Things could not have worked out better. Just working with Vance, sitting across from each other in the office like when we started… I'm so pumped up by this." He paused. "Think I should dye my hair?"

"Get the hell out of here. Where's your integrity? You have a role here." Dee chuckled.

"I have no integrity. And the only role I have around here is hitting the cash register. I am very happy with that. Now give Pete a call and make his day. And tell him for me if he wants to sport in the geriatric Golden Gloves tournament, I'll sponsor him."

Dee laughed and got on the phone to call Pete.

"Pete. It's Dee. What are you doing tonight? Cancel your supper with Greta Garbo. We're going to the Garden to see the Knicks. I got floor tickets. We'll have a quick bite first and then see the game. Roll out the cot. I'll be staying at your place tonight. We'll hit some Scotch talking over the plays."

All Pete said was, "Thanks, see ya later. Thanks a real lot." And just the sound of his rough voice warmed him, like his mother tucking him into bed as a little boy.

"Dee?"

Dee looked up from the *Wall Street Journal* and turned toward Brian Devlin. "What's up?"

"We got a new kid coming in today. Son of a Merrill Lynch guy I know. Nice, clean-cut kid. He could help us around the desk. Here's his resume. Take him under your wing. Teach him the ropes."

Dee took the resume and scanned it.

"Bryce McKenna? Is that Harry's boy?"

"Yes."

"Brian." Brian turned to Dee and looked at him. "Shall I...?"

"Oh," Brian said, "by all means," and laughed.

When Bryce came up and was introduced to Dee, Dee shook his hand warmly. Bryce's hand was ice cold.

Dee sized him up and said, "I do like your resume," and looked at him head to toe. Dee frowned a bit when he gazed at Bryce's shoes. "You have a pair of brown shoes? Tie shoes? Wing tips?"

"Beg pardon?" Bryce said.

"Am I speaking Swahili? I thought my question was rather clear."

Confused, Bryce's eyes showed a bit of fear. "I a..."

"Well? Do you or don't you?"

Bryce began to fidget a little. "Ahhh. No."

"In that case then, we're really not getting off on the right foot."

"Mr. Felico. I don't understand."

"I'll make it simple. We have a culture and tradition here of wearing brown wing-tip tie shoes. You don't wear shoes like that, you get booted out of the firm. The only person that's exempt is T-Bone, our mailman, but he does have a pair in his locker just in case we press the issue." Dee turned back to continue to read the Journal.

"But...but Mr. Felico what should I do?"

"Buy a pair."

"I... I...," he stuttered, wrenching his wallet out of his back pocket. "I don't think I have enough cash."

"Here," Dee said, "here's a C-note. Go down to the end of Rector Street. There's a shoe store there that's been going out of business since the year of the Flood. Get a good pair that fit and are comfortable. Don't want you walking around here like you're tiptoeing on thumb tacks. Brown wing tips with laces. Savvy?"

Bryce took the hundred-dollar bill, looking at the money and then looking at Dee.

"So what the hell do you want, an engraved invitation? Beat it. And I want change."

"Yes, sir," Bryce muttered and scooted for the elevators.

"Is the bond stretcher next on the agenda?" Brian said, laughing.

"You bet."

"Felico. You are a sadistic bastard."

"I learned from the best. Everybody needs a rite of passage." He then turned and picked up the phone to make a call.

21
CHAPTER

They found Pete McKelvey by his stench.

He had died roughly three days earlier in his easy chair peacefully, a half-finished glass of Scotch on the table next to him, and the ashtray next to him stuffed with squelched butts. The television was still on when the police came in scattering the cockroaches and the mice.

Dee found out when Vance Barlow came personally to his desk.

Pete had no family or much in terms of personal possessions. His life insurance with the firm was bequeathed to his Army unit to be used at their discretion, but he had given Vance Barlow a box housed in a black satin bag to be given to Dee Felico upon his demise. It was a revolver, a single action Army Colt .45 with an ivory handle. In it was a short note. It read, "My eternal thanks for your superior marksmanship at killing those three banditos. You saved my life. The best thing that God ever created was a good soldier. And you are one." It was signed, "Lt. George S. Patton Jr., USA."

It took a little doing with Vance Barlow's political connections to ascertain Pete's military records from St. Louis archives. When all the paperwork came through and were presented to the National Cemetery at Pinelawn, Long Island, Pete got a military funeral with a nine-gun salute and a rendering of taps that would rip the heart out of the most stoic soul on Earth. The folded flag was given to Vance Barlow.

It had been a tough week for him. He went directly home after work, ate lightly, and went to bed. He slept fitfully. On Saturday, he felt he needed something to engage his mind, distract him from the black curtain that Pete's death was giving him. He needed some outlet other than work to ease his spirits. He decided to walk to the Strand Bookstore on East 12th Street near Union Square to check the shelves for a little comic relief as well as some serious study.

He wore an old pair of bell-bottom jeans, a loose-fitting cotton shirt tucked in, a little frayed at the collar, a pair of brown driving moccasins without socks, and a long necktie he used as a belt. It was somewhat motley, but it worked in that area of town, and he was very comfortable.

When he entered the bookstore, the smell gave him a cozy feeling and brought back memories of the Mendoza Bookstore on Ann Street where he used to pick up obscure tomes for Bea, but that quickly faded when he heard the piped music the manager was playing. It was a great Bach piece for solo violin called "The Chaconne," a musical prayer dedicated to Bach's recently deceased wife. It was written when he came back from a trip and shockingly found out she had been buried two weeks earlier, yet when he left for his journey, she had been in good health. It was written with an unrestrained feeling of anguish, of lost love, a trembling tenderness that mourned and whimpered in each measure. It depicted her last breath, the softness of the notes ebbing…and then rising, slowly the music taking on an overwhelming sense of hope, capturing her soul's blessed resurrection…into heaven.

He stood transfixed listening to the piece with two other men. He saw the notes dance before him and for the full thirteen to fourteen minutes allowed the music to skin dive into his very being. One's sensitivities didn't have to be acute to enable the rapture of the piece to move one to tears. It was not a sentimental swatch of romanticism. It was the essence of human feeling pushed to its brink. And with Pete recently dead, it added a new feeling of hope and resolution in Dee.

His eyes were a bit watery when the piece ended, not from the music but more so out of a funny thought that popped into his head seeing Pete entering heaven smoking a lit Chesterfield dangling from his lips, passing a large sign on St. Peter's gate spelling "Smoking Prohibited," and then flicking an ash.

After the Bach piece ended, an older gentleman who was listening to it looked at Dee, smiled close-mouthed, and just said, "Yes." It was an all-inclusive code, a connection Dee understood. He responded with a nod, his eyes closed in reverence and mutual adoration. However, next to Dee, a few feet away was an elderly man braced on his cane actually weeping silently, his belly jiggling, his strength all but gone holding back the emotion of a loud outcry.

Dee went to him. "Can I get you a chair?"

The man looked up at Dee and shook his head "No."

"I know," Dee said. "That music moves me too."

The man said, "Look!" His right hand came up. "Look!" He showed Dee a hand with fingers crooked with arthritis, the top knuckles almost at a forty-five-degree angle to the right. "You heard that violinist?"

"Yes," Dee said.

"I used to play like that. I was that good. I had the Chaconne down pat. And now," he said, switching hands on the cane, "this," he continued, showing Dee his left hand, the fingers terribly gnarled. "I can't even hold up a violin," he said in a low grating voice, and then begrudgingly snickered, "I can't even wipe my ass right."

Dee saw the pain in the old man's eyes and said, trying to console, "Few get the grace…to play God's music." Dee reached out for his hand, but the old man pulled his back. "At least you did."

"Leave me alone. What the hell do you know?" He snorted.

The old man then turned and hobbled out of the bookstore, muttering in bitterness.

Dee felt like following him to help. He felt very sorry for him but then thought against it. His meddling might do more harm than good. He stayed where he was for several minutes then walked toward the poetry section. He hankered for some light verse, something funny, even ridiculous to ease his frame of mind. He suddenly thought the poesy of Ogden Nash might fit the bill, and for some serious stuff, he contemplated picking up a book on haikus. He had a desire to put together some powerful seventeen-syllable Japanese eye-openers, something he hadn't done since college.

When he came to the poetry section, he saw a voluptuous red-head with long curly hair in a yellow dress viewing the shelves with some degree of intensity. She was tall, had no makeup on to his pedestrian eye save a daub of red lipstick, and had, what he thought, was an exquisite face. She turned, not seeing him, and he noticed the most delightful paint brush flick of muted freckles around the bridge of her straight nose.

He was quiet, and removed enough from the scene to be as unnoticed as any other browser might be, and began to pleasantly enjoy just watching her. It was a feeling that had been quite foreign to him for a long time. He felt secure in the anonymity, his remoteness very civilized.

And then it happened.

It was so unusual, so unexpected, and so rare that he couldn't believe his ears.

Somehow, somewhere, the manager of the Strand Bookstore got a hold of an old recording and began playing "If I Could Be with You One Hour Tonight." It was the exact, original rendition that Dee had played and still played interminably on his old phonograph. He shivered as though he was splashed with ice water. He saw her rhythmically sway unconsciously with the beat of the music as she perused the bookshelves.

He impulsively went to her. "Miss," he said as she looked up at him. "This is my favorite song. And you never hear it played. Ever. I was just wondering…maybe…" He looked at her directly, a wanting tenderness in his eyes. "Would you please dance with me?"

She was totally shocked at his approach and stepped back. She sized him up quickly. She didn't think he was crazy. His face seemed very pleasant. He was motley attired but not in an overdone way, and the necktie as a belt intrigued her. She knew that was a fashion set by Fred Astaire. She was attracted immediately to the olive complexion, the long sleek mustache, and the sheepish smile. There was a jagged scar on his forehead over his left eye that dipped into his eyebrow that bothered her. But it was the gentleness and kindness in his eyes that seemed to win her reservation. And then he said, like a little boy, "Please."

She acquiesced and received him in her arms. His moves were graceful and subtle, leading her with his thighs and smooth hand pressures. She was, having studied dance, quite impressed with his style. He was moving her with the music almost not as a dance but as part of the music itself. There were no toes being stepped on or awkward bumping movements she had encountered with other men. This person knew what he was doing and was doing it exceptionally well. In fact, she was actually enjoying the dance. She knew where he was going with each step except when he twirled her and did what she saw to be an unusual, eccentric tap step, and then, on beat came back to her effortlessly. She liked that touch.

She looked at him, but it seemed he didn't see her. He had a faraway look, yet his eyes moved dreamily as if reading something. She felt his right hand on the small of her back, his fingers moving very gently, on her spine, as if he was actually fingering the notes on the sax and the cornet playing the instruments. And when a note was sustained, she felt the ball of his finger wiggle, mimicking the vibrato.

She was thoroughly enjoying the dance, their movements fluidly graceful, elegant, as if they had practiced together. She had never heard the song before, and there was something about its relaxed delivery she was taken by. It was, she thought, like good friends playing cards more engrossed in the conversation than the game at hand. A Disney thought of *Lady and the Tramp* in Tony's Italian restaurant sucking on the same strand of spaghetti until they finally kissed came to her mind. She hadn't thought of that romantic cartoon since she was a kid.

The dance was sensual as the jazz lines were smooth like a caressing hand on the back of the neck and lips sliding across a cheek searching for the mouth. And then, he dropped his left arm and let it dangle on the side. She followed his move. It gave her goose bumps. It was a Fred Astaire move. No one, not even her dance instructors, ever did that. And she had studied ballroom dance. She was so engaged in the dance that she felt like Ginger Rogers and when he twirled her to its subdued finale, executing a mild dip, she actually curtsied to him when she righted herself.

They looked at each other; she smiling widely, he with a closed-mouth grin, his eyes alert, no longer far away. He noticed that she didn't have a dimple. And a moment or two later, they heard some applause from several bookstore patrons who had witnessed their dancing display.

They both laughed a little embarrassed.

"Thank you," he said. "I never did that before. You see—"

She cut in, 'That was wonderful. What a treat." Her voice was husky and lower pitched than he thought it would be. He thought it fit well with her. "Wait'll I tell my friends. No one will understand. I certainly don't."

"It's that music."

"No. It's not just that music—it's you. Especially you." She stood for some time looking at him, and for a reason she had no idea why, she said, "My name is Carlotta McGovern."

"Carlotta. Carlotta," he said slowly, formulating each syllable with his tongue as if taste testing something for the first time. "What a beautiful name." He dwelled on it. "Unique. Exotic." He concluded with, "That's a name you don't hear often in this day and age."

"Actually," she was compelled to say, "I am named after my grandmother. Carlotta is my middle name. My real first name is Shelia."

"Shelia. That's a pretty name." He smiled and said, "Anybody ever call you Sheesh?"

She took a step back. "Why, no. No one."

"Like it? Sort of as a nickname?"

"Yeah," she said, almost not to him but to herself. "It has a bit of character."

"My name is…prepare yourself…," he said, her eyebrow going up in anticipation, "is Democedes Felico. They call me Dee."

"Wow. That's a lot of name. But it does have music to it." She laughed nervously. "Greek?"

"A portion, amongst other things."

"You dance," she said, taking a deep breath, "magnificently. Where'd you get that skill?"

"I had an excellent dance instructor." He changed the subject. "What are you looking for?"

"Something light. Funny. Refreshing."

He spotted an Ogden Nash tome and pulled it out of the shelf. "I was looking for this." Then he said to her, "Ever read Robert Service?" He looked for it, awaiting her answer.

"No. Never heard of him."

He found what he was looking for and handed her *The Spell of the Yukon and Other Verses*. He said, "Just read 'The Cremation of Sam McGee.' See how you like it. It's a ballad."

"Okay," she said.

She checked the table of contents, paged to it, and took several minutes to read it, and as she did, he watched the corners of her mouth turn up at times and once in a while chuckle at a witty turn of phrase. She belly-laughed when she finished it. He adored the sound of her laugh. "This really is good," she said. "I really like it."

"May I buy it for you…as a thank-you for the dance?"

She peered at him and then checked the penciled price on the inside cover. "That's okay. I think I can spring for four dollars without having to eat dog food till next payday." Then she asked, "By the way, what was the name of that song we danced to? I liked that sound."

He gazed at her chestnut eyes, pausing as if in thought but more in admiration of her facial features, and slowly said, almost as an afterthought, "'If I Could Be with You One Hour Tonight.'"

A chill came over her face, her lips pressing into a stiletto slash. She squinted. "You know," she said, "you play a pretty smooth game, Mr. Dee Felico. That line might work on…an idiot! Do I look like some kind of bimbo to you? Is that your way of planting a seed?"

"But, Sheesh—"

She spoke over him. "Don't Sheesh me! Don't you dare call me Sheesh!"

"But that's the name of the song," he stated.

"Bullshit!" she lashed out.

"You think I'm kidding? Do I look like the kind of guy who'd pull an asshole stunt like that? If you don't believe me, come with me to the manager and ask him. Ask to see the record!"

She was silent, frowning, and confused. Her uncertainty troubled her.

"'If I Could Be with You One Hour Tonight' is the name of the song," he said.

She searched his face. Her cheeks were hot. She just glared at him unable to say anything for that moment. "I just thought…"

"I meant no disrespect. I'm not that type of person. You simply misunderstood. Nothing more, nothing less."

"So," she said, fingering the book she had in her hand, "that really is the name of the song?"

His smile was genuine, sincere. "Yes."

Her eyes were downcast in disbelief, but then coyly, she gazed up at him. She changed the subject, trying not to show that she was in salvage mode. "Have you found what you are looking for?"

He quickly scanned the shelves and picked out a book of haikus. "Yes. I have my lot now."

They went to the cashier and she paid for her book but asked, "There was a song you played a little while ago, a jazzy piece, I think with a saxophone and trumpet." she looked at him for approval of the instruments mentioned.

"Cornet," he corrected.

"Cornet," she said.

"Yes. A real sweet one, wasn't it?" the cashier said.

"What was the name of that song?" she asked.

"I'll show you." He then picked up an old 78 rpm record that was lying next to the record player. "Here. 'If I Could Be with You One Hour Tonight.' See?" He showed her the record.

"How ironic," she whispered just loud enough for Dee to hear. She turned to him. "I am sorry."

He said, "That's okay," as he paid for his books.

Approaching the door of the store as they were heading out, he said, "I was wondering…"

She looked at him and said, "Yes." It wasn't a question. "You can be with me an hour tonight." A devilish smile crossed her face.

Caught off guard, he stood speechless.

"Was that what you were wondering?"

He smiled. "You read palms too?"

"We'll see. I live on West 22nd Street. There is a little bistro two doors down from the corner on the west side of the street on Eighth Avenue. Is seven okay?"

"I'll be there," he said. And as she smiled and turned to walk away, he said, "You're wearing a fragrance. What is it?"

"Andiamo. Borghese. Like it?"

"I do."

She then turned and said, "See ya tonight," walking away.

He didn't move until she was out of his sight. He enjoyed watching her.

He arrived early at the bistro and decided since it was such a lovely evening to sit at an outside table.

Exactly at seven, she rounded the corner strolling in a casual black-and-white dress that complimented her figure. He particularly liked the shoulder straps that seemed to be made to drape off the shoulder. It gave an alluring look. She smiled when she saw him.

He stood up and shook her hand and waited for her to sit down before he took his seat.

"Seven," she said, "on the dot. Greenwich time. You have one hour."

"Thank you. Sheesh? May I?"

She nodded. "I like the ring to that name."

"I like prompt."

The waitress came. They ordered coffee and Monte Carlo sandwiches which she said was a bistro specialty.

"So. What do you do, Dee Felico?"

He put his tongue in his cheek and said with amusement, "Well. Since you read my mind this morning, you tell me. That is," he qualified, "if your powers don't wane in the evening."

She sucked in her bottom lip peering at him, and the sweet sound it made as she released her bottom lip gave him a quiver. He was enjoying this. "You put me on the spot. Oh, by the way, I read some more of those Service poems. I'm hooked. Really great stuff."

"Don't digress. I'm on the clock, so...let's proceed."

She laughed. "You are a funny one."

"Need a palm?"

"No," she said. "We are going to place our left hands as close together without touching. If they touch we break the spell."

He did what she said as she reviewed his face with the utmost of intensity. After a moment, she, with her right hand, very gently ran her fingers over the scar on his brow down to his eyebrow. He saw concern registering in her chestnut eyes.

She wore the same fragrance she did in the morning and Bernadette Paulson popped into his mind. He scanned her face. He was captivated. She was enticing, delicious, as fresh as reading a new musical score. Her face suddenly sang out to him an old beautiful standard, "It Had to Be You." He heard it as he gazed at her.

The sandwiches and coffee came and she pulled back her hands.

He took a swig of the coffee. "Do we have any results in?"

"Yes. I will tell you what I feel. Just promise me you won't laugh."

He took a bite of the sandwich and, chewing, said, "I promise. Shoot."

She took a deep breath. "Once," she said, "you were a soldier. And you now work on Wall Street." She looked at him, a little trepidation in her eyes.

Blinking his eyes as quickly as a hummingbird's wings, he swallowed quickly the piece he was chewing and put his hand to his mouth. A strange look came over his face, and he quietly said, "Guilty...on both counts."

"You're kidding." She was astonished.

"No. You bull's-eyed them both. How the hell—"

"Dee. I swear. I was kidding. I guessed."

"Well," he said in earnest, "if you can guess like that, whatever you do, I'll double your salary and you can work for me. Just let me know what the Federal Reserve is going to do before they do it and we'll be billionaires in less than six months."

They both laughed heartily and then dug in to their food and engaged in exploratory talk that led to a long crackling dialogue. It was for the both of them like eating ice cream and never getting full. When they were politely asked to leave, since the bistro was closing up for the night, Dee said, "Is there any time left to my hour?"

"You are a funny one. As a matter of fact, there is. Just time enough for you to walk me home. It's just a couple of blocks," she said.

They walked on West 22nd Street. He did not hold her hand nor did she lock her arm in his. "Sheesh," he said while they were walking, "what kind of time do you work with? My watch is well past what I thought my cutoff would be."

Not looking at him, she grinned, saying, "If you studied your physics, you'd know that the greater the gravity, the slower the time."

"By my guess, I'd say we were on Jupiter."

"If that satisfies your curious nature, I will not sidetrack it."

When they reached her stoop, she said, "I had a wonderful hour. Would you like to come in? I do have a roommate."

"No," he said honestly. "It's late. I have stuff to do tomorrow. And the lateness of the hour calls for me to say a good night to Carlotta. I'd love to call on you again if I may."

"I would like that very much." She opened her small purse and wrote down her home phone number on her business card. She then took the card and kissed it leaving a lipstick print. She handed it to him.

"This goes next to my heart," as he placed it in his shirt pocket, "not my wallet."

"You really are a funny one." He held her hand and made no attempt to embrace her. She waited the extra second but then stepped close to him. There was something about him that gave her a feeling of warmth that until that moment she had found in no other man. She impulsively kissed him on the mouth. "Thank you," she whispered.

"Sleep well." He touched her cheek tenderly, caressing it as if looking for something. She then pulled away and ran up the stairs as he watched her safely get into the house. She waved to him before she closed the door behind her.

He walked all the way home to Bank Street, "It Had to Be You" playing in his head, her visage before him in his mind's eye. If it wasn't for the racket of two fighting cats breaking his musings on her, he would have never realized he passed his block.

He made a mental note to light a candle at Mass the next day for his newly found good fortune.

He married her two years later.

22
CHAPTER

The memories flashed in and out like sheet lightning. The emotional upheaval taxed his body. He hadn't felt this strange since the Vietnam days.

The conversation was delightful and robust, strictly professional. Although peppered with some wit and gentle humor, it would fall well beneath any barometric reading that might deem it flirtatious.

From the corner of his eye, Dee saw Bryce walking toward his office. "Well," he said, standing up and extending his hand, "this was certainly a pleasure."

Mary Jo got up also and shook his hand warmly, covering it with her left. "I really enjoyed this. Thank you, Mr. Felico."

"By the way, just a passing thought. What do your parents think of you seeking work on Wall Street? It's a rough-and-tumble business."

She smiled. "My mom's a crossing guard on Myrtle Avenue and is director of our parish's CCD program. My dad was a truck driver."

Dee was just about to speak when Bryce came in. "Finished?"

"Just ending our talk." Dee pressed, somehow asking even though he felt he shouldn't, "Is your dad retired?"

"He died," Mary Jo said. "Two years ago. He was driving his rig on Bruckner Boulevard when, I guess, he felt something coming on. He pulled over, parked, and that was it. Massive heart attack."

Dee felt like a horse's ass. He was so embarrassed with his faux pas that he rubbed his chin with his hand and touched her shoulder very gently. "I am so, so sorry. I would never have…"

"You didn't know, Mr. Felico. It's okay. Mom and I make do." She paused. "And as far as Wall Street is concerned: all options are open."

Bryce keyed in changing the topic quickly. "Mary Jo, I want you to meet some of the guys, and if lunch is okay with you, it's a deal."

She smiled widely, Dee admiring her dimple and the sweetness of her face. "Bryce, in case she's a vegetarian, make sure the place has an ample array of vegetables."

"Not me, Mr. Felico. I can chow down a rib-eye like a lumberjack."

They all laughed as Dee nodded his approval to Bryce, and then Mary Jo Barnes and Bryce McKenna left.

Dee Felico sat in his plush leather chair, turned to look at the Brooklyn Bridge, and exhaled as if punched in the stomach. "My god, my god. Oh my god."

His mind was jumbled. He couldn't concentrate. He watched the river traffic in a daydreamy way. He couldn't snap into focus. He never did explore the waterways on a John McAllister tug boat.

Why is this happening to me? I'm no good to myself or to anybody else like this.

He got up and told his secretary that he had something important to do and would be back in a while. He walked out of the building toward the Battery. Even conjuring up music in his mind as a distraction wasn't working. He just walked in a limbo. He was on a path but unaware of his surroundings. His mind was a blur. He wandered into St. Elizabeth Seton's tiny chapel near the Seaman's Institute. He blessed himself and sat in a rear pew. There were several men there dressed in business attire, probably out of work seeking solace or a blessing for a forthcoming interview.

He sat hunched over trying to pray. The words came, but there was no meaning, no feeling. It was dry as parched grass. He tried to force it, but God was out for a walk that day. And then his mind cried, *Mom, please help!* For a second, he saw her. She looked at him, a cigarette dangling from her mouth, the smoke curling up, partially closing her eye—and then she vanished like the smoke. He became jittery, his palms sweating, his mind suddenly recalling a sensual tap dance Bea had showed him. He saw it in its entirety. Flashy, beautifully delivered, her smile directed specifically at him as if in a taunt. Abruptly, he got up. He wanted no part of this and rushed out bumping into a man coming in.

"Hey, take it easy," the man said.

Stunned, Dee said, gripping the man's arm almost as an after-thought, "I'm sorry."

"Maybe you should stick around a little longer and calm your-self, pal."

Dee heard the words and just acknowledged with a slight nod and said again, "I'm sorry," and walked up the stairs to the street.

He began to walk briskly toward Broadway and worked his way up the street until he got to Trinity Church. He always loved that beautiful soot-black house of prayer at the foot of Wall Street. He walked in. It was completely empty. He sat in a middle pew as an organist started to practice Bach's "Air on the G String," an enchant-ing piece written specifically for the violin's G-string.

As the organist began, Dee saw the notes, his mind suddenly fresh and fertile for music only. He was joyous that his mind was free and he didn't force or challenge what was so naturally coming. He welcomed it without uttering a thank-you lest the experience evapo-rate back into the maelstrom that so beset him.

The notes, so artistically arranged, flowed before his eyes, majestic, simple, elegant. He perceived the dynamics, the intonation, and then he saw Bea, dressed in scanty clothes, white feathers being plucked one by one in a suggestive, alluring way, a striptease. He buried his face in his hands. He muttered, "Air on the… G-string! G-string! Goddamnit!" It was something that should be happening at night! He got up and walked out of the church, his neck clenched with stress. The last time he had a daytime nightmare was when he was in the war.

The first thing he heard was the screech. Flares of heat rushed up to his face. His body tingled.

The car stopped several inches before it would have hit him.

Dee had not even realized he was trying to dash across Broadway in the middle of oncoming traffic.

"You stupid fuck!" the man coming out of the car screamed. "You fuckin' idiot! I coulda killed you!" The man went face-to-face with Dee. He smelled of vomit. The scare of almost running someone over had spewed out his half-digested breakfast all over his shirt and pants. "Look at me! I puked all over myself because of you!"

Dee felt like a hermit crab retreating into its shell. All that came out of him was a very weak, "I'm sorry…sorry." Seeing the mess on the man's clothes, he said, "I'll pay… I'll take care—"

The man screamed, "I wouldn't take a dime from any of you Wall Street guys! You're all a bunch of fuckin' whores!" He turned and went back to his car trying to wipe the mess off his clothes with his handkerchief. "Wanna kill yourself?" he turned just before he got into the car. "Jump off the fuckin' Brooklyn Bridge! Asshole!"

The light was in Dee's favor, and he rushed across the street shaken and ashamed trying to blend and then get lost in the forming clusters of people coming out of buildings heading out for an early lunch.

When he crossed Broad Street, he was doubly careful regarding the traffic. Once he was on the sidewalk, he allowed his hand to brush against the Morgan Guaranty building, head down not making eye contact, just scanning the feet of pedestrians scurrying by.

He stopped, his hand caressing the pockmark in the building caused by a terrorist explosion in 1920. He heard his name being called. "Hey, Felico. Dee. Dee."

He looked up from the pavement and saw an old friend who worked at Goldman Sachs, Solly Greenberg. "Solly," Dee said softly.

"What are you doing? Looking for pennies on the sidewalk?"

Dee had to smile. "No. Just…"

"You okay?" Solly's voice, colored with concern, said, touching Dee's arm.

"I almost got hit by a car crossing Broadway."

"C'mon, buddy. Let's take a walk down by the river and get a whiff of the fish stink down by the Fulton Fish Market. That'll clean out your head and your sinuses too."

Dee still felt a little bewildered and agreed. "Okay."

They walked slowly together, Solly's arm over Dee's shoulder, leading the way.

At Water Street, Solly said, "Let's go to Sloppy Louie's for a little oyster stew. Just like the old days after those compliance committee meetings when we were young and our backs didn't stoop."

Dee looked at him. "My back doesn't stoop."

Solly laughed. "Good. You're back with me. For a moment I thought you were somewhere beyond the outer limits."

Dee slurped down the oyster stew with gusto. "Solly. Boy, am I enjoying this. Haven't had this in a dog's age. Thanks, buddy."

"So," Solly said, "what's going on with you? If you don't want to say, that's okay. But I've known you since we were both coupon chimps."

Dee smiled. "Coupon chimp. Nobody even knows what that is anymore."

"Well? You going to spill? Or do we leave it at that?"

Dee's brows furrowed. He was silent, not really deliberating or deciding whether he could trust Solly, which he knew he could. He was just wondering how stupid he would look to his friend, exposing himself as a sentimental slob or as his grandfather would say, "There's no fool like an old fool." "Okay, Solly. I'll tell you." And he related the experience he had that morning viewing Mary Jo Barnes and how buried memories came out and ravaged his very substance.

After he had told Solly everything, timidity enveloped him. He feared Solly's response. "And," Dee finished, "that's where I'm at."

"It's not unusual. It may be coincidence. It may be more. I've had something akin to your story, but not as involved. I was a new Wall Street kid, back in the Goodbody & Co days, and I'd ride the subway from Brooklyn. Remember the old straw seats back then?"

Dee smiled and nodded.

"Well," Solly continued, "two stops after me—and the car was never full till about the fifth stop—this girl comes in and sits a few seats away from me. I always read the paper on the way in, and that was the end of my paper reading on the subway. She was the most beautiful thing I ever saw in my life. I couldn't take my eyes off her. And every day I'd see her and gaze at her in awe. She never saw me or looked in my direction. I wasn't as forward then as I am today, and I never struck up a conversation with her. I saw her every day for about six months, and then the last time I saw her, I saw that she was troubled and she held back tears. She had this little handkerchief with lace around it and she dabbed her eyes. I wanted so much to go to her to comfort her to rid her from her problems, but I didn't. Woulda shoulda coulda oughta. And I never saw her again. And that was a lifetime ago, and, Dee, I swear to Christ, there isn't a day that goes by that I don't think about her."

"Like the scene in *Citizen Kane*," Dee said.

"Yes." Solly reached over and patted Dee's hand.

"But, Solly, *Citizen Kane* is a movie. Yours was a memory. Mine has blood and marrow. It's fucking alive!"

"Dee. Let it go. Your wife isn't even gone a year. Your insides are like loose cement. It hasn't hardened yet. It may never become totally solid again, but it's still too early in the game. Let it go, Dee. You'll only drive yourself crazy. And nobody needs that. Sometimes there are no answers."

"But the questions are still there, Solly."

"I know. And, for that matter, they may always be there. But sometimes there just are no answers. Go back to work. Do your music. Delve into what you know best. You can't rearrange the past. It'll go away. It'll recede into that place we all have in us called lost and forgotten."

Dee took a deep breath. "Thanks, Solly." Dee reached into his breast pocket for his wallet.

Solly reached over and snatched the bill. "I'll blow. My treat. As far as the psychological counseling, you'll get my bill in the mail. I am, as you know, very, very expensive."

"Eat shit, you bastard," Dee said.

Laughing, they both got up and left Sloppy Louie's.

They roamed around the Fulton Fish Market for a while and then Solly said, "I best be getting back."

"Me too, Sol. I got a private placement I'm working on." Dee shook Solly Greenberg's hand. "Thanks, Solly. You are a good friend."

"Go to work…and let it go."

They parted and Dee walked back to the office.

Dee plowed back into his work structuring the private placement so the lawyers could review it and give it their okay.

He never heard the knock on the glass window of his office until some metallic object was used to get his attention. When he looked up, he saw her smiling and felt like an earthen dyke ready to give. He almost resumed his work, but he knew that would be supremely rude, so he waved her in.

He got up to greet her, the dimple creasing in her cheek, giving more to him than she'd ever know, and simply said, "Hi."

"I'm so sorry. I had to pop in. They offered me the job and I accepted. I am thrilled. I start tomorrow and I just wanted to thank you once again. I know I never met you before, but you made me feel so comfortable… I feel like I know you from…somewhere."

"Well, welcome on board. We'll work you hard. And you'll learn a lot, but I assure you, you will have fun. It's not a lot of people who can say they have fun at work," he paused, "and get paid as well."

She laughed. "I can't wait." She shook his hand.

As she was about to leave, he said something that he couldn't believe. There was something about her face that moment, the eyes brightening as if anticipating an intricate dance step which she knew she could nail flat, and the way her lips partially pouted and then relaxed, parting naturally to hint a glint of teeth. And in the back of his mind, he kept hearing Solly's voice dwindling into nothingness. "Let it go…let it go—for Christ's sake, let it go." And grandpa's old saying, "There's no fool like an old fool," drifted in his mind like night fog over the water. He felt so useless now, unable to focus and concentrate. The gods were playing him, saying, "See that guy? Get him and get him good." Maybe Solly was right—the cement was still sloshing around. There was no grounding, no foundation. It was unsettled.

And then he said something so stupid, so ridiculous that hearing himself actually utter the words had him questioning his own sanity. "Would you care to join me at Harry's around seven for a celebratory drink? Something to christen your new venture with us?"

Are you crazy, Felico? What are you doing? You're getting older. You're getting slower. You're getting dopier. But you still have a good appetite. Above and below the belt? Is that what you think? Is this some kind of grand gesture? A spurt of the old you? You think this is a gentlemanly thing to do? This is not solidifying a deal! This is not a courtesy! This is the mark of a fool. An old fool!

He battled himself. And, in so doing, became the winner and the loser.

She looked up at him, smiling, that smile working him like a deep tissue massage. "I'd love to. But I must help my mom with some paperwork. I'll try to be there. If I'm not there by seven thirty, means I'm stuck. Okay?"

"Sure," he said.

Solly was right! I nailed my tongue to a telephone pole. What an asshole! I should have let it go. What a horse's ass I've become.

He dicked around for the remainder of the day doing little odds and ends, and then toward five regained focus and reworked a few details on the private placement. At six forty he called it quits, washed up, and headed for Harry's at Hanover Square. And walking there slowly, hands in pockets, suddenly got a nervous twinge. He felt like a young kid calling a girl for a date nervously hanging up on the fourth ring, chickening out.

Walking down the few steps entering the watering hole, he was greeted by a waiter he knew and was ushered to a side table where he sat and ordered a merlot.

Waiting…waiting…waiting. He was used to it. He had waited in the war and he had waited in peace.

Waiting was a strange thing. With some, it drove them crazy. With others, a boredom that tortured so much so that they would confess to anything, even being the shooter on the Grassy Knoll. Dee called it "trapped time." It was there. You were in it and couldn't get out of it. But it was yours. And if you had the right mind for it, you could make it work for you.

He had put through many melodies in trapped time. He had daydreamed marvelous thoughts in trapped time. He had even put through some trade strategies in trapped time. But this trapped time was different. It was something he felt out of control with. It was like expecting an opening event to happen but then becoming confused as to whether you were at the right place at the right time for the right event.

He took a small sip of merlot.

He scanned the restaurant, observing the patrons, picking up snippets of conversation, hearing rousting laughter from the other side of the room and the clinking and clatter of utensils on dishes, the squeaking slides of chairs on the wooden floor and the occasional triangle sound of a butter knife on a half-filled glass announcing a toast.

And the trapped time passed, and passed...and passed...well past seven thirty.

At five to eight Dee hailed Sal, a waiter he knew for years, to come over.

"Mr. Dee?"

"Just put it on the tab, Sal, I think I'll be getting along."

"Your guest detained?"

"No, Sal. I think I've been stood up." He smiled at Sal. "Better still," he continued taking out his wallet, "I'll pay for it now." He gave Sal his credit card. "Gotta hit the head." He got up and walked to the men's room.

When he returned, he sat in a chair facing the inside of the eatery for better lighting and signed the check and the credit card slip.

"Mr. Felico! Thank God!" an exasperated female voice said behind him. Looking up he saw Mary Jo Barnes, her face flushed, a sheen of perspiration on her brow. He felt his heart beat like a school boy getting the courage to ask a pretty girl for a date.

He got up and pulled out a chair. "I ran...ran from the subway." She was limping.

"Please calm down."

"I think I broke a heel."

He laughed. "Car service will fix that. Take it easy. Just sit. Take a breath."

"I'm sorry...the subways... I must look a wreck."

He checked himself. He felt a ripple in his chest. "You look...," he hesitated on the word but used, "fine. Just fine."

She smiled at him, and in his eyes it was enchanting. He was, that second, trapped in another time, but only for a second. It was fleeting. He snatched the beauty and beheld it. It was all his. "We'll wait a minute or so, okay? Relax."

She nodded, her hair tousling.

And then, in the stillness of a moment as only a stillness could bring, a white-haired lady appeared at his right, looking at him, smiling, saying, "Hiya, baby," as he suddenly caught the scent of apple blossoms.

About the Author

Richard Layh was born in Manhattan, raised in Astoria, Queens, and is now living on Long Island. He worked thirty-two years for fixed income trading firms on Wall Street. After retiring from "The Street," Richard worked eleven years for the hospital system serving patients in need of financial assistance. To salve his soul, he cooks, paints in oils, writes poems and stories, plays jazz violin and trumpet, and writes music. Currently, his full-time job, along with his wife Vickie, is helping raise their two grandsons from their daughter, Kristin, and two granddaughters from their son, Philip.